Matthew Hughes is the best-kept secret in science
fiction."
                                   ROBERT J. SAWYER

"Matthew Hughes has accomplished something unique:
he has written a novel, without illustrations, that
conveys the tone and feel of comics published during
their Golden Age."
                                   RED ROOK REVIEW

"A funny and surprisingly endearing book, with some
interesting discussions about the role of sin and our
reactions to it."   KEITH BROOKE, THE GUARDIAN

"A supernatural adventure that blends a rich and
unpredictable story, with a tone and wit that provides
plenty of laughs along the way. A great balance of action
and comedic situations, with some romance thrown in
for good measure… This is a great read. 5*****"
                                   CELEBRITY CAFE

"This story starts out as a tongue-in-cheek humorous
parody of the relationship between humans and
demons, until a sharp twist turns religion upside down.
The premise is bold, thought-provoking, and original."
                                   TANGENT ONLINE

MATTHEW HUGHES

TO HELL AND BACK
Hell To Pay

**ANGRY
ROBOT**

ANGRY ROBOT
A member of the Osprey Group

Lace Market House,
54-56 High Pavement,
Nottingham,
NG1 1HW, UK

www.angryrobotbooks.com
Chapter and verse

An Angry Robot paperback original 2013
1

A catalogue record for this book is available
from the British Library.

ISBN: 978 0 85766 162 3
Ebook ISBN: 978 0 85766 164 7

Set in Meridien by Argh! Oxford.

Printed and bound by CPI Group (UK) Ltd, Croydon, CR0 4YY

HELL TO PAY

ONE

Arthur Wrigley was a truly awful little man.

He had started out as a truly awful little boy: willful, selfish, grasping even, to the despair of his parents and the frustration of his primary school teachers. But as the years rolled on, Arthur learned to disguise the worst parts of his nature, or at least to confine them to specific circumstances when they could get him what he wanted at negligible risk to his own comfort.

He was, in short, a psychopath, but of the intelligent variety. Broadly speaking, psychopaths come in two kinds: the smart ones and the dumb ones. The latter clog the lower levels of the criminal courts. They are the kind of offenders who commit crimes without much planning, often with no evidence of any forethought at all. They see what they want and they grab it, indiscriminately smashing a window or a skull if it's in the way, and giving no more thought to the consequences than does any hungry predator leaping upon its prey.

Eventually, they end up tucked away for a long-term sentence. Or dead, because there comes a fateful day when the thing they impulsively crave turns out to be the property of someone capable of disputing ownership in the most forthright manner.

But the intelligent variety of psychopaths learn to control their impulses, at least when it really counts. They plan their approaches and their getaways in detail. They also learn how to mimic the attributes of normal people, and can fake compassion and friendship at a level that could land them on the red carpet at the Oscars, if their career choices led them in that direction – as occasionally does happen.

A substantial number of intelligent psychopaths go into politics or the corporate milieu. Their ability to connive and backstab one moment, but to smile and glad-hand the next, makes them perfectly suited for an environment that rewards those who see the faces of those around them primarily as stepping-stones.

A small yet significant number of intelligent psychopaths – mostly men, but some women – choose the life of the confidence trickster. It's a profession that particularly appeals to those who get no great thrill out of harming their fellow citizens, but just want to appropriate other people's property and use it for their own pleasure. Arthur Wrigley was that kind of fraudster, and after more than twenty years' practice, he had become very good at it.

He came to town just as the golf courses were drying out from the Midwest spring melt, rented a furnished apartment and leased a Lexus. He drove around and marked the locations of Protestant churches in affluent neighborhoods. Arthur generally preferred Baptists, but understood that in areas that historically had attracted substantial German immigration, Lutherans could offer substantial promise.

He attended Sunday services at each of the churches he identified, though he paid no attention to the sermons. Instead, he devoted himself to a close assessment of the parishioners, noting the quality of their clothes, the burnishings of the wives' faces, the makes and ages of the automobiles parked outside. After two weeks, he had selected his church of choice and began attending regularly.

He also became a regular at the most upscale golf club in town, playing three times a week – often by himself, though he was always willing to make up the missing member of a foursome. He professed a modest handicap and played with moderate skill, winning as gracefully as he lost, never welshing, and accompanying everything he did with smiles, rueful shakes of the head, shrugs, winks and nods, as appropriate to the tenor of his game.

Within six weeks, he had become a recognizable part of the environment in the social circles that interconnected between the Praise Baptist Church and the Merivale Golf Club. People saw him shopping at Bonano's, the upscale supermarket, and he was spotted eating lunch or dinner at Boardman's Steak House and The Coq d'Or.

It was at Boardman's that Praise Baptist's deacons gathered once a month, ostensibly to deal with church business, but mostly just to eat a good lunch and gossip. They dealt with the church's affairs over the appetizers and were moving on to discussing Mayor Greeley's proposed redevelopment of Canting Park when Head Deacon Pete Eberley spotted the maître d' leading Arthur Wrigley to a table for one.

"Hey, George!" Pete called. "Want to join us for lunch?"

Arthur, who was George Colville to these people, approached the group and said, with a carefully deferential smile, "If I'm not intruding."

He had played golf with three of the six men at the table, and chatted briefly after church with two others. They assured him that he was welcome in their midst. He sat down and accepted a menu from the maître d' while the others made room and a waiter hurried over with a place setting.

Introductions were made. Arthur already knew all their names, and now they knew one of his. The discussion returned to Canting Park while he selected his steak and vegetables, but when he handed back the menu and rested his hands on the tablecloth, the group's attention came back to him.

Pete Eberley noted the Rolex, the gold ring with the inlaid diamond – at least one carat – and the cut and quality of the new man's suit and tie. Pete was a real estate developer who'd started small and become medium-large, and was used to assessing people's net worth by their appearance. He put George Colville in the several-millions category. People like that were always of interest to a man who put together financing packages.

"So, George," he said, "how's business?"

A wink and a nod from Arthur. "Ups and downs," he said, "but I'm not complaining."

Terry Melchert, seated at Arthur's left elbow, said, "What line are you in, George?"

Arthur turned his mild blue eyes on the questioner, let them crinkle a little at the edges. "Used to be banking."

"Wall Street?"

Arthur made a little noise of confirmation. "Now I mostly just manage my portfolio."

"Retired?" said another of the deacons.

A gentle shrug. "Pretty much."

Pete said, "But you still keep your hand in?"

Another shrug. "Now and then, if the glove fits."

And so the hook was set.

Pete Eberley had got George Colville's phone number before they rose from the table. A few days later, he called and invited him to lunch and a round of golf. They made it a foursome with a couple of Pete's friends. Nobody talked business, and when one of the cronies mentioned the ninety-nine percenters occupying Wall Street, George just smiled and made a gesture that said all of that was behind him now.

Pete cultivated George. Over the next few weeks, they got together for a couple of lunches and a dinner. They played golf and had drinks at the club. They talked sports and politics and movies. The developer gradually came to realize that he and the retired Wall Streeter had a lot in common. They liked the same things, they saw the world the same way. That was particularly gratifying, because Pete was coming to understand, from remarks that George had dropped, that his new friend had moved in some pretty elevated circles.

"Really?" he said. "Donald Trump? What kind of deal was it?"

George gave a little shake of his head and showed Pete a pair of palms raised in denial. "I can't say, Pete. Confidentiality."

"But it was big, right?"

George's eyes twinkled. "The Donald thought so."

By now it was summer, and Praise Baptist was holding
its annual picnic and social in the park down by the river.
George came and everyone was glad to see him.

Especially glad was Jean Tappehorn, aged forty-
something but clinging with increasing desperation to her
thirties. She had been left financially comfortable after a
divorce from the high-school sweetheart who'd thought
that making it big in retail electronics entitled him to a
blonde trophy. Jean was nobody's idea of a trophy, plump
and with her features somehow clumped into the middle
of a too-round face. But lately, the new member of the
congregation had been taking time to smile at her after
services and say good morning. He was an odd little man,
an inch shorter than she was if she wore heels, but he
had a kindly, worldly smile, and she had the feeling he'd
like to say more than good morning, but was just a tad
too shy.

Jean Tappehorn intended to get the shyness out of the
way so she could see what lay behind the leprechaun's
twinkles and nods. For the picnic she wore flat heels
and a dress that made no effort to disguise her curves,
two of which were augmented by the first push-up bra
she'd ever owned. When she saw George talking to Pete
Eberley by the punchbowl table, she drifted over, picked
up a cup and reached for the ladle.

Immediately, the little man spun and said, "Please,
allow me." He gently lifted the ladle from her hand,
took her cup, filled it, and gave it back to her. The
motions twice brought his flesh briefly into contact with
hers. She saw by his eyes that he was aware of it and of

her reaction.

"I don't know if you two have met," Pete said. "George, this is Jean. George is retired from banking."

"How do you do?" George said. He took her offered hand but didn't shake it. Instead he held it in his while his eyes met hers and held them too.

And so it went. As the evening came on, Jean told the couple who'd given her a ride that she wouldn't need one home. Once they'd left, she made a show of looking for them. George noticed and asked if she was all right.

"I think I've missed my ride," she said.

"I'd be happy to take you home."

That led to a drink in the living room, with music on the stereo – he liked the same singers as she did – and then another drink and some talk about the wrongs that had been done to her.

As she sipped her third scotch, Jean said, "George, we're not kids, are we?"

He smiled and nodded ruefully. "That's for sure, Jean."

She looked into his eyes and was glad to see that he didn't look away. It took her a moment and another sip before she could say it. "I've only ever been with one man in my life."

He said nothing but continued to look at her. It seemed to Jean that a warm kindness filled his eyes. He put down his glass and took hers from her. Then he held both her hands in his. She felt more warmth flow from his fingers. For the first time in more years than she could remember, she realized that she was wet.

"I don't know you well, Jean, but I already know that you're a woman who deserves better than she got."

He leaned forward, his eyes closing, one arm slipping

around her. She felt her breath coming fast. It was like being a girl again. It was absolutely glorious.

And so, from then on, it was George and Jean. "Keeping company" was how the ladies of Praise Baptist phrased it, though the lifting of their carefully plucked eyebrows telegraphed a wealth of meaning. But they were glad to see one of the congregation's divorcées nailed down. The Tappehorn woman was no femme fatale, but husbands were husbands, and a divorcée was always of interest.

As the summer wore on, Jean blossomed as never before. A new hairdo, a new wardrobe, and a new energy lifted her out of the ordinary. George was clearly devoted to her and, from the very few hints she'd dropped, he was a skilled and attentive lover. Some of the other wives entertained thoughts of seeing if the little man was temptable. But when Marie McAllister tried flirting with him at one of the golf club's cocktail evenings, he gently but definitely discouraged her interest.

In late August, a wedding date was set for early December, with a Caribbean honeymoon cruise to follow.

Pete Eberley's original plan had been to try to interest George in a condo development that would have fitted nicely into the Mayor's urban renewal project at the old Canting Industrial Park. But as he got to know the other man better, a new and wider vista began to unfold itself before the developer's inner eye. The retired banker had never said anything explicit, but from a remark here and a comment there, the real estate man had gathered the impression that his new friend was connected to a world of high finance whose horizons stretched far beyond any deal Pete had ever been part of.

That world – those far, golden horizons – glimmered just out of Pete's sight, vague and indistinct, but with glints of luster like the reflections off George's diamond ring whenever the banker made one of those offhand gestures that implied so much while saying so little. Pete wanted to ask, but didn't know how to broach the subject. He wanted in, but couldn't find the door.

Then came an afternoon at the golf club. They'd played a round and Pete had won. George had paid up promptly, as he always did, and offered to stand the victor a drink. They sat together at a table by the wall of windows that overlooked the eighteenth hole, and Pete examined the smile on the other man's face as he watched a foursome sink their last putts. He'd been seeing that smile a lot over the last couple of hours, and he read it as the smile of a man who has just pulled off a good score.

"You've got a 'cat that ate the cream' look, George," he said.

The smaller man moved his eyes sideways. It reminded Pete of Herman Cain's expression at the end of that strange campaign ad: a knowing look that somehow invited the viewer to be part of the knowledge. "Do I?" George said.

"Come on," Pete said. "Spill it. What have you done?"

A self-deprecating shrug, a little ducking of the head, then the smile again. "You won't tell anybody?"

"Mum," said the developer, resisting the urge to lean forward, "is the word."

"Well." George took a sip of his bourbon. He said nothing for a few seconds, and then, as Pete was thinking that the moment was going to pass by, he said, "Since we're friends," and shrugged again, and continued, "a little syndicate I put together has paid out nicely."

"How nicely?"

"A net of forty per cent in under ten days."

Pete whistled softly, then he couldn't help leaning forward. "Forty per cent? Of what?"

George looked left and right, then lowered his voice. "Ten million."

The developer blinked, his glass frozen halfway to his lips. "You made four million in less than ten days?"

"Good grief, no," said the smaller man. "The syndicate made four million. I was only in for ten per cent."

"But that's still four hundred grand in about a week."

"Yes."

"What's the tax exposure on a gain like that?" Pete said.

George's eyes twinkled. "Well," he said, "if the transaction occurred in the US, I imagine it would be substantial."

Pete sat back. Some of the murk and shadow lifted from the vista. The far horizons were now kissed by golden sun. "Cayman Islands?" he guessed.

"A little more subtle than that," was the answer, accompanied by a wave of the hand that said no more would be said on that score.

Pete sighed. It was all there before him. He'd found the door. Now he just had to get it to open. "What can you tell me?" he said.

He saw that it was the right way to ask. George looked around again and his voice stayed low. "Bankers," he said, "are occasionally asked to provide short-term funds on a, shall we say, highly confidential basis."

He paused and Pete saw it was time for him to nod,

although he wasn't sure what he was agreeing with.

"The funds also have to be non-attributable," George said, pausing again to see if Pete was following.

Pete wasn't. "I'm sorry, I–"

George leaned forward and whispered. "In cash and off the books."

That drew Pete's eyebrows together. "What are we talking about?"

Another look to left and right, making George look like a conspiratorial elf. "Say there's a pipeline project in Kazakhstan, or it could be a gold-mining lease in Mali. The minister in charge of issuing the licenses initiates an add-on to the formal bidding process."

Pete understood that one. "He wants a sweetener."

"Exactly. But a US or European company that wants to get the project can't just build the extra money into the budget." Another little shrug. "At least, not anymore. There are new laws, and your CEO can end up going to jail."

"So what do you do?" Pete said.

Another glance around. "The company approaches a private bank. The private bank also can't use its own money, so it approaches one or two people its principals know and trust. Those one or two people put together a syndicate of folks they know and trust, and they come up with the cash."

George paused to let it sink in. Pete thought for a moment, then said, "How does the bank make money?"

"General management fees, or a fee for consulting advice."

"So they use other people's money, off the books? Suitcases of used hundreds?"

George took another sip of his bourbon. "Delivered by men with guns and military tattoos."

"Sounds risky."

"It is," said George, "which is why it's all about dealing with people you've known for years and can trust implicitly."

Pete sat back and remembered his scotch. "Forty per cent," he said. "In about a week."

George put up a hand to calm him down. "Forty is unusual. Ten to twenty is more usual."

"But this one was special," Pete said.

"Oh, yes," said the retired banker. He emptied his glass and smiled.

A silence came over them. George held his glass up for the waiter to notice. The man fetched him another drink and he took a satisfied sip.

Pete said, "George."

George looked at him. "I know what you're going to ask."

He said nothing again and Pete reined himself in. "Do you know and trust me?" he said, keeping it calm and level.

"Let me see what comes up." George's smile said he wasn't promising anything. Pete knew he should leave it there and wait.

Jean's romance with her new man was everything her marriage had not been. He was attentive, but not smothering. He had strong opinions on some things, but they generally dovetailed with hers, and he was always willing to hear her out when she had something to say. And the things he did with her in the bedroom had opened a door in her that she had never known existed. Nor had she known about the she-animal that lurked behind it.

She'd asked him what he did, and he'd told her he had retired from banking to manage his own investments. He had worked in New York and London, but had come back to the Midwest because he liked to be among real people.

He gave her an engagement ring with a diamond that had an old-fashioned cut. "It was my mother's," he said. "She would have wanted you to have it."

He didn't move in, though after a month she would have let him. "We don't want tongues wagging," he said. "Time enough after the wedding."

He never mentioned money, hers or his. Obviously, he had plenty. She'd been concerned about her finances. In the divorce settlement she'd won the house – free and clear – and a half-million in blue chips and municipal bonds. Her ex had been a louse, but he'd been a louse who invested conservatively. Even so, the recession had taken a bite out of her net worth so one afternoon, after George had once again convinced her that there really was such a thing as a G-spot, she'd asked him to take a look at her portfolio.

He went carefully through the quarterly statements and her accountant's recommendations. He tucked the papers back into their file folders and said, "You're fine, dear. Good solid stuff."

"But I've lost almost ten per cent of my capital since 2008."

"Temporary," he said. "It will all come back and more as the economy reinflates."

•••

In the church parking, lot after services one morning in early October, George said to Pete, "I'm going in on another deal. Do you still want to be part of it?"

"I'm in."

"It's not a big one, but we'll make twenty per cent." He put a finger to the side of his nose. "Of course, there's always a chance we'll make nothing, even lose it all."

Pete discounted the possibility. George did not look like a man who'd ever lost it all. "What's the project?"

George explained that the deal concerned a shipment of Chinese-made smartphones into India. The man who ran the port authority had retired and his successor had gazumped the "processing fee."

"He wants a hundred thousand and he wants it now. Otherwise the phones don't get to the customers. They might even get damaged if they have to wait around too long."

"Jeez," said Pete.

"It's the way they do things."

"How much on my end?"

George showed him a calming hand again. "Easy," he said. "I was going in for ten thousand, but instead I'll let you take half of that. It will allow me to introduce you to the rest of the syndicate. I have to vouch for you, you know."

"Five thousand," said Pete. "When do you want it?"

"Tomorrow's fine."

"At the club?"

"Let's meet there for lunch." George turned toward his Lexus, then turned back. "Not a word to your banker or your accountant. We don't want any IRS entanglements."

"For sure," said Pete.

He brought the five thousand to lunch. George took the envelope and tucked it into his inside jacket pocket. "About a week," he said.

True to his word, six days later he handed Pete seven thousand dollars. "All's well," he said. "You're in."

"When's the next one?"

"Don't know," said George. "They often come up unexpectedly." He gave Pete a searching look. "We haven't discussed how much... involvement you'd be comfortable with."

But Pete had already thought about it. "I can do fifty grand."

"OK," George said. "I'll let you know."

In late October, Jean's accountant sent through her adjusted quarterly statement. Her principal had shrunk a little further, although bond yields were up. She tackled her fiancé again. "I'm losing money, George."

"Only on paper, my love," he said. "Patience."

"I spent my whole life being patient," she said, "and look where it got me. If I'd been patient with you, would you have ever made a move?"

His smile and the motion of his silver-coiffed head conceded the point.

"Well, then," she said.

"If you want me to handle it for you," he said, "I'll draw up the papers. But I won't put you into anything risky."

And he didn't. He sold her blue chips and cashed in most of the bonds, but moved her into oil and gas. The shifting capital value of the preferred shares during a time of economic uncertainty made them more volatile, but they paid guaranteed rates of return, so her cash flow definitely improved. He also arranged for her to receive a monthly payout, instead of quarterly. He did not tell her that some of the extra money she was now seeing came from the mortgage he had taken out on her home, using the power of attorney she had signed.

She was grateful and showed it, in a way she had never gladly done for her ex. Afterwards, looking up, she said, "I'm getting better at it, aren't I?"

"You are, indeed," he said. "It's a shame all that talent went neglected for so long."

"Well, we'll have plenty of years to develop it further."

He smiled and patted her head.

George told Pete, "Your end is thirty thousand, if you want in."

"I can go more."

"Thirty is all there's room for. There are a lot of players in this one."

Pete delivered the cash the next day. Eight days later, George handed him thirty-nine thousand. Pete and his wife took George and Jean out for a happy and boozy evening of lobster and steak at Boardman's.

George kept attending church and playing golf at the club. It was the surest way to discover if Pete had told anybody about their arrangement. But none of their mutual acquaintances ever sidled up to him and hinted that they'd like to get in on Pete's sweet deal.

George remembered reading a book by a psychologist who specialized in people like him – this was back when he was still Arthur Wrigley and planning his career. The doctor had said that churches and social organizations were to someone like George what watering holes were to lions: a place to assess the gazelles and zebras and pick out dinner.

George did not see himself as a lion, though. As a teenager, he had seen a TV documentary about insect adaption. There was one insect that mimicked the appearance and even the mating pheromones of its prey. Some bug would come spiraling down, eager to fulfill its biological destiny, only to find nothing waiting for it but an appetite behind a set of mandibles.

For a while, teenage Arthur thought of himself in comic book terms as "The Predator," a costumed superdude who blinded all around him with his superior powers. But the more he read about people like himself, the more it was made clear to him that he was better off acting like one of those stick insects that so closely resembled a twig that they went unnoticed. The thing that did in the Arthur Wrigleys of the world, he learned, was that they tended to overreach.

Arthur took that lesson to heart. In a career now stretching over more than thirty years, he had never come close to being caught. He had rules and procedures, from which he never deviated, and which had made him a happy and successful man.

A week after he paid Pete the thirty-nine thousand, George told him during a round of golf that something big might be coming together.

"How big?" Pete said.

"Don't know yet. Big."

"Can I get in on it?"

"I think so," George said. "I'll tell you now, the first two deals were your testers."

Pete paused in putting a tee in the sod. They were about to play the eighth hole, a difficult dogleg. He looked a question at the other man.

"To see if you were the kind of guy who could keep a secret," George said. He smiled. "And you passed, with flying colors."

Pete pushed the tee in, placed his ball, then drove it a good three hundred yards down the fairway, positioning himself perfectly for the approach to the green.

"Nice one," George said.

"I'll have to go to Chicago for a couple of days," George told Jean, "probably next week."

"I'll come too."

"You can't."

Her face clouded. It was the first time he'd ever denied her anything. Then he took her in his arms and said, "I'm arranging a surprise, something special. I want to make sure it's done right."

She brightened again. "What is it?"

"Now, now, don't make me tell you, sweetheart. You'll spoil it."

"Just a hint."

"Mum's the word." He kissed her.

He let another few days go by then told Pete, "It's tomorrow. The buy-in is twelve hundred thousand."

The developer went pale. "One-point-two mil?"

George looked mildly surprised. "I thought you were ready for the real thing."

"I am, I am. But, jeez, a million-two. I haven't got that kind of liquidity."

"Can you get it? By, say, end of business tomorrow?"

Pete's gaze turned inward as he made mental calculations. They were sitting at a table near the wall at Boardman's. George was treating Pete to lunch.

"Well?" said George. "If you can't, I have to tell people now so they can slot in someone else."

"Let me think. I thought I'd have more time."

"I told you last week it might be coming up."

"A million-two."

"Thirty per cent yield."

Pete did another calculation. "That's $360,000 profit."

"Yep."

"How long?"

"Before the payout? Minimum six, seven days. Maximum two weeks, maybe fifteen days."

Pete was thinking hard. He had no more than sixty thousand in cash. He held mortgages on several commercial properties he had developed but to convert them to cash would take time. On the other hand, there was another nine hundred thousand held in trust, part of the financing package he was still putting together for the Canting Park project. If he took that, and got a quick mortgage on his own place…

"I can do it," he said.

"Good," said George. "I'll need it in cash or a cashier's check by five tomorrow. I have to drive it to Chicago and turn it over to the courier. It goes by private jet to Geneva, where the rest of the package comes on board. Then on to Kabul."

Pete's expression tightened. "Kabul? Afghanistan?

What kind of deal is this?"

George looked from side to side, although no one was within earshot. He lowered his voice. "Lithium."

"Lithium? Like in batteries?"

"Like in just about every kind of handheld technology. In your cell phone, your laptop, your camera, your Taser."

"It's a mineral, right, you mine it?"

"Some people do. We're just helping them do it."

"So, it's a lithium mine?"

George shrugged. "It's probably more like a dozen mines." He leaned forward, speaking quietly. "We're not in the mining business. We're in the money business. We're raising and delivering the" – he quirked his fingers in the air – "'fee' that will deliver the mineral leases to a consortium of American companies. Instead of to the Chinese or the Europeans."

"Jeez," said Pete.

"It's the big leagues, Pete. Now, are you in or not?" George took out his phone. "Cause if you're not, I've got to make some calls."

"Three hundred and sixty thousand profit, in two weeks?" Pete said.

George shrugged again. "Unless World War Three breaks out in the meantime."

Pete's gaze went inward again for a few seconds. George opened his phone. Pete said, "I'm in."

At 5.15pm the following day, George accepted a briefcase from Pete Eberley and placed it in the trunk of the Lexus, next to a case of his own. The developer was showing signs of stress. George knew that sympathy and reassurance would not serve, and he said, "If this is too big-time for you, Pete, you can pull out. Nobody's going to think any less of you for it."

"I just feel…" Pete said, then paused, "…a little unreal. Like we're not in Kansas anymore."

"I suppose we're not. But who wants to be in Kansas?"

Pete was staring at George's briefcase. Without comment, George bent over the open trunk and undid the case's snaps, lifted the lid. Inside, packed tight, were banded stacks of currency, each one with a hundred-dollar bill on top. George reached and pulled loose one of the packets – the second from the right at the front of the case – and held it up for Pete to see. He riffled the bills so that a succession of pictures of Benjamin Franklin flickered before the developer's eyes.

"Was that worrying you?" he said.

Pete put up his hands. "No, no," he said, then, "Well, not really."

"It's all real," George said, replacing the stack and shutting the case, then the trunk. "It's all good."

In the rearview mirror, as he drove off, he saw Pete Eberley raise a hand in farewell. George waved a cheerful goodbye and headed for the interstate. Ten minutes later, with the cruise control set just under the speed limit, he was on his way. He tuned the radio to an oldies FM station – Jean had been a diehard country and western fan – and sang along to Dust In The Wind.

In seven hours he was in Chicago. He left the Lexus in a hotel parking lot and took a cab to an address he had visited before. As arranged, he delivered Pete's briefcase to a man sitting at a table in the back room of a social club on the city's south side. On top of the case he placed a cashier's check for the value of Jean Tappehorn's portfolio plus the remaining funds from the mortgage she had yet to learn about.

The total value of Pete's and Jean's assets came to just under two million dollars. George waited while the money was counted and the check verified online. There was no negotiation with the man at the table; the terms had been set long before, and this was not the first time they had done business. For the almost two million, he received almost one million, eight hundred thousand dollars, transferred by phone to a numbered account in Switzerland.

He also received a package that contained a passport and two credit cards in the name of John Gatwick, who had died as an infant at about the same time as Arthur Wrigley was learning to walk.

As soon as George's telephone call to his bank verified that the funds were secured, he shook hands with the man at the table. "See you in a couple of years," he said.

There was an all-night pawnshop across the street. George crossed over and sold the Rolex and the gold and diamond ring for four thousand dollars. He still had about ten thousand left from his original stake for this operation – the money he had riffled in front of Pete's eyes, the rest of the briefcase being filled with stage money bought at a theatrical supply house.

He got another cab and headed for a restaurant he favored when he was in town, had a fine meal, then got a cab to O'Hare airport. He used his cell phone one more time to check that the money that had been sent to his Swiss account had now been transferred, per standing instructions, to a Channel Islands bank, from which it would be moved by a series of subsequent stages through Hong Kong, the Marshall Islands, and the Caymans. It would end up in the account of a Bermuda investment company of which he was all three registered shareholders. From there, it would be transferred tax-free to George's operating company in the US Virgin Islands.

The Channel Islands bank told him that his money was safe. At that point, he threw away the phone and with it the last trace of his time as George Colville. Using John Gatwick's passport and credit card, he bought a ticket to Miami on a flight leaving at dawn. He would sleep at an airport hotel then catch a shuttle to the Virgins tomorrow afternoon. Those transactions would constitute the short second life of John Gatwick, who would also cease to exist once Arthur Wrigley was safely home.

He went to one of the airport bars and ordered a snifter of their best brandy. He preferred it to bourbon, which had been George's drink. Now, with more than two million to his name – although that name was neither John Gatwick nor George Colville, and certainly not Arthur Wrigley – he could return to live comfortably at his elegant house on a forested slope that overlooked the harbor and the old Danish fort at Charlotte Amalie. It would be at least two years before he'd have to put on another disguise and do it all over again.

A week later, a worried Jean Tappehorn went to George's condo. The door was open. Inside, a cleaning crew from a janitorial firm was getting the place ready for a new tenant.

"Tenant?" she said, when she asked the building manager what was going on. "But George owned his apartment."

When the woman told her the place had been let on a month-to-month tenancy, Jean went home, confused. She tried calling George's phone again, but as with the last twenty times, she was redirected to voice mail – and told, again, that the message box was full.

It was then that she thought she had better call the police. Something awful must have happened to her fiancé.

She was wrong about that, of course. But the chain of events she set in motion meant that something truly awful was about happen to Arthur Wrigley.

TWO

"What do you know about con men?" Detective Captain Denby asked Chesney Arnstruther.

"Probably not enough," the young man answered. "Why?"

They were seated in the grand living room of what had formerly been the palatial mansion of Billy Lee Hardacre, ex-labor lawyer, ex-bestselling novelist, ex-television preacher, and current boyfriend of Chesney's mother, Letitia. Hardacre had passed over all his worldly goods to Chesney and his girlfriend Melda McCann, while he acted as mediator and editor for the new version of the Bible being co-authored by Satan and the historical Jesus, Yeshua bar Yussuf. The Prince of Darkness, the former Messiah, Hardacre and Letitia were holed up in the Garden of Eden, wrestling with the first draft.

"There's this case," said the policeman. "A middle-aged woman seduced and stripped of everything she had. The guy left her with an empty bank account and a mortgage she can't pay."

"Who is he?"

Denby shook his head. "No idea. These guys shed their skins like chameleons." He paused to think. "Is that right? Do chameleons shed their skins?"

The life habits of chameleons were not one of the subject areas Chesney had mastered. He was better with numbers. "Never mind," he said. "You're saying you can't find the guy."

"No trail. He was last seen heading for Chicago. They found his car there. We've got his prints, out of the place he rented, but he's never been arrested, never been in the military. He's a total blank."

"Is that usual for con men?"

"Oh, yeah," said Denby. "This guy, he's in his mid-fifties. He's probably been doing long cons for thirty years. Never been caught."

"So let's catch him." Chesney turned to the empty air in the sumptuous room and said, "Xaphan!"

Instantly a figure appeared, hovering in the air above the Afghan rug. It mostly had the appearance of a half-sized, stocky man in a Twenties-vintage pinstriped suit, complete with vest and watch-chain, and cloth spats buckled over patent-leather shoes. Except that, where a face reminiscent of Edward G. Robinson's should have emerged from the replaceable collar, there was the head of a weasel – but a weasel with eyes like saucers, and a pair of down-pointing canine fangs that would have looked more fitting on a sabertooth bearcat.

In one hand the demon held a tumbler of tawny rum, in the other a smoldering Havana Churchill. It downed half the former, puffed the latter into a healthy glow, then said, "Something you wanted, boss?"

"The captain's looking for a con man."

The fiend turned its lambent gaze upon the policeman, who barely flinched. Until only recently, Denby had been under the impression that Chesney – or at least his alter ego, the costumed crimefighter known as The Actionary – was a time traveler from the future. He had lately been getting used to the idea that the young man was instead the controller, part-time, of a demon from Hell.

Denby's process of adjustment was aided by the fact that John Edgar Hoople, the Chief of Police, was about to announce his early retirement, nominating the captain to be his successor. Chesney and his infernal helper had played a major role in the chain of circumstances that were leading to the detective's impending promotion to the very apex of the departmental pyramid.

Xaphan did not ask for more information about the subject of Denby's investigation – demons instantly knew whatever their employers needed them to know. Now it gestured with the stub-fingered hand that held the cigar. Its smoke cohered in one place, spreading to become a gray screen that hung in the air. An image filled the screen: a small, silver-haired man stood facing an old-fashioned, brass-headed bed in a white-walled room. He was also facing a naked, red-haired woman who knelt on the mattress in front of him. The man's pants were around his ankles and he was taking full, though leisurely, advantage of his situation.

Chesney and Denby watched for a moment, then the young man said, "Go and get him."

"You want I should bring him here?" the fiend said.

"Yes."

Xaphan took a moment to finish the rum in its glass. "You want I should let him finish?"

"No."

"Wait," said Denby.

The demon and the young man turned their gazes his way. "There's a problem," the policeman said. "I can't just arrest him."

"Why not?"

The detective sighed. "You know what guys like him get? First offense, white-collar crime – two years maximum. Real time, maybe a year in a minimum-security country club, then he gets parole. They always get parole. They're model prisoners."

"What are you saying?" Chesney said.

"And you don't get the money back. Maybe some of it, but they know how to squirrel it away so you need an army of accountants–"

"Do you want him or not?"

"Oh, yes," said Denby, "I want him. The woman he ripped off is my cousin's husband's sister. A decent, church-going Baptist lady, and he made her feel like something you'd scrape off your shoe."

"But?" said Chesney.

The policeman made a face and a gesture that together said that life was not a wide, straight road, and sometimes you had to take side streets that led you through neighborhoods you wouldn't want to linger in. "It's gotta be off the books," he said.

Chesney looked at him. A few weeks before, the metaphor would not have held much meaning for him. He had spent almost all of his nearly thirty years as a high-functioning autistic. His world had consisted of a few clear pools of light, most of them to do with numbers, in which he felt absolutely competent, surrounded by vast tracts of pure darkness in which nothing made sense. As a child, he'd had to be trained by therapists to read human facial expressions, so he would be able to tell when people were angry or pleased with him.

But in recent weeks, he had spent some time in the presence of Yeshua bar Yussuf of ancient Nazareth, who now went by the name Joshua Josephson. Joshua's divinely granted healing powers had cured Chesney's defect, leaving him for the first time capable of navigating the spectrum of gray reality that had formerly been invisible to him.

At first, Chesney had welcomed the change. In his old state, he had either known things instantly or had been incapable of understanding them at all. But now the new Chesney could examine situations and figure out right from wrong, could even choose between two evils to identify the lesser one. Yet, as the weeks had gone by, the novelty had begun to wear off, and he was wondering if being able to deal with emotions – others' as well as his own – was actually a gain.

Life had been a lot simpler before Joshua.

"Off the books? How far off?"

"Well," Denby said, with a shrug, "obviously, we got to get the money back. For Jean – that's my cousin's sister-in-law – and there's another victim, a real estate developer who's looking at…" – he mimed an index finger to one temple while the thumb flicked up and down like the hammer of a pistol – "…as his way out. Insurance will still pay out even if it's suicide."

Chesney turned to Xaphan. "Can we get the money back?"

The demon tapped cigar ash that disappeared before

it reached the Afghan. Chesney and the fiend had had a discussion about tidiness. "Sure," it said, "I can get the dough. That's jake."

Beside Xaphan, on the screen of smoke that still hung in the air, events seemed to be moving to a conclusion. The young man came back to the policeman. "So, then what?"

"The developer's OK if we get his money back, but Jean's been hurt deep. These guys, they make the woman fall in love, treat her like she's a queen, then dump her in the ditch."

"So?"

"So I talked to her. She needs some payback. Emotional score-settling."

Chesney understood. It was still a novel experience for him. "How high would that score run?"

"You mean, would she kill him?"

Chesney nodded.

"Would that bother you?"

It was a question that, a month before, would have been meaningless to the young man. Bad guys killed, good guys arrested wrongdoers and handed them over to the police. It was an elegantly simple dichotomy, largely based on his appreciation of the adventures of Malc Turner, a mild-mannered UPS deliveryman who developed special powers after handling a strange package gone astray from a parallel universe. Turner became The Driver, and his standards became the model for Chesney's crimefighting career as The Actionary.

"I don't know," the young man said. "It might." He picked at the concept. "I'm thinking it ought to." He wondered if it would bother Melda, and suddenly he had a strong desire to ask her.

But what if she ruled against it? How should he respond? Or suppose she was all for Jean the Baptist disemboweling the con man, and volunteered to hold him still? How would Chesney feel about that? And how should he feel?

He decided not to involve his girlfriend. The situation was already diffuse enough. "Xaphan," he said, "go and get him and take him down to our place in Hell. Tie him up or something then come back here."

"Sure thing, boss." The demon disappeared. The gray screen lingered for a moment, then began to come apart. Before it did, they saw the little man suddenly disappear from the scene in the bedroom. The redhead turned with a puzzled look on her face to see where he had gone, then the image faded to nothing.

A moment later, the demon reappeared, its glass of rum replenished. "I put him in the corner," it said. "He ain't goin' nowheres."

"That sounds fine," said Chesney. He turned to the policeman. "Now what?"

Denby opened his phone and punched a number. "I'll see if the victim is free." He spoke into the phone. "Jean, it's Captain Denby. You remember that question I asked you, last time we spoke?"

Chesney could hear the woman's voice very faintly as her response caused Denby to hold the phone a little way from his ear. She sounded excited.

"Yes, we have," the detective said. "Would now be convenient?" Chesney thought the tiny voice on the other end of the connection was growling. "We'll be there in a little while," Denby concluded. He closed the phone.

"She can't know about..." Chesney said, indicating Xaphan.

"I've thought about that," Denby said. "Here's my idea."

They picked up Jean Tappehorn in the captain's unmarked blue Crown Victoria. She had dressed in old clothing – a loose checked shirt and denim bib overalls, with a pair of sturdy boots – the kind of thing she probably wore for gardening, Chesney thought.

The policeman introduced the young man as "my associate," without providing a name. When he had held the door to let the woman into the car's rear seat, he handed her a strip of black felt and said, "As we agreed."

Jean took the cloth and tied it tightly around her head as a blindfold. She sat up pertly in the back of the car, head erect. Chesney did not have to use his old acquired skills to see that she was full of anticipation. There was a tight little smile on her lips.

"Here we go," Denby said, and backed out of her driveway. They drove for about fifteen minutes, until they came to a lonely stretch of road that ran through woods on the outskirts of the city. When Chesney judged them to be unobserved, he signaled to his demon, floating alongside the passenger window. Instantly, the car disappeared from the mortal world and reappeared in the outermost circle of Hell, where Chesney kept a room.

Technically, the car did not appear inside the room, but in what appeared to be a closed garage. Chesney and the policeman got out and opened the vehicle's rear door, the policeman telling the woman she could remove her blindfold. She did so and looked around. "What's that noise?"

She was referring to the constant howling wind that endlessly swept across the barren emptiness outside.

"Forced-air furnace," Denby said. "It needs some work."

Beyond the car's hood was a pair of steps and a plain wooden door. Chesney went and opened it. He stepped into his infernal toehold: a mid-sized room, with ceiling beams of ancient, dark oak and a crimson carpet. The furnishings were sparse, just a heavy wooden table and matching chair with brass accents. One wall held a wide fireplace in which a heap of embers smoldered; opposite was a drinks cabinet boasting a full complement of crystal decanters and a cylindrical humidor.

Since Chesney's last visit, two items had been added. One was a stout iron hook driven into a ceiling beam in a corner near the fireplace. The other was the naked man hanging by his ankles, his hands trussed behind his back.

"Xaphan," Chesney spoke to his demon in a manner that only the fiend could hear. "Why is he naked?"

"It's Hell," the demon said. "We're big on tradition."

Arthur Wrigley's face had been strained when they entered. As he focused on Jean and saw her come toward him, his eyes widened. So did his mouth. He made a sound, but it wasn't a word.

Fists on ample hips, she stood and examined him. "Well," she said, after a while, and rubbed her palms together. She looked about her, as if taking in the room for the first time, and her eyes alighted on the liquor. "Is some of that vodka?" she said.

"Yes," said Chesney.

"And is there any vermouth?"

"I'm sure there will be."

"Then would one of you gentlemen mix me a vodka martini, very dry. And chilled, if you have ice."

She turned her attention back to her former fiancé. Chesney spoke privately to Xaphan and a moment later he carried a chilled glass over to the woman. She took it from him without changing the direction of her gaze and downed half of it in one swallow.

"Mmm," she said, the sound hardly making out of the back of her throat, then took a savoring sip. "That's really very good." Then she handed the glass back to Chesney and addressed the hanging man. "You introduced me to vodkatinis, didn't you, George? 'A sophisticated drink for a sophisticated lady,' you said."

"Jean, darling," the man said, "there's been a terrible mistake–"

"Oh, yes, 'George'," she interrupted him, lifting one foot to gently spin him around in a slow rotation. "Terrible."

He was saying other things, but she wasn't listening. She turned to Chesney and the policeman. "I'm going to need some things."

"In the garage," Denby said, indicating the door they'd come through.

They had made a list for Xaphan, specifying that none of the implements should be lethal in the hands of a middle-aged woman. But Chesney wondered, as Jean Tappehorn went over to the bench along one side of the garage and began inspecting this and that item, if they might have underestimated her capacity for inventive mayhem. In the end, she gathered up a braided horsewoman's quirt, a dressmaker's pincushion, profusely and colorfully studded with glass-headed pins, a limber switch cut from a willow tree, and a carpenter's sandpaper block – a medium-coarse grade of abrasive. With these objects in her arms, she turned to the two men and said, "Would you mind waiting out here? Some things are private."

"You mustn't kill him," Denby said. "We talked about that."

"I won't," she said, with a reassuring smile. "Not even if he begs me."

She went through the door and closed it quietly behind her.

"I suppose," the policeman said, "that, if she does any real damage, your demon can fix it?"

"As long as he's still alive," Chesney said.

"Well, then, how about we let Xaphan keep an eye on things and we go back to your place. There's something I need to talk to you about."

"Xaphan," Chesney said. "Do it."

Immediately, they were back at the mansion, the demon hovering over the Afghan rug again. "That skirt, she's got a real good eye," it said. "Knows how to build the tension, too. Coulda used her back when Alphonse was sweatin' Bugs Moran's boys."

Denby looked puzzled. "Alphonse?"

"The last time Xaphan was up here," Chesney said, "he was working for Al Capone. The time before that, he was helping out Blackbeard."

"The pirate?"

"Hence his fondness for rum."

The policeman took a moment to integrate the information into his worldview, then came back into focus. "Have you recovered the money?" he said.

A duffel bag appeared on the floor. "All in there," the

fiend said, "separated into two piles, his and hers."

"All right," Chesney said. "Go back down and keep an eye on things." When they were alone again, he said to the policeman, "What's on your mind?"

"The Twenty."

He was referring to the small group of powerful people who actually ran the city he and Chesney called home. It had begun in 1932 as a score of wealthy and well placed citizens who had banded together to take forthright action that drove Prohibition-era organized crime out of town. Afterwards, the Twenty – now grown to an actual membership of forty-seven – had gradually eased into many of the activities that had been the province of the rumrunners and speakeasy operators they had so roughly evicted. Captain Denby, as an honest but knowledgeable cop, resented their hidden rule over the community, and wanted to break their power.

"What about them?" Chesney said.

"I want to take them down."

"All of them?"

"As many as I can get," the detective said. "And the ones I can't get, I want to make them pull their horns in."

The old, pre-Joshua Chesney would have said, "How can I help?" The new, ostensibly improved Chesney stroked his chin and said, "It's tricky."

"How tricky can it be? You've got a demon that can go anywhere, any time, gather evidence, find where the bodies are buried." He meant the last remark literally. Back when he still thought Chesney was a time traveler, he had been taken back several years to see the accidental, but highly inconvenient, death of a TV news reporter in the offices of a law firm connected to the Twenty. One of the people who had helped dispose of the body was now the Chief of Police. It was Denby's use of his demonically acquired knowledge that had won him his promotion to captain and a free hand to investigate whatever he wanted to.

"There are limits to what Xaphan can do for me," Chesney said.

"What limits?"

"'Hell doesn't fight Hell'," the young man quoted. "My demon can't interfere with anybody else's deal with Hell."

Denby paused, taking it in. "You mean someone on the Twenty has a deal with the Devil?"

"Yes."

"Who?"

"I don't know."

"And you can't ask the demon?"

"I can ask," Chesney said, "but it won't tell me." He held up a hand as he saw the natural question forming in Denby's face. "And it won't tell me who doesn't. The whole subject is off limits."

The detective swore, imaginatively, then stood silent, tugging at his lower lip. Chesney could see him thinking it through. After a while, Denby said, "But it doesn't mean that we can't do anything, does it?"

"It means we can try this or that, but anything that conflicts with the other guy's contract will get us nowhere."

"After a while, though, we might build up a picture, get some idea who's who."

Chesney said, "Yes, but there's another tricky part."

"Well," said Denby, "it's Hell, so there would have to be."

"The tricky part is that I'm covered by 'Hell doesn't fight Hell'," Chesney said, "but you're not. Neither is Melda."

"Ah," said the policeman. "So it could be 'Bug, meet huge foot.'"

"I'm afraid so."

"I gotta think about this," Denby said.

At that moment, Xaphan popped into view, puffing a Churchill between its saber canines. It removed the cigar, inspected the ash, and said, "That dame's moved on."

"Moved on to where?" Chesney said. "She couldn't get out into Hell."

"Nah, I mean she done all she wanted to do with the whip and the pins and so on. Maybe she got a little bushed, all that effort. So she mixed herself another cocktail and sat there for a while, thinkin'. Then she started eyeballin' the fire."

"What's she done?" Chesney said.

"You know that thing they say," Xaphan said, "how you're gonna hold somebody's feet to the fire?"

"We'd better get back down there," Denby said. "Let's bring the money. It might distract her."

The young man addressed the demon. "Do it."

They arrived in the garage and made for the door. They could hear Arthur Wrigley's screams before they opened it. Inside the room, Chesney saw that Jean Tappehorn had lowered the bound man to the floor. She stood with one foot planted firmly on his chest so that he could not wriggle away from the heaped embers in the fireplace, which were slowly cooking the soles of his feet.

The rest of Arthur did not look much healthier. The woman scorned had obviously made hellish use of the switch and quirt, with a judicious application of the medium-coarse sandpaper, so that his hide was more red than pale. She had transferred every one of the pins from the cushion to a particular part of his anatomy, which now might never be of service to him again.

"Jean," Denby said, "I think we're probably done now. By the way, here's all your money back. Plus Pete Eberley's."

She looked down at her former fiancé, who had stopped screaming and was now only emitting low moans. Chesney surmised that the nerves in the soles of Arthur's feet had been cooked into oblivion. When she took her foot off him and went to inspect the contents of the duffel bag, the young man took hold of the battered fraudster by the armpits and dragged him away from the fire.

"It's all there?" she said, stooping and poking a finger through the stacks of currency.

Xaphan communicated something to Chesney, and he passed on the news that there had been more in Arthur's accounts than his recent takings, so the demon had split the overage between her and the developer. "Call it partial compensation," the young man said.

She smiled at him then glanced sideways at the moaning man. "And not the greater part," she said. Then she shook her shoulders, as if preparing herself to open a new chapter, and said to the detective, "Would you please take me home now?"

Denby picked up the bag. "Will do."

She took one last look at Arthur Wrigley, and her face assumed a reflective cast. "I've heard," she said, "that there are men who… like this sort of thing." When she saw Denby's expression, she added, "I don't mean to this level.

But the general approach."

"I've heard that, too," said the policeman, as he led her through the door.

"Where," she said, "would you find such men?"

"The internet, I suppose," said Denby.

She made a small confirmatory noise and allowed him to open the rear door of the Crown Victoria. Without being asked, she put the blindfold back on. Denby put the money in beside her and she gave the stacks of bills a gentle pat.

Back in the room, Chesney said to Xaphan. "You'd better fix him and bring him back to Hardacre's. Then we'll figure out what to do with him."

"You want I should pull out the pins? It makes his dingus look kinda pretty."

"I doubt he shares your view."

The fiend shrugged. "Everybody's a wise guy."

Chesney went to the garage and got into the car's front passenger seat. He signaled to the demon, visible through the open door. Denby started the engine and immediately they were back on the deserted woodland road. They drove towards Jean's house and along the way Chesney told her she could take off the blindfold.

She looked around at the suburbs they were passing through. After a while, she said, "That place where we were, it's not on the map, is it?"

Denby said, "Better not to talk about it."

"I suppose." She was quiet for a moment. "What will happen to him, whatever his name is?"

Chesney answered. "We haven't worked that out yet."

"You can't let him go. He'll just do it to someone else."

"We'll have to see."

•••

"She was right, you know," he said to the policeman as they drove back to Hardacre's estate. "We let him go, he'll go right back to work. And all the sooner, because we took all his money."

"What do you want to do?" asked Denby. "Kill him?"

"What else is there?"

The detective made no answer, and they drove the rest of the way in silence. When they got back to the estate, a dark blue Mercedes-Benz sports car was parked on the gravel apron at the end of the circular driveway. "Melda's back," Chesney said.

Since Chesney had acquired Billy Lee's power of attorney, Melda had quit her job as a nail-care technician at a beauty salon in the city. She was now managing the more-than-forty million dollars in assets that the lawyer-turned-novelist-turned-televangelist had accrued over his triple careers. Chesney had helped at first, until it became clear that she had a natural talent for dealing with money. Then he had stood back and let her rip.

As he and Denby came through the front doors into the wide foyer, she was standing by the entrance to the sitting room. "There's a naked man tied up and gagged in there," she said, gesturing with a thumb over her shoulder.

"We know," said Chesney, crossing the floor and giving her a peck on the cheek. These days, being able to afford any perfume she wanted, Melda smelled even better than before. He took a moment to tell her so.

"Thank you," she said, "but..." She gestured toward the open door behind her.

Denby explained. The young woman's eyes narrowed as the policeman outlined Arthur Wrigley's profession and the effect he had had on Jean Tappehorn and, presumably, a string of other women. When he told her of the last victim's revenge, Melda's chin went up and down in approval.

"I was feeling sorry for him," she said. "All those scars. But not now."

"Scars?" Chesney said. He went into the living room, where the con man lay trussed on the Afghan. He saw at once that Xaphan had healed all of Arthur's wounds, but had allowed each one to be replaced by a corresponding scar. The crosshatching made the smaller man look like a photographic negative of a Victorian etching.

"What's with the polka-dot motif on his johnson?" Melda asked. When told what had caused the myriad little round scars, she gave another nod. "Some women," she said, "you just ought not to mess with them."

She crossed the floor to where the man lay and nudged him with a thoughtful toe. "So what are you going to do with him now?"

"That's what we were wondering," Denby said. "If we let him go, he'll just do it again."

On the floor, Arthur Wrigley was shaking his head in an emphatic no, while making urgent sounds through his cloth gag. When Melda looked down and showed him a face that wasn't buying it, he stopped.

"Xaphan gets rum from a cargo ship about fifty fathoms beneath the Caribbean sea," Chesney said. "If we said, 'Take him there and leave him'…" He thought for a moment, then said, "Xaphan!"

The demon appeared, its stubby hands grasping the usual accouterments. "What's all the rumpus?" it said.

"If I asked you to kill this man…"

The fiend waved a hand in a way that said *Hold it*.

"Nuh-uh," it said. "Demons can't bump youse guys off. One of the rules. We can only help youse do it."

Chesney looked at the bound man. He didn't need to consult Malc Turner. "I'm not killing anybody," he said.

Melda had been thinking about it. "It's not like he'd be missed," she said. Then a small cloud formed on her brow. "No. Just because you can do something doesn't mean you ought to."

"I'm glad you said that," Chesney said. "It's still kind of new to me, this gray-areas thing."

"I suppose," Denby said, "that the Garden of Eden is out of the question."

"It's already got a snake in the grass," Melda said.

But an idea was blossoming in Chesney's mind. On his inner screen, Chesney could see the stony slope above the mud-brick house in which he had found Yeshua bar Yussuf. It had been preserved unchanged, endlessly repeating one last day, because it was part of an early draft of reality that had since been revised. The divine Author, like many of his mortal, uncapitalized imitators, kept his discarded drafts. And a demon, empowered by the will of a mortal being, could move between those drafts.

"Remember Nazareth?" he asked the demon.

"I remember everything."

"Are there other places like that? Pieces of earlier drafts of the great Book?"

"You bet."

"How many?"

"Four thousand, three hundred and seventy-four." The demon's saucer eyes widened. "How about that?" it said and took a long swallow of rum. "I didn't know that until you needed me to know it." It took another sip and looked as philosophical as a sabertoothed weasel could look while puffing on a cigar.

"Wait a minute," Melda said. "Are you telling us there are more than four thousand other worlds that used to exist but got edited out?"

"No," said Xaphan. "There are trillions of worlds. I'm telling you about four hundred thousand, three hundred and seventy-four former universes." It puffed reflectively on its cigar. "Of course, a lot of them were pretty simple."

"What do you mean, simple?" Chesney said.

"Well," said the fiend, "used to be, the universe was only a couple of thousand miles across, and it had this solid dome for the sky with two big lights in it. Up above the sky was water, and same thing down below the ground. That's how rain and wells used to work."

It searched its newfound information store and said, "Huh, that's interesting. Back in the time of the Chikkichakk–" Then the saucer eyes blinked and the fiend suddenly seemed to find the contents of its rum glass fascinating.

"Who were the Chikkichakk?" Chesney said.

"Forget it," said the demon. "You mugs ain't supposed to know about that."

"What do you mean?"

Xaphan looked down at its spats. "I ain't sayin'."

"What if I order you?"

The fathomless eyes came around to Chesney. "That wouldn't be good."

"Satan's already told you to give me whatever I ask for," Chesney said.

"This is different." When Chesney started to argue Xaphan cut him off. The fiend hitched its padded shoulders and shot its french cuffs like Jimmy Cagney about to nail a scene. "Listen, to start with, I was just to give you two hours a day, only in your home town, and only to do with your crimefightin' malarkey. If I gave you exactly what you asked for and it wasn't what you really wanted, hey, that was all part of the standard service, get me?"

"Got you," Chesney said.

"Then things get complicated, and the Boss says, 'Give the kid some leeway, let's see where this thing goes.' So then it's different, and that's OK, cause there are, whattaya call it, compensations." The demon lifted its glass and flourished its Churchill.

"But there's leeway and there's leeway," it said. "I didn't even know about the Chikkichakk until you needed me to know about the other universes. Or put it this way: I used to know there was other universes but I didn't know about that one. Then suddenly I knew about that business. But as soon as I started to talk about them, I knew I wasn't supposed to spill the beans, see?"

"Says who?" said Chesney.

"Never mind. All I know is I ain't supposed ta, so I ain't gonna. You can lay off the third degree. It ain't gonna get you nowheres."

With that, Xaphan drew on the cigar until it was red hot then blew a series of smoke rings toward the ceiling. Chesney felt for a moment the way he used to, when he would wander into one of those fields of darkness he could never make sense of. He wanted to ask Melda's advice, but he noticed that her attention was fixed on the scarred naked man on the rug.

"Let's not get sidetracked," she said. "What we need

to know is, can we drop this guy off in some dead end where he won't come back to haunt us?"

Chesney focused on the practical question. "All right. Xaphan, what's available, like say, the Tower of Babel or Noah's Flood?"

The demon consulted whatever inner resources it had, and said, "That could be arranged. We could drop him off just when everybody starts babbling or when the waters start to rise. Nobody's gonna notice another poor sap."

Chesney made up his mind. "Let's do it."

"Which one you want, Tower or Flood?" Xaphan said. "Or we could put him in one of Pharaoh's chariots just when the sea comes back. That way, you're not icin' him. It's, you know, Himself is doin' it."

Melda shook her head. "It would be like drowning a puppy." She looked down at Arthur, who had begun to wriggle and make noises again. "Not a nice puppy," she said, "but still…"

"Tower of Babel," Chesney said. "Who knows, he might make some kind of life out of it." He looked at the others. "Anybody else coming?"

Melda said she had to get dinner on and Denby said he needed to drive the Crown Vic back to the city.

"Xaphan can whisk you there," the young man said.

The cop waved a hand to say no thanks. "I want to think about some things while I'm driving."

"OK." Chesney turned to his demon. "Tower of Babel it is."

The room disappeared from around him and he found himself in a dusty, rubbish-strewn street lined by two- and three-story houses made of mud brick. Xaphan hovered in front of him, the still-trussed Arthur Wrigley slung over one shoulder.

"Don't point that thing at me," Chesney said, and the fiend floated around to hang beside him. The young man looked down the street and saw that it ended in a wide, open space, floored in more dust. From the center of the plaza reared a dun-colored stepped pyramid, broad at the base but gradually narrowing as it ascended to a seemingly impossible height. An endless file of near-naked men filled a ramp that wound its way, level after level, around the outside of the huge edifice. The thousands of slaves, encouraged by whip-wielding overseers, passed new bricks hand-to-hand up the ramp.

Chesney saw that the top of the building reached to a layer of cloud that spread to either side of the highest level, though the rest of the sky was clear blue to the horizon. As he looked, the cloud darkened and a crackle of lightning passed through the vapor. For a moment, all motion ceased and all eyes looked up. Then someone shouted a command, the whips cracked, and the flow of bricks resumed.

Chesney saw another flash of lightning. "It's coming soon, isn't it?" he asked the demon.

Xaphan clamped its cigar between its teeth and used the freed hand to take out its gold pocket watch. "Five minutes," it said.

"Then let's go." Chesney looked up and down the street, saw only a woman carrying a terracotta water jug on her head, and some urchins squabbling over something in the dust. "Can they see us?"

"Nope." Xaphan set off toward the square, gliding through the air. Chesney followed.

They came out into a vast space, most of which was

taken up by a brickworks. Basket-carrying slaves were hauling mud through a gate in the high city wall beyond which a sluggish river was visible. They dumped the muck into a gridwork of wooden forms, nine bricks to a form, that lay on the ground, then other slaves brought straw from a huge hay mow and trampled the fibrous material into the mud. When the supervising brickmaker judged the work well enough done, he shook and lifted the form so that the bricks lay on the ground under the hot sun. Far away, across the plaza, what Chesney assumed were yesterday's products, now dried and ready for use, were being collected and brought to the base of the spiral ramp.

Chesney watched for a moment, then said, "Better make him blend in." Instantly, Arthur Wrigley was clothed in coarse rags, and a pair of woven grass sandals appeared on his feet.

"That'll do," said the young man. "Lose the ropes and gag."

Xaphan set the man on his feet and motioned with his cigar. The restraints disappeared.

Arthur swallowed, looked around at the busy throng, and said, "Listen–"

But Chesney shook his head and told Xaphan to make the fraudster visible. Almost immediately, a burly overseer noticed the new arrival. He came bustling over, eyes wide in outrage, and said, "What are you doing, standing around, you horrible little man?"

Chesney recognized the language. It was the same one they spoke in Heaven and was understandable to all ears.

The overseer's whip flicked expertly and Arthur acquired the makings of a new scar. He yelped and fled in the direction the man drove him, down toward where a line of slaves wielded wooden spades to dig more mud from the riverbank.

"What now, boss?" Xaphan said.

"Home."

Melda was in what had been Billy Lee Hardacre's study when Chesney arrived in the mansion's spacious foyer. He dismissed the demon and went in to see her. She had converted the study into a home office, from which she managed the former televangelist's fortune. She was seated at the desk, looking at something on the computer monitor, one corner of her mouth askew as she chewed thoughtfully on the inside of her cheek.

He paused in the doorway and looked at her. She was dressed in a black skirt-and-jacket combo with an understated white blouse. The outfit made her look sharp and competent.

"I'm worried about something," he said.

She turned from the screen. "That's not like you," she said.

"I know," he said. "That's one of the things I'm worried about."

THREE

Life began to change for Chesney Arnstruther when he accidentally summoned up a demon and refused to trade his soul for whatever Hell could offer. The incident occurred during a delicate time in the evolution of the infernal realm, and led to the entire rank and file of demondom, both the tempters and the punishment corps, launching their first ever strike. Chesney, as the unknowing instigator of the whole business, had found himself in a difficult position. Satan himself had personally expressed his anger at the young man.

Needing guidance, Chesney had gone to his formidable mother, and she had taken the matter to Billy Lee Hardacre. The former labor lawyer-cum-novelist-cum-TV preacher had deduced that the situation validated the theory that had been the basis of his Doctor of Divinity thesis: that the universe was a book that the deity was writing. The reason for the divine project was summed up in the words of Hardacre's prologue: *The best way to learn some things is by reading a book; but for other things, the best way to learn is by* writing *a book*.

God was writing a book, Hardacre maintained, in order to understand morality. And, like many an author, He was revising the tale as He went along. In the present draft, He was doing something He hadn't done before: allowing some of the characters to become aware of the true nature of what they thought of as reality. God wanted to see – again, as many an author has done – where they would take His story. Which had now become *their* story.

None of that had been of any concern to Chesney. As a high-functioning autistic actuary for a small midwest insurance company, his world had revolved around numbers that, he sometimes said, sang to him in a symphony of order and predictability. He was also a devotee of what he always referred to as "comix" even though the world had long since moved on to calling them "graphic novels" – especially the adventures of Malc Turner, aka The Driver.

But when he became, for a short time, the lynchpin on which the entire structure of reality turned, Chesney saw an opportunity to fulfill a dream. As his price for resolving Hell's labor dispute, he became The Actionary, a costumed crimefighter with a demonic helper. He then set about cleaning up crime in his native city, although the results of his efforts were not always what he anticipated.

Still, he usually managed to keep himself within the pools of light in which he felt secure, and to ignore the surrounding fields of darkness. But then had come the association with Joshua, rescued from an earlier draft of the great book. Joshua couldn't help healing those who came in close contact with him. He had healed the actuary's autism. All those fields of darkness had now become, at least in theory, comprehensible to Chesney

Arnstruther. At the same time, his pools of light had disappeared, blended into the general illumination.

And he wasn't at all sure he liked it this way.

"I've been thinking about Poppy Paxton," Chesney told Melda, coming into the study and sitting in one of the chairs.

He noticed right away that she sat more upright and a little line formed between her brows. The old Chesney wouldn't have read the meaning of those changes, but the new version did, and understood the sharpness in his girlfriend's voice when she said, "Why are you thinking about that b–"

She cut herself off and softened her tone. "Why?"

"What happened to her, it was pretty awful," he said. Nat Blowdell, a political consultant her father had engaged when he was planning to run for governor – and, maybe someday, president – had kidnapped her and carried her off to Hell. Blowdell was using her as bait to draw in The Actionary for a final confrontation.

Chesney, aided by Melda, had rescued the young woman, but the experience had been traumatic. Xaphan had removed her memory of the events, but demonically-induced amnesia represented a rough-and-ready intrusion into a fragile human psyche. Poppy Paxton was today only a shadow of what she had been.

"You had a crush on her," Melda said.

He shrugged. "It's gone now."

"All of it?"

"All. All gone."

Now it was her turn to shrug. "She got what she deserved."

"Did she?" Chesney considered the idea. Poppy had been vain and willful. She was used to getting her own way, spoiled by a doting father. He understood that now. But did that mean she deserved to be dragged down to Hell, even the outermost circle, then to have her brain addled by a fanged weasel-headed demon? "No, I don't think so," he said.

Melda softened a little more. She could be tough, Chesney had come to understand, but she could also be tender. He liked that he could now recognize such qualities in her. It was like suddenly being able to see in color after a lifetime of knowing only black and white.

"All right," she said. "She got a bum deal. But what can we do about it? Xaphan fixed her as good as it, a demon, can, right?"

"I suppose," Chesney said. "I guess I want there to be another option. No, I feel like there *ought* to be something I can do."

"You could take her to see Josh."

He shook his head. "I thought about that. Trouble is, he has no control over his healing power. It's not like something he does; it's more like something that happens through him. So he'd fix her, all right, but it would be with her memory fully restored. Then what would we do with her? We can't keep stacking people up in the Garden of Eden."

"Besides which," she said, "she might not want to go there."

Chesney realized, not for the first time, that he hadn't yet got the hang of seeing all sides of a question. "Maybe we should get some advice," he said.

"Who from? Your mother? Your demon?" She looked

at Chesney until he caught on that she wasn't offering serious suggestions. Then she said, "No, we'll have to figure out Poppy all by ourselves. In the meantime, let's just leave her on the shelf, OK?"

"I'm still going to worry about her," he said.

"So you should. It's what nice people do when they've messed up somebody's life. Even when the somebody helped quite a bit."

"It was a lot easier," Chesney said, "before."

"For you, maybe," his girlfriend told him. "The rest of us had to do a lot of working around."

When Xaphan went back to Hell, it did not report to its supervisor. It hadn't reported in for quite a while. That was because the Devil himself had instructed the demon to give the young man whatever he asked for, whenever he asked it. Xaphan reasoned, in the simple, self-serving way that demons do their reasoning, that meant being on call all the time. Which meant it could not resume its former duties as foreman in charge of a platoon of tempters.

Of course, while it was on call, it could legitimately spend its non-working time maintaining Chesney's toehold in the outer circle of Hell. And it could define said maintenance as sitting in one of the room's armchairs, drinking overproof rum it had rescued from the cargo hold of a storm-sunk freighter, and smoking Cuban cigars taken from the inventory of a Havana factory that was in the process of burning down.

The demon was performing both activities to its complete satisfaction when the air was suddenly split and almost the entire volume of the room was filled by a demon the size of an elephant, although it had the general appearance of a mouse – if you allowed for the elongated snout that was overfilled with the curved, conical teeth of a Nile crocodile. Xaphan recognized Satan's first assistant, Adramalek, a demon on which the ruler of Hell had personally conferred the rank of archduke.

The relative sizes of the huge archduke and the not-very-big room meant that Xaphan found itself closer than was comfortable to the other's fangs. It dropped the cigar and tumbler of rum – they disappeared before they reached the stone floor – and eased itself up the back of the armchair until it was perched on the top of the seatback. "Help you?" Xaphan said.

"You haven't reported in."

"I'm working fulltime with my insignificance." The fiend used the common infernal term for what humans called a soul.

Adramalek's pink mouse hand suddenly held a piece of parchment covered in hand-written sentences grouped into clauses. It bore the signatures of Satan and Chesney Arnstruther. "The contract says you're to work with him only two hours out of twenty-four."

"There was an amendment," Xaphan said. "I'm on call twenty-four hours a day now."

The huge mouse's back hairs bristled. "We don't amend contracts. A deal is a deal."

"Not when the Boss and the insignificance shake on it."

"The Boss let a deal change? In favor of the insignificance?"

"That's about the size of it. Besides that, I now report directly to Himself."

There was a silence, marred only by the faint sounds coming through the stone walls of the howling winds that constantly scoured the outer circle of Hell. Then the archduke said, "The Boss told you to report to him only?"

"Yep."

"Personally, face to face?"

"Uh huh."

"Just where exactly did this conversation take place?"

"You don't know?"

"If I knew, I wouldn't be asking, would I?"

The question put Xaphan in a difficult position, which had to do with the fundamental underpinnings of the universe. The prime driver of all Creation was the quality that humans called "will", especially "free will". Humans had it, because the deity had given it to them. Satan had it too, and from the same source, though the divine thinking behind that decision had never been explained. But angels and demons did not have will of their own; they had to borrow it from those who did.

Angels borrowed theirs from the prime source, and so they could do whatever God wanted done, and were absolutely incapable of doing anything He didn't want. The same applied to knowledge: Heaven's operatives knew whatever the deity wanted them to know, and nothing else. Beyond whatever information they were allotted, they were incapable of working out any other knowledge. They were simply not equipped to think.

Demons were in much the same condition, except that their borrowed will came from Satan, who had a huge supply of the commodity, and from humans who chose to league themselves with the forces of darkness. Thus Xaphan could come and go in the world as long as Chesney willed it to do so; and Xaphan would know whatever it needed to know to fulfill Chesney's will. And it could think a little, but only within the boundaries of fulfilling its insignificance's will.

So if Adramalek did not know that Satan was holed up in the Garden of Eden, trying to work out a new book of reality with the man who used to be Yeshua bar Yussuf of ancient Nazareth, there was only one conclusion to be drawn: the Devil didn't want his first assistant to know what he was doing.

"What makes you think," Xaphan asked the monstrous mouse, "that I would know something you wouldn't?"

The archduke turned its head so that it was regarding the weasel-headed demon from one lustrous black eye. Xaphan could see its own reflection looking back. "Something," said the senior demon, "is going on."

"Something," said Xaphan, "is always going on."

"There's talk," said Adramalek, glancing around as if it was possible for someone else to be in the now overcrowded room, listening in, "of a book."

"That so?"

"You know anything about that?"

"Maybe. Depends on what book we're talking about."

The elephantine mouse moved in closer and dropped its voice to a whisper – a loud whisper, because it was coming out of a huge set of vocal cords, but a whisper nonetheless. "A book that changes everything."

"That would be some book," said Xaphan.

"A book that could make a case for a whole new set of rules."

Xaphan resembled a sabertoothed weasel struggling to understand a new concept. "A rule book?"

"Not a rule book, you idiot!" The archduke drew back and studied the smaller demon, as if trying to decide whether it was dealing with genuine stupidity – which was not uncommon in the lower ranks of demonhood – or feigned ignorance. It decided to push on. "A book that we're all part of, that everything is part of."

"Like I say," said Xaphan, "that would be some book."

"A book," the other demon said, "that sometimes gets rewritten."

Xaphan shrugged. "I guess that happens to books."

"And when it does, we all get rewritten, too. Except we don't know it."

One thing Xaphan knew from his long existence as a demon in a hierarchically organized underworld: always shift responsibility upwards. "You oughta take that up with the Boss," it said.

"I'd like to," said Adramalek, "except I don't know where he is."

"How bout that?" said Xaphan.

"But it seems you do."

Another silence now settled on the scene. Satan's first assistant was waiting for a response, and the junior fiend had the impression it might not wait too long.

Xaphan was, by its demonic nature, not a thinker, but it could recognize a situation where some figuring out was called for. "The way I see it," it said, "if I know where the Boss is, it's cause he wants me to know it. Right?" The fiend paused and spread its stubby-fingered hands until it got a nod from the archduke.

"And if you don't know where he is, that's because he don't want you to know. Am I right again?" The mouse eyes narrowed until Xaphan couldn't see its reflection at all. The archduke made no other response.

"So if he wants me to know and don't want you to know, he probably doesn't want me to tell you, right?" Xaphan held up one index finger in inspiration. "Tell you what, hows about I go ask him if he wants me to tell you? And, while I'm at it, do you want I should tell him why you're askin'?"

The silence that followed was even deeper, or maybe the winds outside had grown louder. Adramalek's eyes were mere slits now, but the little bit of black that showed between the lids gleamed as hard as obsidian. "No," it said.

A moment later, Xaphan was alone again. The fiend slid back down in the armchair and arranged for its hands to be filled once more. It drew a thoughtful lungful of cigar smoke, blew it out, then swallowed some rum.

"That mug's right, though," it said to the empty room. "Something's going on."

Something was definitely going on at Police Central. Chief of Police J. Edgar Hoople had called an unexpected news conference on only an hour's notice. Reporters and camera crews were still finding their way into the first-floor briefing room when the Chief strode in and positioned himself behind the lectern adorned with the Department's coat of arms: a pair of crossed nightsticks beneath which was the Latin motto, *habemus vos in manos*. It was supposed to translate as "we have you in our hands" and convey the meaning that the public was being safely protected, but the Department's rank and file preferred the alternate translation: "Gotcha!"

Hoople was wearing his "serious public business"

face as he scanned the room. He had timed the event carefully, waiting until both Mayor Greeley and Police Commissioner Hanshaw were out of town. The former was at a conference of big city mayors, where his participation was limited to voting against any measure he didn't fully understand – which was most of the agenda – unless he was confident it would lead to more state or federal funds ending up in the city treasury.

The Commissioner was visiting a highly discreet establishment in a neighboring state where he could indulge himself in certain harmless sexual eccentricities that, were they ever to become public knowledge, would end his career and marriage, and make it difficult for him to walk down the street without seeing fingers point or hearing snickers, if not guffaws. Hanshaw always checked into the place under an assumed name that he assumed, wrongly, gave him anonymity. In fact, every member of the Twenty, that cabal of the wealthy and powerful who actually ran the city, knew of his odd preferences, which had won him the nickname, behind his back, of Babycakes.

"Ladies and gentlemen," said the Chief of Police. "I have a brief announcement. I have decided that the time has come to spend more time with my family. I am therefore taking early retirement and will be resigning as your Chief of Police, as of 5 o'clock this afternoon. My last official action will be to appoint my successor."

Hoople looked to the side door through which he had entered thirty seconds before. He was about to beckon to the man standing there, but he was interrupted by a veteran police reporter seated in the front row.

"Uh, Chief," the man said, "do you actually have the

authority to appoint the next Chief of Police? Isn't that the Commissioner's job?"

Technically, the man was right: it was Hanshaw's responsibility to name the new head of the Department. In practice, though, the Commissioner made no decisions more significant than where he would have lunch without getting the say-so from Boss Greeley. But at this moment, Chief Hoople was not operating on the basis of technicalities nor practices; he was acting out of necessity. If he did not resign and name Captain Denby to replace him, the detective would tell what he knew about the Chief's role in the disappearance, eighteen years before, of a young woman who had been assistant producer of a local TV newscast.

Cathy Bannister's death had been accidental, but it had occurred in the offices of Baiche, Lobeer, Tressider, an establishment law firm closely connected to the Twenty, where she had gone to get damning information on transactions the Twenty did not want brought to light. Chief Hoople, then a detective lieutenant, had helped dispose of her body – one of several useful services he had performed for the oligarchy that had steadily moved him up the promotion ladder.

But now Denby knew all about that. Worse, the Chief believed that the detective was working with a time traveler from the future who could deliver evidence that would see the Chief spend his retirement in prison. Worst of all, the time traveler had personally hauled Hoople to a desolate place where the air stank and freezing winds had chilled his flesh. In a voice like that of the Wizard of Oz – the amplified one, not the little putz behind the curtain – the man from the future had promised to abandon the

Chief there. By comparison, the Gray Bar Hotel was a paradise.

So now J. Edgar Hoople fixed the impertinent reporter with his best *I take no nonsense* gaze, the one he practiced in the mirror, and said, "Article 14, Section 12, Paragraph 3, Subparagraph (a) of the Department's Charter says, and I quote, 'The Chief of Police is empowered, at his sole discretion, to appoint officers to all ranks of the Department, based on merit.' Last I looked, Chief of Police is a departmental rank."

He waited to let that one sink in, then said, "The man I am appointing is a senior officer with an unequaled record. He personally apprehended The Taxidermist, and he found Cathy Bannister." Hoople was proud that he was able, because of practice with the mirror, to say the next few words with a straight face and a clear voice. "He is one of the finest officers that I've been privileged to serve with."

He gestured now toward the man in the doorway, and as Captain Denby came to join him at the lectern, wearing his own serious-business face, the Chief spoke his name and began a round of applause that spread through the room.

Denby said, "Thank you, Chief Hoople," and turned toward the reporters. "I've got nothing to say at this time, except that it's an honor to serve the people of our city and I will do my best. In the next few days, there'll be a news conference at which I'll answer all your questions."

With that, he shook the Chief's hand, holding it while the still photographers snapped their shots and the reporters shouted questions, just in case they got an answer. Then Denby led Hoople back to the door through which they'd entered. Beyond it was a hallway that ended in an elevator well. The two men got into the private car and the Chief pushed the button for his office floor.

When the door closed and they were alone, Denby said, "The other part of the deal is you give me all the private files."

Hoople had sagged the moment the elevator door had closed. He handed Denby a small steel key, the kind that unlocked a safe that doubled as a secure filing cabinet. "You got 'em," he said.

When they emerged, Hoople crossed to the desk and collected a briefcase that stood on its polished top. He looked around at the cups and plaques and framed photographs on the shelves and walls, then turned toward the elevator.

"You don't want your stuff?" Denby said.

Hoople pushed the button and the car elevator opened. Without turning back to the new Chief, he raised a hand in a gesture that said, *Who gives a shit?* and stepped into the car.

Denby looked at the key in his hand, then at the tall, steel-doored cabinet in the corner. "OK," he said, "here we go."

An hour later, he was deep into the files when the phone rang – not the multi-buttoned, beige model on the Chief's blotter, but a red instrument in a compartment behind a little door in one leg of the pedestal desk. It had no dial.

Denby brought it out, set it on top of the desk and lifted the handset. "Hello."

The voice that spoke in his ear was smooth and relaxed, the voice of a mature man for whom it has been a long,

long time since he encountered any situation of which he wasn't the master. "Chief Denby?"

"Mr Tressider," said the policeman.

"You were expecting my call." It was not a question.

"I was."

"We should talk."

Denby looked at the papers spread before him. "I think so," he said.

"What," said the voice in his ear, "do you think should be the nature of our conversation?"

The detective paused. He knew what he was going to say, but sometimes it was better to let the other side of a conversation wait for a few heartbeats. After a few moments, he said, "Problems. And opportunities."

Tressider did not play the same waiting game. He said, "And which of those are you to me?"

"Oh," said Denby, "I'd like you to see me as an opportunity."

Now there was a pause, then he heard a chuckle. "That," said the man on the other end of the line, "is what I've just been telling His Worship the Mayor, as well as the Commissioner of Police."

"I suppose they saw me as a surprise," said Denby.

"They did," said Tressider. "I didn't." The policeman waited again. After a moment, the other man said, "We should meet."

"Sure. Come on over."

"Better not. My office?"

It was Denby's turn to chuckle. "Better not."

"Neutral ground, then," said Tressider. He named a restaurant on the city's west side, a place where the menu listed no prices and the wine came up from the cellar in dusty bottles.

"All right," said Denby. "Let's say eight, tonight. You'll make the reservation?"

"I already have." The line clicked in the detective's ear as Tressider broke the connection.

"Xaphan!" Chesney said, and the demon was instantly floating in the air beside him, rum and cigar in place.

"What?"

"How is Poppy Paxton doing?"

One oversized weasel eye squinted through the cigar smoke. "Hard to say," it said.

"Why?"

"Depends on what you wanna know. See, her plumbing's working fine, hair and nails growing at a normal rate, blood sugar's good and liver function hunky-dory. She's lost a little weight, but she was wantin' to do that anyway. Her last period–"

Chesney held up a hand to stop the flow. "Psychologically," he said. "How's her state of mind?"

The demon disappeared and reappeared immediately. The short-fingered hand that held the cigar now held a manila file folder. "Read for yourself," it said.

Chesney took the file, opened it. Inside were several pages of paper covered in neatly typed notes. He scanned them quickly, words and phrases jumping out to catch his attention: *post-traumatic stress disorder, lacunar amnesia, repression, fugue state, resistance, panic attacks*. Then he went back to the beginning and read more slowly. The young woman had been examined by a raft of experts, from neurologists to psychiatrists, and their joint conclusion was that she had suffered some kind of emotional shock that was so intensive that she had wiped it from her mind. So far, no brand of therapy – and her father seemed to be working his way through all the schools of treatment – had had any effect.

At the moment she was on a course of anti-anxiety drugs, with twice-weekly sessions of therapeutic hypnosis. Neither one was helping. One of the doctors was suggesting that she be placed in a medically induced coma for two weeks, to see if she would "reboot" when they brought her out of it.

"That's not good," said Chesney, closing the file and handing it back to the demon.

"I seen worse," Xaphan said.

"Hell is not really a proper standard of comparison."

"You want I should monkey with her some more?"

Chesney put up both hands, palms out. "No! You might make it worse."

"I could put her back the way she was," the fiend said. "I mean, before the monkeying."

"Except then," Chesney said, "she would remember going to Hell and everything that happened there. Which would probably mean she'd still have post-traumatic stress disorder and I would be in big trouble."

"It ain't post-whatsit," said Xaphan. "It's what happens sometimes when one of youse gets too close to us. Some of our juice seeps into you. It can make you kinda shaky inside."

"You're saying that contact with pure evil weakens the soul?"

"Yeah, if the s–" It interrupted itself then started again. "If the insignificance is already a few shades darker than usual."

Chesney didn't see how the information helped. He thought for a moment. "What if I took her to see Joshua Josephson? She touches the hem of his jacket and she's healed."

The fiend shrugged. "He's got the moxie, all right. But then you gotta explain him to her, plus he's in the Garden of Eden, so you got to explain that, too. Not to mention the Boss, who's probably not gonna take kindly to a couple buttinskys when he's tryin' to work."

"But after she's over the touch of evil, you could remove her memory again."

The weasel head shook emphatically from side to side. "Nah, once she's had the treatment from that Nazareth guy nothin' I do is gonna stick."

Chesney frowned and thought again. Thinking was still new to him and he wasn't entirely sure if he was doing it right.

"I take it," said the demon, helpfully, "that just bumpin' her off is out of the question. Alphonse used to solve a lot of his problems that way."

"You may," said Chesney, "take it that bumping off Poppy Paxton is not only out of the question, it's out of the paragraph and the whole chapter."

"Then whatta ya wanna do?"

"I want to fix her without restoring her memory. Make it like none of it ever happened."

The demon clamped the cigar between its fangs, shot its cuffs and hitched its pinstriped shoulders. "Tricky," it said.

Chesney waited to hear more. When nothing was forthcoming, he said, "But? There is a but, right?"

Xaphan took the cigar out of its mouth and tapped the

ash off it, the gray powder disappearing before it touched the carpet. It drained the rum from its glass and said, "There was this bird, see, long time back."

"What bird?" Chesney said.

The demon's weasel brows drew together. "Maybe I oughta ask the Boss if I can tell ya."

"Why?"

"This guy, he was kinda a big deal."

"What do you mean?"

The weasel eyes blinked. "Now that you ask me, I got the straight dope. This guy, he could do things – make it rain, heal the sick, make stuff catch fire, even fly a little."

The young man thought he saw the connection. "He had a demon working for him?"

Xaphan shook its head. "Nah, that's why he was a big deal. The mug had magic, the real McCoy. The Boss asks him did he wanna make a deal, the guy tells him twenty-three skidoo."

"I don't get it," Chesney said. "Where'd he get magic powers from, if not from a deal with your side?"

The fiend puffed its cigar into a healthy glow then tapped the ash from the end again. "Well, if it ain't from our side, there's only one side left, know what I mean?"

Chesney pointed a finger upwards. "You mean…?"

"I mean… yeah."

"How did that happen?"

"I only know what I know," said the demon, "and here it is: bout the same time as your friend was goin' around throwin' mugs like me out of our homes–"

"You mean when Joshua was casting out demons that had possessed innocent souls."

"Tomato, tomahto," said the fiend. "But, yeah, bout

the time You-know-who figured He'd give your friend that kind of moxie, He gave this other bird another kind."

"Why?"

"Now you're askin' me somethin' I don't know," said Xaphan, holding out its empty glass and watching as it spontaneously filled with amber rum. "Maybe the Boss knows. And maybe I oughta have asked him before I told you."

"And maybe he wouldn't welcome the interruption," reminded Chesney.

"You got a point there." The demon drank half the glass.

"So who was this guy who had the power? And is he in Heaven or Hell? Cause he's got to have been dead two thousand years."

"No, he don't," said Xaphan.

Chesney waited for an explanation until he realized one was not forthcoming. "Explain," he said.

"He's in one of them other universes, like your friend was."

"And he could heal Poppy?"

The demon consulted its store of knowledge. "Yeah," it said.

"Can we go get him?"

"Uh huh."

"Then let's do it." Chesney rubbed his hands together. He felt almost the way he used to, when he was safe within a pool of light. "What's the man's name?"

The demon said a word that sounded to Chesney like *shmoon*. Then it said, "You'd call him Simon – Simon Magus."

•••

Archduke Adramalek was scanning a list of demons newly available for duty in the punishment corps. A gradual reorganization of Hell's demonic personnel was taking place, now that modern management techniques were being applied to the business of tempting humanity. It had been brought to Hell's attention that instead of assigning demons to tempt each and every human being, the effort to lead mankind astray could be concentrated on those persons identified as opinion leaders. Public relations practitioners, many of whom ended up in Hell, knew that if you turned a relatively few charismatic individuals in the direction of darkness, the rest of the human herd would follow. The new thinking meant that demons formerly tied up in the tempter brigades could be reassigned to the punishment corps, to relieve the overstressed fiends that had to cope with the constantly swelling population of the damned.

Adramalek was transferring names from the general list to specific punishment cadres in the several circles of Hell when it came across an anomaly. It called its clerical aide before it and pointed a vast mouse hand to a name midway down the roster.

"Why is Melech on the reassignment list?"

"It must have just become available for reassignment," said the assistant, a demon shaped like a rooster, but with down-curving curved horns sprouting from below its comb and its tail feathers replaced by a hairless appendage more suited to a sewer rat.

Adramalek shook its great gray head, the wiry whiskers swaying with the motion. "That's not what I'm asking," it said. "I'm asking why Melech has been reassigned. We're converting rank-and-file tempters into punishers. But

Melech is – or was – high-grade. It was assigned to work one-on-one with humans who formally signed away their insignificances."

"Oh," said the horned chicken. "Then I don't know."

The huge mouse nodded. "Which raises the question: why?"

"Why don't I know? Because I don't need to."

"Exactly," said Adramalek. "Tell me, when was the last time a high-grade tempter was demoted to…" – the archduke checked the rank notation next to Melech's name and its voice took on an even more pronounced note of suspicion – "all the way down to level one?"

The clerical aide knew the answer. "That's never happened."

"And how could it have happened and we – I – didn't know about it?"

There was only one possible answer, the same one the archduke had so recently heard from Xaphan, and Adramalek was in no mood to hear it again. Satan's first assistant made a decision. "Get Melech in here. Now."

The lower-ranked demon focused its awareness, found Melech in a marshaling area in the sixth circle and issued a command. A moment later, the summoned fiend appeared in the archduke's chancellery. Melech was twice the height of a man, its limbs and torso rail-thin and clothed in tight-fitting black garments. The face resembled a human skull stretched lengthwise, the eye sockets filled with dull black lenses. From the nasal cavity emerged a cluster of wriggling, blind worms.

Adramalek was consulting a document and did not at first look up. Then it raised its mouse head and bared its crocodile teeth in what passed in Hell for a smile.

"Melech," it said, "where have you been?"

"First assembly area, circle six," said the emaciated demon.

The archduke's eyes narrowed. "Before that."

Melech's narrow shoulders shrugged. It raised its eyes to the chamber's stalactited ceiling and said, "Originally, I was in seraphim choir number six hundred and forty-one stationed to the left of the Throne, midway between choir six hundred and–"

"Where were you," Adramalek said, "immediately before you were in the assembly area?"

The fiend hesitated before answering. "I don't know."

The more Adramalek heard that answer, the less enjoyable the experience became. Its voice now carried a tone that caused Melech to take a step back. "How can you not know where you were?"

"I was…" The elongated demon looked about as if an answer might lurk somewhere in the chamber's shadows.

"Spit it out!" said the archduke, heaving its vast bulk in Melech's direction.

The demoted fiend backed itself against a wall, while the horned chicken found a corner to cower in. "I was… disincorporated," Melech said.

The archduke paused with its long, toothy muzzle only inches from the other's face. Long experience in the treacherous hierarchies of Hell had taught Adramalek never to show surprise. Now it said, "Of course you were. And deservedly, too."

It let Melech wait and wonder what was coming next, while its mind tried to grapple with the implications of what it had just heard. Melech had been disincorporated – blown to motes of the spirit-stuff from which demons and angels were made. There was only one power below Heaven capable of doing that to a high-ranking fiend: the autocratic monarch of Hell. And Satan had not found it necessary to do such a thing since the early days of their arrival down here when, in the time just after the defeat of their rebellion, the Devil had needed to establish just who was in charge.

So now the ruler of the underworld had thought it necessary to blast one of his followers to fragments, leaving Melech to undergo the unpleasant experience of gradually recoalescing its substance and regaining its awareness. Temporary disincorporation had always been the ultimate punishment – not even Satan could eradicate spirit-stuff – and it had been reserved for the ultimate crime of rebellion against the First Rebel.

Adramalek was unaccustomed to thinking through a chain of events; demons knew what they needed to know, after all. But the implication here was simple enough: Melech had been disincorporated; therefore Satan had blasted him. Satan only blasted demons for raising their fists against his authority; therefore Melech had rebelled against the Devil's rule. Which ought to have been unthinkable. Yet here was the recoalesced criminal.

Something was definitely going on, the archduke thought. And whatever that something was, Lucifer didn't want his first assistant to know about it. That realization should have ended the matter, but, somehow, it didn't. Adramalek wanted to know what was going on, even though that desire must put the fiend in conflict with the will of the Boss. Which could earn not only a demotion from the rank of second-in-command, but the experience of being blasted into near-nothingness, followed by the lengthy and deeply unpleasant process of reforming itself, then the ignominy of reporting to a marshaling area to be reassigned, probably to work with the least significant of the insignificances.

Demons were slow to think, but quick to make up their minds. The archduke's giant mouse head swiveled toward its assistant. "Get out!"

When it was alone with Melech, still trembling against the wall, Adramalek said, "All right, rebel. Now I want to hear it. All of it. From the beginning."

A few minutes later – the story had to be dragged out of the errant demon, step by step – Adramalek knew what Satan did not want his first assistant to know. Although, it occurred to the archduke, there was possibly a difference between the Devil not wanting him to know a particular set of facts, and the Devil wanting him not to know them. If Adramalek now knew those facts, was that not a prima facie indication that Lucifer's will was not set against his assistant knowing them?

It was a decidedly narrow piece of ground to stand on, but the archduke was willing to try to balance on the edge of the precipice. It regarded Melech and let what it had just learned arrange itself in its mind once again. Melech had been assigned to one Nathaniel Blowdell, a human who had traded his insignificance for a panoply of superpowers that he believed would ultimately allow him to rule the world.

So far, the arrangement had been standard. Hell had been making deals with would-be world-rulers as far back as the late Neolithic, when all there was to rule were mud huts and fields the humans dug with sticks. But then had come the twist: Blowdell had convinced Melech that an immense change was coming soon – something about a great book and the writing of a new chapter that would alter everything. Obviously, Melech was the source of the rumors that were filtering through the underworld.

The truly amazing thing about this was that Blowdell's arguments had been enough to induce Melech to break the cardinal rule: Hell had fought Hell, in the form of Melech attempting to destroy Xaphan and Xaphan's charge, Chesney Arnstruther, in whom Lucifer, for reasons known only to himself, took a deep interest. Satan had intervened, blasted Melech to atoms, and sent Nat Blowdell down into the bowels of Hell – where he remained, suffering exquisite punishments.

Then a new thought suddenly burst into Adramalek's awareness. "Wait a moment," it said to the still trembling former rebel. "This fight between you and Xaphan, where did it occur?"

"The outermost circle."

"Where Xaphan has its hideaway?"

"Yes."

"And the human Blowdell was there?"

Melech nodded. "I'd given him a suit that protected him against the cold and the wind."

"But he died there?"

"Yeah. The Boss was having some fun with him, but Xaphan's human snapped Blowdell's neck."

"And then?" said Adramalek.

"Then the Boss sent him straight from there down to be punished."

"You're sure?"

"It's what I know," said Melech.

Which meant, Adramalek was thinking, that it was

what Satan wanted the fiend to know. But it couldn't be true. The rules said that humans could only be consigned to Hell after death, and death could only take place in the mortal world, between Heaven and Hell. Blowdell's neck may have been snapped, but in Hell that wouldn't have killed him. He had to be still alive. It was a clear violation of the rules, yet the Boss had done it. After blasting Melech for breaking one of the cardinal rules, Satan had knowingly broken one himself.

Something was definitely going on. And Adramalek needed to know what it was, even if Lucifer himself didn't want it known.

The archduke eased away from Melech, went back to the spread of papers on the lectern. It plucked a document from the heap and scanned it, then took up a quill pen, dipped it in an inkwell, and made a notation. "I'm assigning you to Punishment Battalion 92."

"Ninety-two?" said Melech. "Isn't that forgers and counterfeiters?"

"Yes."

The ex-rebel looked as confused as its featureless face could manage. "That's easy duty."

"Yes, it is," said Adramalek. "And you might want to keep that in mind."

"Ah," said the thin fiend. "So what do I need to do for you?"

"I'm glad you understand," said the huge mouse, offering a toothy smile. "Two things you will do: first, you will tell no one of your transgressions nor of this so-called book. If I hear a whisper about it, you will be immediately reassigned to the worst job I can find."

"Agreed. And the second thing?"

"Locate Blowdell and bring him here." As the fiend made to leave, the archduke said, "And do it quietly."

FOUR

The food was foreign, everything covered in its own sauce. Denby had let Tressider order, his command of foreign languages being only good enough to tell him that the menu was all in French. The lawyer also chose the wines, and after his first sip the policeman realized that the kind of wine he had always thought of as a good red was probably what a real connoisseur wouldn't even use to scrub out his garbage cans.

Throughout the meal, their conversation was about the food, the weather, where they had gone to school and where they liked to vacation: Tressider was a Yale Law School graduate who liked the south of France; Denby was a product of North Side High who had been to Cancun once and Vegas twice. The new Chief of Police had read somewhere that gentlemen waited until the port was served before talking business. By that definition, Tressider must be a gentleman, because it wasn't until the smoothly deferential waiter had laid a wooden salver of cheeses and crackers on the table and filled two small glasses from a carafe of blood-dark liquid that the lawyer said, "Well, I suppose we should get down to it."

Denby tasted the port, found it an education, and cut himself a small piece of a cheese he couldn't have named. He chewed it with a bite of cracker, sipped a little more of the fortified wine; the combination amounted to a post-graduate seminar.

He had decided that this encounter was the kind of tennis where he was wiser to let the other man serve. "Go ahead," he said.

Tressider delicately dabbed his lips with his napkin. Denby noted the cloth was spotless. "We were talking about problems and opportunities," the lawyer said.

"Yes, we were," the policeman said.

"What sort of opportunities are you looking for?"

"What have you got?"

Tressider steepled his fingers and regarded Denby for a moment. Then he said, "As we see it, being Chief of Police is an opportunity for you to be of service, from time to time."

"Whenever problems come up," Denby said. "So essentially a reactive rather than a pro-active role."

The lawyer inclined his head. "It's also an opportunity for you to earn our gratitude."

"Just how grateful would that be?"

"Chief Hoople—"

"Ex-Chief Hoople," Denby corrected.

Another slight dip of the silver-maned head. "Ex-Chief Hoople received a quarterly stipend, deposited into an account in the Cayman Islands."

Denby's face remained impassive. He'd figured on that kind of arrangement, but there had been nothing in his predecessor's files. Hoople apparently was not as dumb as he looked. "How much of a stipend?"

Tressider named a figure. Denby doubled it and handed it back to him. The lawyer's eyebrows scaled his forehead. "That's a lot of money for someone who's only been in the position for a few hours."

Denby moved his own eyebrows in a facial shrug and reached for the carafe of port. He was finding that he liked the stuff. "For someone who eased your incumbent out from under your noses," he said, "it's not so much."

He poured himself a refill and one for Tressider then waited for the other man to respond. The lawyer drank half of his without taking his eyes off the policeman then said, "All right."

"Fine," said Denby. "Now there's just one thing."

"What would that be?"

"I like to know who I'm working for."

"You're working," said Tressider, "for the Twenty."

"Yes," said the policeman, "but who is the Twenty working for?"

The lawyer turned his head to one side and regarded Denby as if he were a strange and unexpected specimen. "The Twenty," he said, "are a group of public-minded citizens who guide the affairs of our city in a way that avoids unneeded upsets and disruptions. They are the wise old heads that a mature community requires."

"I've read Hoople's files, and I've been around for a few years," Denby said. "I know what the Twenty is. What I want to know is who's in charge?"

"What makes you think anyone is in charge?"

Denby didn't answer the question. He just kept looking at the lawyer the way cops look at crooks over the table in the interrogation room. After almost a minute, Tressider said, "Well, it's not me."

"I didn't figure you for the boss," the policeman said. "But it seems to me that there's a guiding hand in there somewhere."

"If there was," Tressider said, "and I hope you won't take this wrong, that knowledge would be above your pay grade."

"Chief of Police was above my pay grade not long ago. Yet here we are."

"Yes," said Tressider, "except we haven't established exactly where 'here' is."

"Like I said," Denby said, "I'm interested in opportunities."

A question formed in Tressider's face and just as quickly resolved itself. "You've not finished your climb."

The policeman raised his half-empty glass in a salute. "There you go."

Tressider gave him a considering look. "You don't get it all in one day, Chief," he said. "There has to be a… shall we call it a seasoning? You need to be weighed and winnowed, as the saying goes."

It was Denby's turn to nod in acquiescence. "Long as it's not too long a season."

"It's not just time," Tressider said. "Which brings me to another, although related, matter."

"What's that?" said Denby, finishing his glass.

"I hear," said the lawyer, "that you're on good terms with a man who, shall we say, has all the time in the world."

Denby's face grew still again. He said nothing.

Tressider waited until he was sure no answer was coming then went on. "Such a man could also pose problems and opportunities."

Denby shrugged. "He's not under my control."

"Are you under his?"

"No."

"What does he want? What is he after?"

Another shrug. "Hard to say. He's not like us."

Tressider nodded, then lowered his voice. "He's from the future."

"Could be," said Denby. "If there is such a thing."

"A parallel dimension?"

"Same answer," said Denby.

"Is he a threat to us?"

"To us? Nah."

"Then is he an opportunity?"

"For us?" Denby shook his head. "He's doing what he does, for whatever his reasons are, and we're mostly just part of the scenery."

The lawyer studied him. Denby maintained his cop face. After a while, the lawyer said, "I need to know more about him, what he's after."

Denby grinned. "Want me to introduce you?"

"No, but I want you to tell me what he does."

The policeman moved his head in a thinking-it-over gesture. "And who will you tell what I tell you?"

Tressider showed a small smile. "Again, Chief, that's above your pay grade."

"My present pay grade."

Another nod of the head, then the lawyer said, "We'll arrange your Cayman account and deposit your stipend for this quarter. Further installments will come on the first day of each quarter."

"Fine."

"We'll need to know where you are. Make sure your office always has your current contact information."

"No problem."

Tressider drained his glass and said, "Then we're done here." He stood up and didn't offer his hand.

Chesney found Melda in the office, financial statements spread across the desk that had been Hardacre's but was plainly now hers. She looked up as he came in and said, "Do you know what credit default swaps are?"

Chesney searched his memory. "Only that they're abstruse financial instruments. Why?"

"I'm wondering if we should diversify our portfolio."

"I don't think of myself as someone who has a portfolio," the young man said.

"Well, maybe you should start, because that's what you are now."

"I think," said Chesney, "that I would like to leave all that to you. I have... other things on my mind."

She had dropped her gaze back to the papers. "Our cash flow is way down," she said. "Billy Lee used to have a steady revenue stream from his TV program, but that's all dried up. And the royalties from his novels are just dribs and drabs."

"How much money can we need?" Chesney said.

Melda gestured at the well-appointed room and, by inference, the mansion they were now living in. "This place has a lot of overhead. Do you know how much it costs just to keep the lawns mowed? Then there's the heating bill, and the taxes..." She went back to the papers, humming tunelessly.

Chesney went and looked out the window at the lawn.

He'd seen a man riding a mower over it a day or so ago, and he was pretty sure he'd also seen someone pulling a big steel roller across the turf. It might have been the same man, or someone different. "I'm still wondering what to do about Poppy Paxton," he said.

"Well, don't," she said, not looking up. "She's well looked after."

He continued to look out at the lawn. "You know," he said, after a while, "if we needed money, I could probably get Xaphan to bring us some gold or jewels. There's plenty of it a mile or two underground."

She looked up at him now, and he didn't need his old training to see that she was puzzled by his remark. "What would be the fun in that?" she said.

"What's the fun in credit default swaps?"

She looked at him for a few moments then said, "Maybe what you need is to go out and bust some bad guys."

"It's not that easy anymore. Xaphan says I've scared the really bad ones out of town."

"Then go out of town after them."

He grimaced. "You know I'm only allowed to fight crime in the city."

"I know that was the agreement," she said, "but so was the business of only having Xaphan for two hours a day. The Devil's given you leeway on time, maybe he'll give you leeway on geography."

"You think?"

"I think it's worth finding out. It would be good for you, and it's gotta be good for the world to have a few less crooks running around."

He let the idea settle into his mind, envisioning bursting onto the scene of some crime-in-progress and foiling the evil-doers, like Malc Turner. After a while he said, "I'll do it."

But when he opened his mouth to call up his demon, Melda said, "Not here. I'm trying to work."

"The old burg ain't the same," said Xaphan. The demon looked around at twenty-first century Chicago and shook its head. "One of the differences between you mugs and us," it said. "Youse guys are always changin' the neighborhood. Our place, it always stays the same."

"Not true," said Chesney. "None of this would have happened if Hell hadn't been changing. You wouldn't have gone on strike, for one thing."

The demon looked up at the Willis Tower visible above the rooftops and curled its lip behind one sabertooth fang. "The place had more class back in the old days."

The young man waved the argument away. "Let's get to business," he said. "Where are the bad guys?"

"Over this way," said Xaphan, stepping out of the shadowed doorway of a sporting goods store in which they had appeared. Chesney was dressed in the gray-toned costume and half-mask of The Actionary, his crime-fighting persona. Moments before, he had been in the foyer of Hardacre's mansion – now effectively his and Melda's – then had come a brief passage through his toehold in Hell, though not too brief for the fiend to acquire a Churchill and a tumbler of rum. Now, demonically rendered invisible to anyone who might be sharing these darkened, night-time Chicago streets with them, they proceeded at a brisk walk – or, in Xaphan's case, a brisk mid-air glide – toward a four-story brick building squeezed between two taller, newer structures.

The shabby low-rise probably dated from when
Xaphan used to ride around these same streets on the
running-board of Scarface Al's armor-plated Packard. In
those days, it would have housed the offices of small-time
lawyers, accountants, doctors or dentists, some of whose
names still appeared in faded gold and silver lettering on
the upper-floor windows. But now those windows were
uniformly painted over from the inside with industrial
green paint, and glowed from within, but dimly and with
a faint light that looked cold to Chesney.

"It's all going on in there, right now?" he asked the
demon as they stopped on the sidewalk outside the closed
front door and looked up.

"Want me to show you?"

"Yes." But as a screen formed in the air in front of the
young man's eyes, he said, "Not that way. Lift me up to
the top floor and activate my x-ray vision."

He had been wanting to try out the new power,
now that he and Xaphan had worked out the initial
misunderstanding that had had Chesney's eyes actually
emitting bursts of high-intensity radiation. Now he
wasn't exactly sure of the mechanism involved, but he
was satisfied to be able to look through walls without
exposing anyone on the other side to a heightened risk of
cancer or birth defects.

Hovering in the air outside a top-floor window, he
looked. A portion of the wall and the green-glowing
glass disappeared, as if he were looking through a round
hole ten feet in diameter. Inside, a high-ceilinged space
had been divided into a warren of cubicles, each just big
enough to hold a small cot, and each cot just big enough
to hold a small woman.

There were women in most of the cubicles, and most of them were with men. They were doing the kinds of things that Chesney, before Melda, used to know only from pornographic videos he rented and carried home in unmarked bags. But even his largely untutored eye could tell that these women were not enjoying their activities as much as the women in the films. The ones that weren't engaged were lying on their cots staring at the ceiling, or sitting on them staring at the walls or at their hands. A few were gathered in a small room in a corner of the floor, sitting on chairs and drinking coffee and soft drinks, talking to each other.

"Let me hear them," Chesney told the demon. Immediately his ears became more sensitive than a bat's. He could hear grunts and moans and rhythmic noises from the cubicles, the soft voices of the women in the break room. Some of them were speaking what sounded like Chinese, a couple were talking in Spanish. One woman who was alone in a cubicle was whispering softly to herself what might have been a prayer, in a language that might have been Russian.

Chesney felt a stirring of emotion. It threatened to grow stronger if he let it, and he knew that would not be useful. So he pushed it down, employing a technique he had recently learned and never needed when he lived in pools of light surrounded by darkness. "Next floor down," he said to Xaphan.

They descended to the third floor, but the sights and sounds there were no different, except that more of the cubicles were busy. He told Xaphan to take them down one more level. When he aimed his penetrating vision at the interior, he saw that here the spaces were larger, the furnishings less utilitarian, and the women younger – in many cases much younger. "They're just girls," he said.

"Yep," said the fiend.

Chesney had been researching trends in crime. He had learned that human trafficking had become a major international criminal enterprise. Young men and women, boys and girls, from Asia, Africa, Latin America, and what used to be called the Eastern Bloc, were smuggled into America to work in sweatshops and brothels. Sometimes, they had been inveigled into taking on debts that they could never repay. Sometimes they were simply beaten into compliance, or the gangs that owned them threatened to take reprisals against their families back home.

When he understood the scope of the problem, Chesney said, "That is evil."

"Oh, yeah," said his demon. "It's a doozie."

And so The Actionary decided to do something about it. The nearest big city that was a major node in the human-trafficking network was Chicago. With Xaphan's help, he would crack open one of the brothels and expose the people who ran it to the light of justice.

"Not gonna be easy," said his assistant. "Guys on the scene, they're just soldiers, maybe the right day of the week, you get a capo or underboss. They ain't gonna squeal. They'll do their time, a little off for good behavior, then they're sprung and they go back to work. For bein' stand-up about it, they could get promotions."

Chesney thought about how they had moved an illegal poker game, graced by naked call girls, into Civic Square so that the racketeers involved could be arrested. The ploy had not worked out exactly as planned because a corrupt police force and district attorney's office had managed to hush things up.

"What about the senior police and DA in Chicago?" he said. "Are they as corrupt as ours?"

The demon had moved its stubby-fingered hands in a see-saw gesture. "They ain't like they was in Alphonse's day," it said, "but it depends on who you're talkin' about."

"But there are honest cops and prosecutors?"

"Sure, if you like that kind of thing."

Chesney thought about it. After a little while, he had a plan.

Now, hovering outside the building full of trafficked women and girls, he said to Xaphan, "First floor."

They dropped down and he looked through the great hole that seemed to appear in the building's front entrance – a plain wooden door with a steel core and a peep-hole – set in a wall of old red brick. He could see an office with a cashier's wicket that opened onto a small, shabby lobby. There was an elevator and a stairwell, but the door to the stairs was sealed shut.

There was a fat Hispanic woman behind the cashier's grill and a big black man with a shaved head sitting on a chair in the lobby, next to the door with a peephole. He was reading a paperback, and not watching the closed-circuit television monitor on a table beside him. Behind the cashier's office was a larger room that contained a pool table, a fridge mostly full of beer, a desk and some chairs. Four men were in the room, two of them playing pool, one studying the racing page of the *Sun-Times*, and the other seated at the desk working a calculator and making entries in a ledger.

"Like I said," Xaphan said, "the guy at the desk is a

capo. The others are just soldiers."

"Then we do what we planned," said Chesney.

"You got it." The demon drank the last of its rum and clamped the cigar behind its fangs. "You want 'em now?"

"Yes. Part one."

"Okey-doke." The fiend disappeared. A minute went by, then another. Chesney heard the elevator descend inside the building. A moment later a middle-aged man came out of the front door. A police car rolled down the street, but the two officers inside paid no attention to Chesney – he was still invisible – and barely glanced at the man exiting the building who pulled an electronic car key from his pocket and clicked it to make a car parked at the curb across the street flash its lights. He got in and drove off.

A few moments later, another car arrived. A paunchy man got out, crossed the street, and knocked on the door – two raps, a pause, then one more, another pause and three in quick succession. It opened and the bald-headed man waved the new arrival in. It was all very mundane, Chesney thought, just a business doing business as usual.

Xaphan appeared beside him, cigar glowing and rum glass refilled. "Done," it said. "I put 'em in the empty cots."

"Part two," said Chesney. He was still hovering about ten feet above the sidewalk. "I'll stay here."

"On my way," said the demon. It vanished again. Time passed, then the fiend reappeared. "Done," it said again.

"You…" – Chesney paused as he sought for the right words; *messed with their memories* didn't sound very nice – "made them think what we want them to think?"

The demon blew smoke. "They all think they been

plannin' this for weeks."

"Then let's get on with it."

"Nuttin more to do but watch," said Xaphan. "Here they come."

Around a corner down the block came a police squad car, lights off and silent. Behind it came another, then a sergeant's command car. They rolled to a stop at the curb a hundred feet short of the building. From the other direction came two buses that might have been used for taking kids to and from school, except that they were painted black and had the logo of the Immigration and Customs Authority stenciled on the sides. They also pulled up well short of the building and of the camera mounted above the door.

Men and women got out of the cars and the buses, and lined themselves up, single-file, against the storefronts. Some of them were in uniform, others in plain clothes but with badges hung around their necks on lanyards or from the top pockets of their suit jackets. The ones at the front of each line wore body armor and helmets; they carried shotguns and automatic weapons.

When everyone was in place, a two year-old sedan came sedately around the corner and stopped in front of the door of the target building. A middle-aged man with thinning hair and wearing a wrinkled suit got out and crossed the sidewalk. He rapped on the wooden surface of the steel door: twice, once, then three times.

A moment later, the door opened, but the big black man filled the space. "I don't know you," he said to the man on the doorstep.

"Pleased to meet you," said the newcomer, raising a can of pepper spray and letting the doorman have a two-second stream of the chemical from chin to forehead. The bouncer staggered back, choking, hands going to his eyes, and the man with the pepper spray stepped in after him, holding the door open for the two files of police and ICA agents now surging forward from both directions.

A bell sounded harshly from inside the building. Chesney was still looking through the wall from his position above the front door. He saw the Hispanic woman take her hand off a red button on the wall beside her and turn to run through the door into the rear room. Back there, the pool players had stopped their game and the man who had been reading the racing page was getting to his feet. Then the back door crashed open, thanks to two uniformed and armored men swinging a battering ram. From the alley behind the building, armed men and women swarmed into the room, swinging their weapons to cover the corners and shouting at the surprised occupants to, "Get down! Get down!"

Back in the lobby, cops were hauling the blinded bouncer out into the street, one of them handing him a bottle of water. Somebody found out how to shut off the bell, while a burly officer with a long crowbar pried open the door to the fire stairs.

A man was just coming down the stairs, his clothes disheveled. He took one look at the uniforms filling the lobby and his mouth dropped farther than his comb-over, which was hanging down to his shoulder. He turned to run back the way he had come, but didn't climb three steps before he was grabbed and pulled backwards. A moment later, handcuffed with a white plastic restraint, he was being hustled outside. A uniformed sergeant on the sidewalk looked the arrested man over and jerked his thumb back over his shoulder to the mouth of an alley across the street, saying, "Holding area."

The Hispanic woman and the four occupants of the back room, now all cuffed, were marched through the front office and out onto the street. The sergeant sent them down the street to be placed in the backs of squad cars. A plainclothes policewoman came out carrying a cardboard box full of passports and national identity cards. The sergeant gave her a thumbs-up and she headed over to the buses where she stationed herself beside the door of the first vehicle.

Meanwhile, police were now swarming up the stairs and through the doors into the upper floors, shouting, aiming weapons, grabbing whomever they found and cuffing them. Chesney, rising through the air to observe the action, saw that the apparent chaos was actually well ordered. A stream of men and women and girls was being escorted down the stairs, the sergeant on the sidewalk directing the males to the holding area, the females to the buses. The policewoman with the collection of ID documents was comparing photos against faces.

Another vehicle turned onto the block: a panel van whose sides were painted with the logo of an all-news television station. A few seconds later, bright lights lit up the action in front of the building, and a well-coiffed woman with a microphone was briskly approaching the sergeant. He waved her toward two men in suits who were standing on the other side of the street. She gestured to her camera operator and turned in their direction. Before she got there, another news team's vehicle was rolling up to the scene.

"This is working well," said Chesney.

"Alphonse always used to say I got a talent for organization," said the demon.

"Top floor," the young man said. He scanned the floors as they rose higher, saw an efficient clearing of the building: some thirty customers cuffed and frogmarched to the alley mouth, maybe fifty women and girls also restrained and bundled into the two buses.

"Here we go," said Xaphan. It gestured toward one of the cubicles, where a uniformed officer was shaking the shoulder of a man dressed in a silk shirt and tailored slacks who was sleeping on a cot, his handmade Italian shoes neatly put together on the floor beneath the bed.

"The shoes are a nice touch," Chesney said.

"Yeah," said the demon.

"Let him wake up now," the young man said. Instantly he saw the sleeper's eyes open. The man sat up, looked about him in confusion, then focused on the officer pointing a gun at him. The man swore in Russian, then in a thick accent he said, "I want my lawyer."

In another cubicle, a uniformed cop and a detective were shaking awake another man. This one, when he came out of slumber, spoke with a born-in-America accent, but came around to saying the same thing as the Russian.

The detective handcuffing him said, "You're an assistant district attorney. You are a lawyer." He held up a finger as if a bright idea had just struck. "Hey, you could defend and prosecute, maybe save yourself a legal bill."

They led their collar out of the cubicle and into the path of another arrestee in the custody of a pair of uniforms. "And this is your friend from Immigration," said the detective. "I'll bet he's looking for a lawyer, too."

"We're here investigating," said the ICA agent.

"Sure you were," said the detective.

"Shut up," said the assistant DA. "Don't say anything." Then he saw the Russian being brought out and his face went pale. The gangster's face was like stone, but the eyes he turned on the two men in handcuffs could have passed for chips of black volcanic glass.

The plainclothes cop said to the two crooked officials, "Which of you is going to be the first? Cause that's gonna be the one that goes into the witness protection program. The guy who talks second, he gets to share a cell with Ivan here."

Two more sleepy, confused men were brought out of cubicles, cursing in Russian and struggling even though they were handcuffed. The first Russian said something to them in their native language that made them freeze then look sharply at each other. Then the cops hustled all of them toward the door.

Moments later, they were marched out the front door and down the street, the three Russians to be crammed into the back of a squad car, while the ICA man and the assistant DA each got their own unmarked Crown Victoria. They were accompanied all the way by a cluster of shoulder-borne television cameras, the lights throwing a gaggle of shadows against the storefronts they passed.

Across the street, the women and girls were being matched with IDs and loaded onto the first bus. The second bus was filling with the found-ins. Chesney, hovering with Xaphan ten feet above the sidewalk, watched with interest.

"This is good," he said. "But you're sure the cops are all going to think they've been working on this for weeks?"

"They already do," said the demon. "Youse mugs, youse have lousy memories. Youse only remember a few things, but your brains make up stuff to fill in the blanks. It's why you're so good at foolin' yourselves. There's all these things that you know for sure that really ain't for sure at all."

"Well, for sure we saved those women."

The demon shrugged and puffed its cigar back to a rosy glow.

"What?" said Chesney.

The fiend hoisted its shoulders again. "Saved, schmaved," it said. "The broads all go into detention, some judge sends them back where they come from. They still owe the Russkies or whoever. They still got to make good on that. Probably get sent over again."

"That's awful," Chesney said. He thought for a moment. "Can't we cancel the debts?"

Xaphan showed the face of a weasel that resented being imposed upon. "I gotta do a lot of paperwork, all those ledgers. And these Russian guys, they want to see it all balance. One kopek out, there's a fuss."

"But you can do it?"

The demon frowned at the ground. "Yeah, I can do it."

"Then do it."

Xaphan concentrated. "OK," it said, "done."

Chesney felt relieved. "No point saving them if they just end up back where they started."

"They still get shipped back to wherever they come from. And they still got whatever problems made them hook up with these mugs inna first place."

"Well, that's no good. Can we–"

The demon held up a hand, the cigar wedged between

two stubby fingers. "Listen, boss, you oughta had noticed by now, but every time you solve a problem, there's another problem behind it."

"Yeah, but–"

"You can yeah-but me all night, but there comes a point I got to go ask the Boss just how much leeway he wants me to give ya."

Chesney's first instinct was to say, OK, let's go ask. But the look on his assistant's face told him that might not be a perfect answer. "What?" he said.

"Thing is…" the demon said, then puffed on its Havana as it chose its next words, "thing is, the Boss, he's been known to change his mind."

"How so?"

"He goes this way, is what I'm sayin', then he goes that way." The demon studied the end of the cigar a moment, then said, "He don't want to think about you, cause he's busy. So he leaves things like they are. I show up, make him think again, maybe he says, 'Nah, ditch the leeway. Go back to the contract.'"

Chesney felt a chill. "What does that mean?"

"I dunno. We never went wide on a contract before. Maybe we let bygones be bygones. Or maybe he goes all hard-ass on ya, says, 'Xaphan, all that stuff you did outside the contract, undo it.'"

"He can do that?" Chesney's chill went deeper. "That's not fair!"

His assistant puffed up a blue cloud. "We're Hell," it said. "We don't do fair. We do contracts, to the letter."

"Jingle beezer bats!" There were times when Chesney wished he could swear, but for all the changes wrought in him over the past few months, the taste of his mother's soap still lingered. Nonsense syllables were still his first and only resort.

Xaphan had more to say. "Now, here, I'm speakin' just for me," it said. "I got myself a good deal. I don't got to be runnin' back and forth, supervisin' other demons' contracts, doin' paperwork – you think Russian gangsters are bad, you should see our filin' system. Instead, I help you out, and I get to enjoy some side benefits."

It tapped ash from its cigar and held up the glass in its other hand, which still held an inch of rum. "I wouldn't wanna lose that, see?"

"So what are you saying?"

"I'm sayin' we go on like we been goin'. You do your crimefightin' thing, I'll help you along; you get your leeway, I get my benefits. We won't rock no boats, OK?"

"But I want to make a difference!"

The demon drank off the last of the liquor. "Well, you sure made a difference to that crooked assistant DA. He's already squealin'."

"So he gets off?"

"But the Russkies don't. And maybe one of them spills the beans on somebody higher up the ladder."

"I suppose." But the young man was not happy. "I just wanted to do good."

"You're doin' good," said his demon. "It's just always gonna be messy around the edges."

Chesney thought about his pools of light. "It didn't used to be like that."

"Always been like that, long as I can remember."

"No," Chesney said, "for me it wasn't."

"Sure it was," said Xaphan. "You just didn't notice."

•••

"He was kind of hard to find," said Melech. "I figured he'd be with the other politicians on Turd Island, but nobody there had seen him. Same with the back-stabbers in the worm pits and the pamphleteers with the red-hot iron pens–"

"I don't need to hear your full itinerary," said Adramalek. "Where was he?"

"That's the funny thing: no punishment drill at all. I finally found him in a stone cell in the outer circle, just sitting there."

"I see," said the Archduke, although it didn't quite.

"He's slightly broken where Xaphan's client did his neck," said the bone-faced stick-demon, "and there are pieces of him missing."

"Go away," said Adramalek. "Report to Punishment Battalion 92. And if you want to stay on easy duty," – an oversized mouse-finger indicated the trembling human – "this business stays between us."

"Fine by me," said the fiend, the last syllable coinciding with its disappearing.

Adramalek propelled its bulk closer to Nat Blowdell for a better look. The human flinched backwards from the crocodilian teeth, causing his head to flip forward on his crooked neck. The demon heard fractured bones grate against each other and Blowdell's whimper.

"We're going to have a talk," the archduke said.

The man pointed at his mouth and made a dry, rasping sound. Adramalek looked closely and saw that the tongue was shriveled to the size of a thumb and the other tissue dry as old parchment. The human hadn't had a drink in weeks; he'd be long dead if he were anywhere else but Hell.

"I'm going to fix you," said the demon. It exerted itself slightly and Blowdell's neck straightened. He grew another right foot to replace the one that was missing. The small round holes in his torso filled in, and all of him swelled generally as tissues rehydrated. He no longer looked like something Egyptian tomb robbers would have found on a bier and flung to the floor. Adramalek decided to put some glucose in his bloodstream and some innocuous nourishment in his long-unused stomach and bowels.

The man drew in a long breath and let it go. He looked about him and the demon saw his gaze sharpen. "Don't think," it said, "that you have any hope of controlling this situation. I can put you back the way you were and add some maggots burrowing through your flesh."

The archduke was gratified to see Blowdell's tremble reappear. "Good," it said. "Now, what I want to know is how you convinced Melech to rebel. I want to know all of it, but I don't want any self-serving embroidery."

"The truth, the whole truth, and nothing but the truth?" said the man.

"That's right," said the giant toothy mouse.

"And after?"

"I may put you back where Melech found you. Or I may send you back into the mortal world – where you would work for me."

"Deal," said Blowdell.

"We'll see," said Adramalek. "Now, from the beginning."

Denby used his smart phone to access the Cayman account, following the instructions Tressider had given him. Supposedly, the contact would be untraceable. He entered in the account name and his password, and the screen showed him a balance of $50,000 and a list of options. He logged off and closed the connection, then sat back in the chief's comfortably upholstered chair.

His new job brought him surprisingly little to do. J. Edgar Hoople had been a consummate delegator, having passed most of his duties on to a captain who served as his administrative assistant. One of the new chief's first actions was to call in the captain and tell him that he could either go back into the Department or take an early retirement with a beefed-up pension. The gray-haired policeman had opted for the golf courses of Florida; his time as Hoople's right hand had earned him some dedicated enemies in the lower levels of the pyramid.

"You'll stay long enough to train your replacement," Denby said.

"Sure. Who's that going to be?"

"He's waiting outside." Denby keyed his intercom and told the buxom young woman at the desk outside his office to send the waiting man in. She would soon be departing too; Hoople had not picked her for her secretarial expertise.

The door to the office opened and Seth Baccala stepped in. Denby made the introductions and sent the two men off to begin the changeover process. "Come back and see me when you've got all the forms filled in," he told Baccala.

The smooth young man was back in an hour. "It promises to be an interesting job," he said.

"As long as you're sure who you're working for," said the Chief of Police.

•••

Chesney and Melda ate breakfast, the morning after the brothel bust, watching the TV news channel. The coverage of the night's events had gone national.

"You did a good job," Melda said, watching the video of the gangsters and their friends being perp-walked toward the police cars.

"But I'm not happy," he said.

She took him back to bed and they did the things that had always made him happy before. But after, when they lay side by side, getting their breath back, she heard him sigh.

"I want to have one thing come out right," he said. "Not mostly right, not almost completely right. One thing done right."

She addressed the ceiling. "Poppy Paxton." It was not a question.

He didn't answer right away. But after a while, he said, "Yeah."

"Well then, you'd better see about it."

He turned toward her. "You're sure?"

"Nothing's sure," she said. "But it's the thing you most want to do right."

FIVE

Even after he got the go-ahead from Melda, Chesney was still not sure how to deal with the Poppy Paxton problem. Xaphan had named a man who could help, but the demon was never totally trustworthy. The young man decided that some research was in order. He sat down at the computer and googled Simon Magus. Immediately, the monitor screen filled with links. He clicked on the first one and began to read.

An hour later, he was no better off. In fact, he felt less sure of the worth of Xaphan's suggestion than before he'd started. This Simon was a controversial figure who had been around at about the same time and in the same neighborhoods as Joshua Josephson. Chesney got the impression that the two had been competitors, both performing miracles and both predicting the end of the world. Each had had a following, although Simon's seemed to have mostly died out after he fell – or leaped; the record was unclear – from a building in Rome while trying to demonstrate that he could fly.

He clicked on more links, read more texts, but the more

he tried to bring it into focus, the less clear the picture grew. Finally, he blanked the screen and said, "Xaphan!"

Suddenly, he smelled cigar smoke and a whiff of sulfur. "What ya know, whatta ya say?" said the familiar voice from behind him.

"I'm trying to make sense of this Simon you said could help Poppy."

"Yeah?"

"And it's not working. I need to know, was he a good guy or a bad guy?"

"Yes."

"What do you mean, 'yes'? Which was he?"

He couldn't see the demon shrug, but he knew that the gesture accompanied the answer he heard. "Both."

"You're frustrating me," Chesney said.

"I can only tell ya what I can tell ya," said the fiend. "Some people said he was the cat's pajamas, some people said he was a no-good rat."

"Was he evil?"

"Some days, yeah; some days, no. Like most of youse mugs."

Chesney could feel his temper fraying. He spun around in the chair. "Was he working for your side?"

"You mean, did he have an arrangement?"

"Yes."

"Nah. I told ya, the Boss made him an offer, he turned it down. He was…" The fiend inspected the glowing tip of its cigar, then said, "…a wild card. Like your pal from Nazareth." It paused as if a new piece of information had just appeared in its mind. "Like you, maybe."

"Me?" said Chesney.

The weasel brows drew down as the demon wrestled

with the unfamiliar process of thought. "I'm not sayin' it's for sure," it said after a moment. "But it looks as if sometimes You-know-who gets tired of the way the story's goin', he shuffles the deck and deals out a wild card or two. Then he sees where it goes from there."

"I'm not a wild card," said Chesney. "I'm just a guy who wants to fight crime."

"Your buddy was just a guy who wanted to tell people the world was going to end," said the fiend. "Look how that turned out."

"And this Simon," said the young man, "what did he want?"

"Like a lot of youse birds, he wanted to be the big cheese, live high on the hog. Everywhere he goes, guys are tippin' the hat, frails are givin' him the glad eye."

Chesney was even more unsure now. "He doesn't sound like the kind who'd want to do a favor for a stranger."

Xaphan rocked its weasel head in a way that said *maybe yes, maybe no*. "He's been stuck in the same day for two thousand years. He'll wanna make a deal that gets him sprung."

"You mean, we'd have to bring him to Poppy?"

The demon nodded. "And then he's not gonna want to go back in the bag."

"What would we do with him?" Chesney said. "After?"

"I think," said the demon, "it's gonna be more a case of what's he gonna wanna do with himself."

Chesney looked around the room. After a moment, he realized that he was looking for a pool of light. There were none to be seen.

He sighed. Doing something had to be better than doing nothing, because the situation had to be changed.

"All right," he said. "We'll do it."

"If you don't mind a suggestion," said his assistant.

"What?"

"When we see the guy, let me make the deal."

Chesney grunted. "Did Al Capone say you had a talent for negotiations, too?"

The demon did its Jimmy Cagney shoulder hitch and cuff-shoot. "The subject never came up. Alphonse was not a negotiatin' kinda guy."

Chesney had expected ancient Rome to have more... he had to search for the right word, then decided it was: *grandeur*. He had been anticipating double rows of white marble columns, fountains and temples, sweeping flights of steps, wide-open plazas with distinguished, toga-clad men walking slowly, deep in conversation.

Instead, he appeared in a narrow canyon of an alley, with brick-and-stucco buildings rising several stories above his head, and was immediately jostled by a small and swarthy man in a torn woolen tunic who was bent double under the weight of a two-handled earthenware pot half the fellow's size that tapered to a point at one end. Behind him came another man with the same burden.

"In here," said Xaphan, pulling the young man into a low arched doorway, as a third and fourth porter trundled past, sweating and breathing hard because the street angled sharply upward. One of the men slipped and almost lost his grip on the jar, which earned him a sharp blow on the thigh from a man who walked behind the porters, carrying only a polished stick carved from some dark wood.

The man had slipped because the footing was

treacherous, the narrow thoroughfare's pavement being covered in various kinds of filth, from rotting vegetable peelings to human waste. No sooner had the little caravan passed than Chesney heard a shout from above and a fresh dollop of something ill-smelling splatted against the previous deposits, right where he would have been standing if his demon had not kept him from stepping out of the archway.

The opening led to a hallway with a door on either side and a wooden staircase leading up. The steps were unpainted but polished smooth in the middle by foot traffic. Chesney moved back from the street and looked through one of the open side doors into a small square room. It was divided by a rough wood counter behind which stood a man, and behind him stood shelves bearing unglazed clay pots. The man was using a wooden cup to dole out dried green lentils from one of the pots onto a balance scale. A thin woman in a shapeless shift was watching the process closely.

Chesney turned and looked through the opposite side door, and saw a man pouring a cloudy oil from a tapered earthenware jug into a small wooden pail. A woman who might have been the sister of the bean-buyer was keeping just as careful an eye on the business.

"Stores," Xaphan said from behind him. "But you don't buy your olive oil here. This mug's sellin the squeezin's from the squeezin's."

Chesney stepped away from the doors, towards the stairs. "Where's Simon?"

The demon gestured with an upthrust thumb. "Top floor. No, I tell a lie – now he's on the roof."

Chesney regarded the stairs doubtfully. They were

steep and dark even in daytime. An odor of old sweat and rotting food hung around the stairwell. "Maybe we should wait for him to come down."

"Won't be a long wait," said the fiend. "In fact..." It looked toward the open arch, and said, "That's him now."

A moment later, Chesney heard a scream that began as faint and distant but became rapidly louder. A dark shape flashed past the doorway – although it was traveling in an unexpected direction – then landed with a sickening splat on the filthy pavement outside. The body, clad in a dark, knee-length woolen robe ornamented with embroidered stars and Greek letters, bounced upwards an inch or so, then lay flat and motionless.

"That's him?" said Chesney. "Simon?"

Xaphan drew on its cigar. "Yowza."

The young man eyed the still form. Blood was flowing from beneath the head and he thought he could see a broken bone poking through the stained cloth. One arm stretched out as if reaching for help, but the legs were bent in impossible directions. "We're too late."

"Nah," said the demon. "Perfect time to make him an offer."

A crowd was beginning to gather, some looking down, some looking up and pointing. The women who had been buying lentils and oil rushed out to see what had happened, although the shopkeepers remained where they were, watching over their wares. The rubberneckers were talking to each other rapid-fire in a language Chesney couldn't recognize. Then a shaggy-haired man in a greasy wool tunic stooped with one ear cocked toward the body, signaling for silence. In the lull, Chesney heard a groan. The body's outstretched hand closed and opened, then pushed at the ground.

A gasp went up from the gawkers. A one-eyed man who'd been feeling along the side of the fallen man's robe snatched his hand back. The bloodied head turned against the smeared pavement and half lifted. The crooked legs straightened.

The crowd evaporated in all directions. Chesney did not understand the words he was hearing, but the meaning was clear: the onlookers were calling on whoever they thought watched over them to protect them from serious magic – serious magic usually being something ordinary folk did not benefit from.

Chesney approached the groaning man on the ground, poked his head out of the doorway and saw the street empty. Even the porters and the man with the stick had got themselves out of range. He looked at Xaphan. "Can you fix him?"

"If you want. But if you take a look you'll see he's doin' a pretty good job all on his own."

It was true. The bone that had been projecting through the cloth – it had looked like a rib – had withdrawn back into the body, although the rent in the back of the robe remained. The legs looked whole now; in fact, the man was getting his knees under him and pushing up with two undamaged arms.

The young man heard a clatter of footsteps behind him. Down the stairs came three men in tunics and sandals. They stopped when they saw the fallen man struggling to rise. Chesney did not need to understand their speech to grasp that he was hearing profanity that expressed anger and disbelief. And he wasn't surprised when two of the men reached into the tunics and produced wide-bladed utilitarian daggers. One of them glanced at Chesney and said something that sounded like an order, backed up by a flourish of the weapon. Then the three of them advanced on the man, Chesney had no doubt they had just thrown him from the rooftop.

"Xaphan," he said. "Ten-ten!" It was shorthand for an instruction for the demon to give him the strength of ten powerful men and to increase his operating speed by a similar factor. Immediately, the action in the hallway slowed to a crawl, the two men with the knives moving toward him in super slow-motion while the third stood immobile behind them. The Actionary went toward the armed pair, plucked the blades from their hands and tossed them to the floor. Then, spreading his arms, he reached up and placed a palm on the sides of their heads and smoothly brought them together.

Experience had taught Chesney not to try to do things too quickly when in ten-ten mode, so the two skulls did not bash together with bone-crushing force. But both knife men opened their eyes and mouths with comic slowness, and he saw their pupils already beginning to grow large as they plunged into unconsciousness. They were falling too slowly to allow him easy access to the third attacker, whom he took to be the boss of the trio, so he thrust his hands through the space between their shoulders – there was not much room in the hallway – and pushed them down and to the side.

To the man bringing up the rear, Chesney thought, it must have seemed as if his two underlings had suddenly disappeared. Then there would have been a flicker of motion before him, a darkening of the daylight from the doorway, followed by a sudden blackout as a fist too fast to be seen connected with his stubbly chin.

"Xaphan," Chesney said, "back to normal."

The third man was still slumping to the floor as Chesney's world returned to regular speed. He turned to find himself being regarded by the man on all fours out in the street. The fellow now pushed with his arms until he was kneeling upright, then began to raise himself, though still unsteadily, to his feet.

He said something to Chesney, a question. One of the words might have been *angelus*. The young man turned to his assistant and said, "I need to know what he's saying."

The demon nodded. "Try it now."

Chesney said, "What did you ask me?"

The man frowned. "I don't understand you. Speak Greek, or Latin. Aramaic if you know it."

"Xaphan," Chesney said, "stop messing around."

The pinstriped shoulders shrugged. "You said you wanted to unnerstand him, not the udder way around."

The young man sighed. "Rum," he said, "and cigars."

"You gotta remember," said his assistant, "I been doin' it one way for thousands of years. It ain't like changin' hats." But he signaled with a stub-fingered hand that the problem was fixed.

Chesney turned back to the man. "You are Simon the Magician?"

"Your Greek is very good," said the man, his eyebrows climbing through the blood on his brow. "So now I'm thinking you're not an angel. They always spoke Aramaic."

"I'm not an angel," Chesney said. "Are you Simon?"

The man ignored the question. He was peering into the hallway where Xaphan hovered above the unconscious

assassins, as if he could perceive the presence of the
demon but not the details. "No," he said. "I suppose
you're not an angel. It was too much to hope."

He brushed at the filth on his robe. Chesney saw that it
was of much better quality than any other garment he'd
seen during his brief stint in Rome. Now Simon drew
himself up and, even with the mud and blood on his face,
he struck a dignified pose. "You're wasting your time," he
said. "And your master's."

"I don't have a master," Chesney said.

"All demons have the same master."

"I'm not a demon. My name is Chesney Arnstruther.
I'm a man, like you. Are you Simon?"

The man's face said he wasn't to be fooled. "Outlandish
name," he said. "Yes, I'm Simon, but you already know
that." He looked again towards Xaphan. "I can't make that
one out. It's like a shadow within a shadow but, really, I
don't need to see it clearly to know what it is. Besides, I
doubt that a clear view would be a pleasant one."

"Hey," Xaphan said, shooting the cuffs of his pinstripe.
"I take pride in my appearance."

"He can see you," Chesney said, "or at least he knows
you're there. How come?"

A shrug of the weasel eyebrows. "I told you. He's a wild
card."

"You're talking to it, aren't you?" said Simon. He was
looking much improved; in fact, except for the mud and
blood smears, he could have posed for the "after" shot in
an advertisement for a wide range of health products.

"All right," Chesney answered him, "cards on the
table."

"I don't know what that means."

"It's an expression where I come from – which is not, by the way, the underworld – meaning I'm about to make a full disclosure."

Again, the other man's eyes rolled. He reached up and flicked some dried blood off one eyelid. "Of course you are."

Chesney had recently had quite a lot of practice in the art of accepting the unlikely. "Listen," he said, "I know there's a lot to take in, but I've come to ask for your help."

Simon offered him a knowing smile. "Which I'll give you because you've saved me," – he waggled his fingers at the three comatose assassins – "from certain death."

"No," said Chesney. "I wasn't expecting them at all. I thought there would have to be a negotiation. You'd want something from me in return."

For the first time, the man seemed interested. "And what could a demon offer me that would be an improvement on my present circumstances?"

"I am not a demon," Chesney said again. He gestured with his head toward Xaphan. "I have one working for me, but otherwise I'm just like you."

"I doubt you're *just* like me. Do you happen to live the same day over and over again?"

Chesney conceded the point. "No, I don't, but–"

Simon interrupted, and now his face was alive with energy. "But you know that I do!"

"Yes," said Chesney. "I've seen it before. Now–"

"How? Where?" The man stepped close to Chesney, clutched at his sleeve, peered into his face. "Do you know a way out? Or even how to die and stay dead?"

The young man said, "Well, yes."

Simon now took to shaking Chesney by the shoulders.

"Which? Tell me!"

"N-n-not the dying!" Chesney said. "But we *can* take you out of here."

Simon let go of him, and looked around the grubby, body-strewn hallway as if fresh wonders might suddenly appear. The oil seller poked his head out of his doorway, saw the three assassins sprawled on the floor, and ducked back into his shop.

"You mean," Simon said, "that I'll never have to see *his* ugly face again? Or smell his rancid oil just before I die?"

"Yes," said Chesney, then added, "provided we can come to an agreement."

The look Simon was giving Chesney now was full of speculation, with calculation peering over its shoulder. "Come up," he said, gesturing to the stairs. "I have some good Falernum." When he saw Chesney's expression, he added, "It's only two floors up, and the air's better."

They climbed four flights of stairs and came out into a hallway with a high ceiling. The walls were of plastered brick and there was only a single door on either side. Simon led them to one of these, made of dark wood with heavy iron fittings. He looked at the closed door then struck his forehead with a palm.

"I've never been back here after..." He waved a hand toward the stairs. "One of them has the key. They always lock it after they take me out, because they're going to come back and loot the place."

He turned toward the stairwell, but Chesney put a hand on his arm and said, "Wait." He looked at Xaphan. "The key."

The item appeared in the demon's hand, a bronze key six inches in length, with complications at one end and a rendition of a bull at the other. The fiend handed it to Chesney who passed it to Simon.

"You're sure you're not a demon?" the man said.

"I'll explain it all."

Simon inserted the key into a hole surrounded by a plate of black iron. He turned the bull end twice to the sound of clicks and clucks from within. Then he swung the door open on a half-pillared foyer whose floor was covered by a blue and white mosaic showing a man losing a wrestling match with two sea serpents.

They passed through an archway into a clean, spacious room, with a checkerboard floor of black and cream marble, and a high plastered ceiling. The walls were red but most of their space was taken up with painted scenes of people and beasts, both real and mythical, in landscapes that drew the eye into false distances. An ornate brass chandelier hung from the ceiling and the place was furnished with low-slung couches upholstered in red velvet as well as a couple of backless chairs. A pair of bronze statues on freestanding plinths and a marble bust of a bearded man, painted in life-like colors, completed the decor.

After seeing the downstairs entrance, Chesney was surprised by the elegance of the room. "If this is one of the lower floors, what must the penthouse look like?"

Simon gave him a puzzled look. "The higher you go, the worse the accommodation," he said. "The top floor is mostly windowless cubicles where day laborers sleep without room to turn over." He folded his arms and studied the young man. "Where exactly are you from?"

"It's a long story," Chesney said.

"Then lie down," Simon said, indicating one of the

couches. "I'll have the girl bring you some wine while I clean myself up. Then you can tell me all about it."

He exited by an inner door, clapping his hands. Chesney seated himself on the couch. He heard Simon calling, then repeating himself impatiently and loudly. A frightened female voice answered him, and a few moments later, a barefoot young woman with a plain, pale face and clear rings of white around her irises came into the room. A tray in her hands rattled with a pewter jug and a pair of silver goblets. She set the tray on a small table then took up the jug, but when she tried to pour her hands shook so badly that the wine spilled.

And now she was horrified. She bit her lip and looked about her. Chesney got up, at which she set down the jug and backed away, trembling.

"I won't hurt you," he said, but she clearly did not believe him, because she turned and ran out of the room, her bare soles slapping on the marble floor.

"Xaphan," Chesney said, "clean up the spill."

Instantly, the puddle of wine on the tray disappeared, and both goblets were filled. The demon said, "I ain't no butler, you know."

The young man took one of the goblets and resumed his seat on the couch. He looked toward the door through which the young woman had fled. "That girl was terrified."

"Slave," Xaphan corrected him. "I seen worse."

"Of course you've seen worse. You're from Hell." Chesney tried the wine. It was golden and heavy-bodied and sweeter than he'd expected. He'd read that the old Romans never drank their wine straight, but always added water; this, though, tasted as if it were full-strength.

"Is he trying to get me drunk?" he said.

"Uh huh."

"So I should watch myself?"

"You'd be better off watching him," the fiend said. "He's a slippery customer."

"Hmm," said Chesney. "Maybe cards-on-the-table isn't the best strategy."

The demon shrugged. "Mind if I join you?" it said, and without waiting for an answer caused a tumbler of amber liquid to appear in its hand. It drained half the glass and puffed on its cigar, then said, "You want my advice, don't try to outfox Foxy here. He's a slick one. Play it straight, see?"

Chesney eyed his assistant sideways. "That's your advice?"

"Yep."

"Is it good advice?"

The demon looked at him coolly. "I told you about wild cards," it said. "Another way of saying it is this is no ordinary mug just off the boat. He's one of what you might call the hinges of the world. He's got some smarts."

"I see," said Chesney, wondering if he actually did.

"You better. Think about it. The guy's been living the same day, over and over again, for near on two thousand years. That's a total of seven hundred and ten thousand, four hundred–"

"I can do the math," Chesney said. Numbers were still his clearest pool of light.

"OK." Xaphan paused to puff up its Churchill. "So after all those times, suddenly he gets a different end to the day. Instead of getting thrown off a roof and stabbed, he's saved by a mysterious stranger. But is he bowled over? Nuh uh. He gives himself a little shake and then he's offering you some vino and puttin' on the glad rags."

"You're right," Chesney said.

"So when he comes back, he'll be cool as a cucumber and ready to take you to the cleaners."

Chesney's mouth felt dry. He took another sip from the goblet.

"So go easy on the hooch," the demon said.

Chesney held the goblet in his lap. "What did Al Capone have to say about dicey situations?"

The demon lifted his shoulders and let them drop. "Rush a gun, but if the guy pulls a knife, run away."

"I don't think that helps."

The fiend spread its hands and said, "You asked. But I can tell you what Dutch Schultz would say."

"What?"

"Don't shit a shitter."

Chesney heard the sound of sandals on marble. A moment later, Simon Magus swept through the doorway in a tunic of blue silk with purple bands at its hem and cuffs that were embroidered in gold thread. He collected his goblet from the table and went to sit on a couch facing Chesney. He regarded the young man for several seconds, then reclined on one elbow. "Very well," he said. "Let's hear it."

Chesney told the story straight: how he'd accidentally called up a demon and refused to sell his soul, and how that had led to a strike in Hell. Then he added the part about how the Reverend Billy Lee Hardacre had negotiated an end to the strike and how it was the preacher's opinion that all of Creation was a book being written by God because the deity was trying to teach Himself morality.

"From time to time," Chesney said, "God writes Himself into a corner. Usually what He does then is to stop whatever side road the tale has led Him down, go back to wherever the narrative started to unwind, and head off in another direction."

But when it happened with Chesney, he said, and everything stopped because Hell wasn't working anymore, Hardacre – who was a pretty experienced author himself – convinced God to try a different approach: give the characters their head and see where it went from there.

"And that's what's been happening. So now Satan and a man you probably heard of, Yeshua bar Yussuf, are in the Garden of Eden trying to see if together they can make up a better story than the one God's been writing. And they've got Billy Lee to help them with the technicalities.

"In the meantime, something I did has led to a young woman being hurt. She was kidnapped into Hell and had a very hard time. Xaphan, my assistant, took away her memories of the experience, but her mind is damaged. When I asked Xaphan if there was anyone who could fix her, he mentioned you. So we've come to ask you if you would be willing to help."

When he'd finished, Simon looked at him over the rim of his goblet. Chesney had noticed that while he was talking, the man had often brought the drink to his lips, but he also noticed that the man's Adam's apple hadn't moved once.

Simon lowered the cup and said, "Is there more?"

"Well, yes, but it's not relevant."

"Let me be the judge of that."

So Chesney told him about how he had always wanted to be a crime fighter and how he'd set a price for his cooperation in ending the infernal strike: the part-time use of a demon to give him crime fighting powers.

"And how has that arrangement worked out?" Simon asked.

Chesney looked at the demon hovering off to one side, puffing on its cigar between doses of rum. "There were some rough patches in the beginning, but we've smoothed most of them out."

"Rough and smooth," the other man mused. "You have an interesting way of talking. Did you study rhetoric?"

"No. Mathematics."

"Not all that Pythagorean foolishness?"

Chesney shook his head. "Mostly probability theory."

Simon was silent for a time. He took an actual drink of the wine. Chesney could see that although the man was looking straight at him, his focus was on whatever he was seeing in his own head. After a while, Simon put the goblet on the floor and said, "Let me see the demon."

Chesney bid Xaphan make itself visible. Simon showed only a slight shock. Then he looked the fiend over carefully, from his spatted wingtips to his saber-fanged weasel's snout. "Odd costume," he said at last.

"I don't notice anymore," said Chesney.

"What's it drinking?"

"It's called rum," Chesney said. "Would you like to try some? You'll find it strong, compared to wine."

Simon seemed to take that as a challenge. He rose and carried the wine back to where the slave had left the pitcher and poured the Falernum back into it. Then he held out the goblet. Chesney instructed Xaphan to fill it with rum, at which the fiend protested and the young man had to repeat himself, while the magician watched the exchange attentively.

Then Simon took a mouthful of the liquor, swallowed, and coughed. And coughed again. "Poison!" he said, when he could get his breath back.

"No," said Chesney. He took the cup and drank some of it. "See," he said, "it just takes getting used to."

Simon tried another swallow. "Hmm," he said. "I see what you mean." He returned to the couch and took another sip, then deliberately set the goblet back on the floor.

"Now," he said. "I have some questions."

"I will try to answer them," said the young man.

"Yeshua bar Yussuf, he was the preacher from Nazareth that his followers called the Messiah. Is that the one you mean?"

"Yes."

"He is dead. I heard of his crucifixion long before I was trapped here. In fact, those were some of his more dedicated followers who threw me off the roof."

"I thought," said Chesney, "that they were all about love-your-enemy."

"Apparently, the rule allows for exceptions." Simon tried a little more of the rum, found the experience more pleasant. "So how did he end up alive in Eden?"

Chesney told him how Joshua had been taken to Heaven in the flesh, where he just didn't fit in, especially when a new version of himself emerged that was divine, God having redefined himself as a Trinity.

"So he got sent back to Earth, but he couldn't be fitted into the current narrative. So, like you, he was stuck repeating the same day in one of the story's dead-end drafts."

"He was living the same day over and over again? Ending with his being crucified?" Simon seemed to find the idea delightful.

Chesney got the impression the idea pleased the magician. When he told him that he'd found the former prophet sitting in a mud-brick house, bored to death, the magician made a disparaging noise in the back of his throat. After a moment's reflection he said, "'Bored to death?' I like that. Inaccurate, though, isn't it, since we three don't actually get to die."

Chesney would have answered but the man held up his hand and said he wanted to think about what he had heard. "Make yourself at ease," he said, "until I return." He stood and walked a few steps toward the inner door then stopped and retrieved the goblet of rum, taking it with him.

"What do you think?" Chesney asked Xaphan, when they were alone again.

"I don't think," said the fiend. "I either know or don't know."

"Then what do you know about what he's going to do?"

The demon drew on its cigar then tapped the ash into the air. "He's going to make a deal," he said. "He *wants* to make a deal, but the rum has thrown him."

"What? Why?"

"He's a wise guy," Xaphan said. "In his world, he knew everything there was to know, see? Seeing me didn't faze him, cause he knew about us already. But the popskull was new. Now he's thinking, what else does this bird know that I don't?"

"He doesn't want to be negotiating at a disadvantage,"

Chesney said.

"Some of that. Mostly, he just likes to know everybody else's cards as well as his own."

"So what do we do?"

The demon moved its head in a seesaw motion. "Give him a taste," it said. "Like with the rum."

"What do you mean?"

"I mean, take him out of here, let him see the sights, give him a good time. Show him what he's gonna be missin' if he don't make no deal." It drained its glass. "Then bring him back here and say, 'So, now?'"

"You think he'll go for it?"

The weasel brows drew down. "I keep tellin' you I don't think," it said. "I know or I don't know. With this guy, this wild card, I don't know. But if he was any other bozo from down the street he'd jump at it. I mean, I dunno what it's like gettin' killed, but from the way you mugs carry on about it, it ain't no fun. And he's been through it now four hundred and ten thousand–"

"I get you," said Chesney. "OK, we'll give him a taste." He thought for a few seconds, then said, "Disneyland?"

The demon shook its head. "Vegas."

The reason Nat Blowdell had got himself into so much trouble was because what he'd always wanted most of all was to rule the world. It was more than just wanting; he was convinced that he would be really, truly great at ruling the world. And on top of that, deep down inside – allowing for the fact that a full-blown psychopath's deepest depths actually run pretty shallow – he knew that he deserved to rule the world.

But having spent some time living in Hell, he now

realized that getting to rule the world was not going to be as easy as he'd originally thought. In fact, most people – that is, the non-psychopathic – in Blowdell's situation would have realized that setting out to rule the world was one of those ideas that sound good voiced in your own head at four in the morning when you're staring at the ceiling, but lose their appeal when you try to make them work in the bold light of day.

But Nat Blowdell was not most people. He still wanted to rule the world, was still convinced he was the man for the job. The fact that he had suffered so much in his first attempt just made him angry. It wasn't fair that he should have been denied his rightful reward. Indeed, from his point of view, which was the only point of view that mattered, he had been done a gross injustice. So now he not only wanted to be the supreme power on Earth; he felt an obligation to punish those who had snatched the prize from him.

One of those deserving meddlers was Satan, but Blowdell was leery of going up against the Prince of Darkness. Once had already been once too many. But the guy who called himself The Actionary? That was a guy who was going to get what was coming to him. As soon as Nat Blowdell could arrange it.

But that couldn't be right away, because the price of getting out of Hell had been to work for Satan's first assistant, Adramalek. The actual specifics of what that work would entail were still being ironed out, and in the meantime, Hell's newest operative had been buffed up and fleshed out and sent back into the mortal world with instructions to find out what The Actionary was up to and report back.

The assignment had evolved from Blowdell's conversation with the archduke after he had explained about the divine book and how he had used his knowledge of its existence to subvert his demon, Melech. Blowdell was happy to keep tabs on The Actionary; that would make it easier to settle the score with the meddler.

But he was still trying to figure out what was what in what he thought of as "this Hell set-up." He asked Adramalek, "Can't you just bring in the asshole's demon and sweat him a little?"

The elephant-sized mouse had snapped closed its crocodilian teeth in irritation, prompting the man to jump back. "Xaphan," it said, "is on direct assignment from the Boss."

"Does that happen often?" Blowdell asked.

The second snap of the teeth convinced him that The Actionary's circumstances were unusual, maybe even unique.

"It's got to have something to do with the book," he said.

The archduke screwed up its mousy face in a struggle to do what it was not made to do. "Probably," it said at last.

"And that's got something to do with The Actionary, right?"

Again the mountainous mouse labored and brought forth a syllable. "Right."

"Now, as I understand it – and I've certainly had a lesson in the underlying principle – you can't do anything to or against this Actionary because Hell doesn't fight Hell."

"Primary rule. One rebellion got us all stuck down here. We don't want to find out where a second revolt will get us sent."

"But nothing stops me from sniffing around and finding out what this guy's game is?"

Adramalek nodded.

"And if his demon comes after me?"

"You're on your own."

It wasn't the safest and easiest assignment Blowdell had ever undertaken, but he was confident he could outsmart a do-gooder and his demonic pal, too. These fiends had powers aplenty, but his experience told him that most of them couldn't think their way out of a T-maze.

"What is your plan?" the archduke wanted to know.

It was clear to Blowdell. "He's got a thing for Paxton's daughter, Poppy. He jumped into Hell to rescue her. If I keep her in view, eventually the boob will show up."

"And then?"

"And then I'll have a conversation with him, and he'll tell me everything I – that is, we – want to know."

"What makes you so sure he'll talk?"

"Because," Blowdell said, "I'm smart, and he isn't."

SIX

It was a warm Indian summer evening when Blowdell rang the doorbell at the Paxton mansion. The butler who answered the door recognized his employer's former political consultant, but did not invite him in. "Mr Paxton is not receiving," he said.

"He'll receive me. Go tell him I'm here."

"Very good, sir."

The servant closed the door. Blowdell stood on the doorstep telling himself not to get angry. He didn't like it when people failed to give him the respect he was due. When the man came back and admitted him, Blowdell added his name to the list of people he would square the accounts with once he was ruling the world. It was quite a long list.

When he'd been advising Paxton on his run for governor – stepping stone to the White House – the old man had always received him in either his study or the big sitting room on the first floor. But now the butler led him up the marble staircase and along a corridor on the second floor. The man opened a door and said Blowdell's name.

It was a bedroom, the lights dim, the air humid and full of a medicinal smell. Warren Theophilus Paxton was sitting up in the huge bed, wrapped in a dressing gown and propped against a Himalayan heap of pillows. A humidifier was bubbling away in a corner, and a sideboard against one wall was topped by a phalanx of bottles containing pills and liquids.

The old man squinted as Blowdell stepped into the room. He opened his mouth to speak, but all that came out was a dry cough. The butler hastened to fill a glass from a pitcher beside the bed and held it to the flaked skin of his employer's lips. Paxton took two gulps then pushed the water away. He looked at Blowdell again, blinked as if at an apparition, and spoke. "Nat? Is that you?"

"In the flesh, W.T." He looked around the room. "You've been sick?"

"Jesus, where have—"

A coughing fit interrupted the question. Blowdell waited for it to subside then said, "I can't talk about it, W.T. National security."

The old man peered at him a moment more, then waved a pale hand, its skin like age-spotted parchment. "Doesn't matter. Nothing matters now."

"You've had a hard time of it." Blowdell knew how to sound as if he cared about people he associated with.

Paxton made no answer. He was staring at something only he could see.

After a silence broken only by the gentle huff of the humidifier, Blowdell said, "And Poppy? How's she doing?"

A tear made its way down the pale cheek. "Not good," the old man said. "Something… happened."

"I heard about that."

"Doctors say…" Again, the limp wave of the dry hand.

"May I see her?"

Paxton's aged eyes came around to him, blinked. "What for?"

"Maybe I could help."

The old man looked at Blowdell as if the younger man had made some foolish but forgivable breach of etiquette. "Help? How could you help?"

"I don't know until I try."

Paxton went back to looking at the bleak vista inside his head. But he weakly signaled his consent and asked the butler where his daughter was.

"The conservatory, sir."

"What is she doing?"

The butler gently cleared his throat. "Not very much, I'm afraid, sir."

The servant led Blowdell back downstairs then down a corridor and across a large dimly lit room to where a set of French windows had once opened onto the mansion's expansive garden. The late Mrs Paxton had preferred to enjoy her greenery indoors and had had a glass-walled and -windowed room built out onto the patio. It was well supplied with plants in pots, many of them now grown tall and full, and with cushioned wicker chairs and settees.

On one of the latter, underneath an overhanging potted palm, Poppy Paxton sat and stared at not much at all. Her maid had dressed her in a shapeless cotton dress, without make-up, and a pair of cloth slippers. She sat with her legs crossed, the knee on top bouncing continuously up and down. The motion had caused one slipper to loosen and fall off. Poppy had made no attempt to put it on again.

The butler stopped at the French windows and said, "I won't stay, sir. Men can make her nervous. I must advise you to speak quietly and calmly and not to approach too closely nor to make any sudden motions."

"I'll take it easy," Blowdell said.

The butler pointed out a hospital-style call button at the end of a cable attached to one end of the settee where the young woman sat and told him to press it if she became upset, then withdraw. The maid, a trained nurse, would come and take care of Poppy.

"No problem," said Blowdell. He stayed where he was until the butler had left, then slowly crossed the tiled floor. Poppy Paxton did not appear to notice him until he was within ten feet of her. Then it was as if she awoke from an open-eyed sleep, with a sharp intake of breath. Her eyes opened wide and she stared at him as if he were an apparition. Her knee stopped bouncing.

Blowdell knew that this was a crucial moment. He had been masked and clad in a full-body costume when he'd dragged Poppy down to Hell. She shouldn't have been able to identify him. But he knew that the mind – especially the deranged mind – could make strange connections. If she recognized him as her kidnapper, he would have to rethink his plan.

She stared at him without blinking, her face blank. He studied her, saw no panic or terror, and began to relax. He took a seat on a nearby fan-backed wicker chair and showed her a smile. "Poppy," he said, his voice soft, "it's Nat Blowdell. I used to work with your father. Do you remember me?"

He wasn't sure if she'd even heard him. She continued to give him the empty stare. He waited, and then it was as if a switch had been thrown somewhere in her disordered psyche. She looked down, then up at him again, and he saw her reaching for a memory, then catching hold.

"Politics," she said.

He smiled again. "That's right. Your dad was thinking of running for office, and I was advising him."

She nodded and he could see her assembling some kind of framework that included him. Then she sighed, shook her head gently as if reminiscing on some folly of her childhood, and went back to staring at nothing. Her knee began to jiggle once more.

"Poppy," he said, still soft, "do you remember what happened to you?"

She spoke without intonation. "No."

"Do you remember a man dressed in blue and gray? He called himself The Actionary."

He saw her briefly strain after memory, then fall back into inertia. "No."

"I remember him," Blowdell said. "What happened to you was his fault." The knee briefly paused its bouncing, then resumed. "If he ever asks to see you," he continued, "don't be afraid of him. He can't hurt you. I won't let him."

The knee paused. She looked at him again, but he wasn't sure how much of what he was saying was getting through, and he had no great faith that she'd remember.

But that wasn't the point of why he'd come here. Back when he'd been advising W.T. on his political ambitions, Blowdell had arranged for a team of technicians to visit the Paxton house between the hours of 3 and 4am. They worked for a private security firm with which he had a long-standing relationship. Blowdell did not trust his clients to follow his advice, so he'd had the techs install listening devices in the walls of key rooms; by a low-powered, short-range signal, the bugs fed whatever they picked up to a central receiver hidden in the gray box on an outside wall, where the house's telephone system connected to the underground phone lines.

Every night, when the Paxtons were asleep, Blowdell's computer used to dial the Paxton's landline number and add a three digit code; the phone would not ring in the house, but the hidden collector would transmit a compressed digital package. The computer would use software borrowed from the National Intelligence Service – the spooks who listen in on everybody's conversations – to winnow the recordings for keywords.

Now that he was back, Blowdell had reprogrammed the system to listen for a new set of words that included *Actionary, Hell, demon, Hardacre,* and anything he could think of that might fit his new assignment. But the technicians who had planted the bugs had not covered the conservatory – W.T. Paxton didn't like the place and never went there. Blowdell now repaired that oversight by placing a listening device in the fronds of the palm that sheltered Poppy.

She twitched when he came near to plant the bug, then froze, staring at her motionless knee, until he withdrew.

"I'll come and see you again," he said.

She gave no sign that she'd heard him. The knee began to bounce again.

At the end of his first day as Chief Denby's administrative assistant, Seth Baccala left his desk neat and tidy before asking his new boss if there would be anything else.

"Nope," said Denby. "How are you settling in?"

"Fine."

"Any surprises?"

Baccala shook his smooth head. "Admin is admin. Only the forms are different." He took thought then said, "One thing."

Denby had gone back to reading through the jackets of selected officers. He looked up. "What?"

"Hoople had a slush fund. He got a piece of every pay-off. His assistant kept a ledger. I found it in the safe."

"So?"

"So a captain from vice squad dropped by and asked if the system was still in place."

"What did you tell him?"

"Business as usual," Baccala said, "until I hear different."

"Good," said Denby. "Just cause it's a new broom, doesn't mean it has to sweep totally clean. Not yet."

Baccala did not go straight home. He walked the few blocks to the office building where, years before, he had accidentally killed the aspiring television journalist Cathy Bannister. It was past quitting time for office workers, but the lights were still on in the offices of Baiche, Lobeer, Tressider, and the main door was unlocked.

He made his way to Tressider's corner office. The door was half open, but he knocked and waited until the lawyer told him to come in. The older man was seated on the couch reading a document on foolscap-sized paper, a glass of aged scotch in one hand. He gestured with that hand for the young man to take a seat, his gaze still on the paper. Not until he'd finished reading the last dense paragraph of single-spaced print did he look up.

"So?"

"Good," said Baccala. "So far, it's business as usual."

Tressider sipped his scotch, looked at the younger man over the rim of his glass. "No new projects? No unexpected enthusiasms?"

"New broom, same old sweeping. But he's reviewing the files of some of the senior officers." The lawyer's eyebrows put a silent question. Baccala said, "I think he's confirming some long-standing opinions."

"He strikes you as thorough?"

"And focused."

"Which could be good," Tressider said. "Or not."

"Time will tell."

The lawyer took another swallow, finishing the drink. "And when it does, you'll tell me."

After Seth Baccala left, Tressider returned the document he'd been reading to its file and locked it away in his private safe. He made a note in his billing diary then got his jacket from the armoire in one corner and shrugged into it. He went out into the firm's main space and checked to see who was working late, saw the lights on in a couple of smaller offices where younger lawyers who hoped to make partner some day were going the extra mile. Then he went back into his own private domain and locked the door from the inside. He closed the blinds and drew the heavy curtains over them, plunging the room into darkness relieved only by a dim spill of light from under the door.

The armoire door was still open. He reached up until a finger found a cavity in the molding between the top and the back. He pressed and heard a click. The back of the armoire swung away from him, revealing a shadowy flight of stairs leading upwards. He stepped through and began to ascend.

An odor surrounded him, of camphor and something sickly sweet. But he was used to it and his face remained impassive. At the top of the stairs was a small square landing before an unmarked door that showed no apparent means of opening. Tressider knocked gently and waited, not looking up at the hemisphere of dark glass over his head. After a moment, the door disappeared silently into the wall. When he passed through the opening, it slid closed behind him.

The room was small and furnished like a parlor in a wealthy man's home, a home of a few generations before. Its air smelled musty, as if it had been breathed too many times. A plush, wingback chair stood in the center of the deep pile carpet, a round table beside it holding a crystal carafe and a glass. Sunk in the chair was a diminutive figure, wrapped in a brocaded bathrobe. The head that protruded from the robe was completely hairless, the face a mass of wrinkles, the eyes like two bullet holes in parchment. But the gaze they turned on Tressider was sharp, and the voice that issued from the bloodless lips, though thin, was full of power.

"Well?"

"So far, sir, nothing to cause concern."

"You're sure?"

"As sure as we can be, at this stage."

"Your agent?"

"In place."

The figure in the chair coughed twice. "And we're sure of him?"

Tressider gave the same answer. Then he stood and waited to see if there would be more. A minute passed, then another. The thin voice said, "Go away."

The lawyer turned, the door opened for him, and he heard its whispery slide closing behind him as he descended the steps. A moment later, he was in his darkened office again, the armoire closed on its secret.

He crossed to the outer door and unlocked it. But before he opened it, he let the shudder he had been repressing convulse his back and shoulders.

"Casual but not plebeian, that's what I wanted," Simon said. "So is it?" He was looking at himself in the full-length mirror in the dressing room of the suite they were occupying at the MGM Grand complex in Las Vegas.

"You're a peach," Xaphan said. "A humdinger."

The magician frowned and turned to Chesney. "Are we all still speaking the same language?"

"Yes. Xaphan has a few verbal idiosyncrasies."

For convenience's sake, Chesney had had the demon give Simon the power to speak and understand modern American English. The man was now examining himself in the mirror again. The demon had clothed him in a cream-colored linen suit, a pale blue silk shirt, and a pair of white loafers. He turned and looked over his shoulder. "I've seen Persians wearing leggings like these," he said. "Very functional."

Then he rubbed his palms against his upper arms. "I see desert out there, baking under the sun. Why is it so cold?"

Chesney started to explain about machines that cooled the air. After a few words, Simon signaled that he didn't really care about the technicalities. "You brought me here to tempt me," he said. "What have you got?"

"Food?" Chesney said. "Drink? Entertainment? Gambling?"

"Yes," said Simon. "And women. How are the flute girls in your world?"

Chesney turned to Xaphan. "Does he really mean they have to play flutes?"

"Depends on what you call a flute," the demon said.

They went down to the casino, which was roaring with light and noise. Simon took one look from the top of the stairs that led down to the enormous room and said, "The lights! The noise! Wonderful!"

Then he plunged into the crowds. He went from table to table as Chesney followed, bewildered by the welter of ways to lose money – blackjack, poker, some kind of clicking-spinning wheel with card suits on it, rank upon rank of electronic slot machines. Simon stopped for a while to watch the croupier spin a roulette wheel, and while he did so a young woman in a short skirt offered him a drink from a full tray. He took it, sipped, and said, "This is not rum."

"It's bourbon," said the waitress.

The magician repeated the word to himself and drank some more. Then his eye caught movement at another table. He sidled over, watched as a large-bellied man leaned over the craps table and threw the dice, then watched again as the croupier apportioned winnings and losses to the people crowded around.

Simon turned to Chesney. "How is this played?"

"Um," Chesney said. Poker was the only form of gambling he'd ever indulged in. "Xaphan? Can you explain?"

"I'll just clue him in," the demon said. It gestured.

Simon's eyes widened. "Ah," he said. Then, "I'll need sesterces."

Chesney looked at Xaphan. The demon told Simon to look in his pocket.

"What's a pocket?"

Xaphan gestured again, then told Chesney, "It's easier this way." The magician was already digging into a side pocket of his jacket and coming out with a wad of bills. He already knew that they were money and that he had to exchange them for chips.

"You didn't steal that, did you?" Chesney asked his assistant.

"Yeah, but I got it from some bad eggs across town."

Simon was placing a bet. The dice flew across the board and bounced. The croupier pushed chips toward the magician's stack. He stacked them on the same oblong space. The dice rolled again, and again Simon collected.

"He's really lucky," Chesney said.

"Luck ain't got nuttin to do with it," his assistant said.

Chesney dropped his voice, even though no one could hear him, or even see his lips move, when he was speaking to his demon. "He's cheating?"

"Reason we want the guy is cause he's got powers, right?"

"But casinos don't like cheats. I've seen movies where they take them in a back room and some guy with a hammer breaks their hands."

A roar went up from the table as Simon raked in another wealth of chips. The croupier picked up the dice and dropped them into a slot under the table, producing a new pair. He gave the magician a humorless smile as he passed them to the big-bellied shooter.

"Let him know about the hammer," Chesney told the demon. A second later he saw Simon blink. He reached down and moved the lesser part of his piled-up chips off the playing grid. The shooter threw the dice again, and Simon shrugged as his stake was raked away. He pocketed the remaining chips.

"How about dinner?" Chesney said.

In the restaurant Simon said he had been in taverns where people ate sitting at tables. "The food is never good. Besides, the digestion is always improved when one eats while reclining."

Chesney assured him the meal would be excellent and had Xaphan make the man literate in English so he could read the menu for himself.

"There's no garum," Simon said, after perusing the offerings.

"What's garum?" Chesney said, which won him a look of astonishment. Then Xaphan put the knowledge in his head and he grimaced. "Really? A sauce made from rotting fish?"

"And no larks' tongues," Simon said. "This is how you tempt a man of culture?"

Chesney signaled a passing waitress. "A double bourbon for my friend here."

Simon looked up at the young woman. "Will you be available after the symposium?" he said, adding in a hand gesture that, though new to Chesney, still left him in no doubt as to its meaning. "What do you charge?"

The waitress gave him a hard look. "Do what now?"

Chesney put up both hands. "He's from out of... I mean, he's come a long way."

"And he's like to go all the way back with a pain in his–"

"He didn't mean to offend. It's different where he comes from."

The woman's eyebrows said she wasn't buying it. "Sounds to me like he's from down the block."

"He had excellent language teachers."

"Well, he'd better get some manners teachers, somebody going to tear him a new one."

"A new what?" Simon said, when she'd gone to get the whiskey.

"Maybe it would be better if you just observed for a while," Chesney said. "Modern interpersonal relations are complex."

"It's a mistake," said Simon, "to be too lenient with your slaves. You've never heard of Spartacus?"

The woman was coming back with the whiskey. Chesney said, "It would be better if you let me handle this."

Simon seemed to catch on. "More men with hammers?"

"She's thinking shears," Xaphan said.

Simon kept his eyes on the menu. Chesney ordered for them both, a steak for himself and lobster for the magician. Xaphan suggested he ask for a bottle of the restaurant's hottest hot sauce, adding, "In this guy's time, they liked grub they could really taste."

Simon's eyes watered when he tried the sauce on the lobster. Chesney had ordered them wine – the costliest on the menu – and the magician drained his glass to put out the fire. But then he said, "I could learn to like that."

"Wait until you discover chocolate ice cream," Chesney said.

The ancient man ate with gusto, following the lobster with a few more entrees from the menu. The day that he had relived so many times – although actually it had lasted only from mid-morning to late afternoon – had included no feasting, he explained. Finally, having consumed enough to choke a hog, in Xaphan's evaluation, he politely asked Chesney, "Where may I vomit?"

"Are you ill?" Chesney said.

"No, just full."

Xaphan said, "Those Romans used to upchuck so they could put on the feedbag again."

"We don't do that," the young man said.

"I wish I'd known," said Simon. He looked a little green.

"You can't heal yourself?" Chesney said.

"I told you, I'm not ill, just full."

Chesney turned to Xaphan. "Can you relieve his discomfort? Delicately?"

"Sure."

A moment later, Simon said, "That's even better than vomiting. Where's the menu?"

"How about we go see a show?" Chesney said.

The other man acquiesced. As they left the restaurant, he said, "I suppose it's too late for gladiators, isn't it?"

"By about fifteen hundred years," said Chesney. "But this place has singing, dancing, comedy, acrobats–"

"I passed an evening at the Palace once," said Simon. "In Caligula's time. He had this trained donkey, and there was a senator's wife who–"

"We have nothing like that!" Chesney said.

"Actually, boss," said the demon, "there's a place a couple miles from here–"

"Enough!" In the main concourse, he saw a placard mounted on an easel next to a wide archway, and said, "Perfect! We'll go see the magician!"

Simon's face said he didn't expect to be impressed. The prediction turned out to be accurate.

The stage magician was billed as Charles Darnay. He was a slim young man with lacquered black hair and a sparkling suit who spoke with a distinctly French accent. The room was terraced, with four levels of tables leading down to a circular stage. Chesney led the way to an empty table near the front. A waitress immediately arrived and took their order. Simon leaned back in his chair and watched the performance, his chin elevated and his eyes half closed.

To Chesney, the act seemed seamless and smooth. Items suddenly appeared in the man's hands and disappeared just as quickly. He produced a pair of doves from a handkerchief and a flash of fire from an empty hand, then stood his attractive female assistant on a bench behind a curtain she held up herself – but when the cloth fell she was nowhere to be seen.

The audience applauded. Simon said, "Huh!" in a tone that conveyed no respect. Darnay turned his head sideways and sent him a cold look.

The assistant reappeared from the wings, bringing two chairs. She and Darnay set them up a few feet apart, their backs facing each other. Then she stood while he made mystic passes before her eyes, which closed. She toppled backwards but he caught her in his arms and lifted her until her neck rested on one chair back and her heels on the other.

Simon blew air over his lips and crossed his legs. He

shook his head as if at some grand folly.

Darnay gave him another sideways look that was sharp enough to cut flesh but continued with his act. His fingers caressed the space above the woman's rigid, supine form. Then he lifted his hands, palms down, and as if she were a puppet on strings, the assistant rose slowly into the air.

"Pah!" said Simon, and turned away in a pantomime of supreme boredom. To Chesney, he said, "This you call a magician?"

The man on stage bristled, but went through with the rest of the performance. Lowering the woman to the chairs, then standing her up and awakening her from the trance. He bowed, she bowed, the band that had been playing accompaniment blew a fanfare, and the audience clapped. But the applause was none too loud; certainly, it was not loud enough to drown out Simon's comment to Chesney: "Piffle! The fellow's a mere mountebank!"

The band played Darnay's exit music and the assistant left, but the man remained on the stage. The room grew quiet with expectation. "Perhaps," the man said, "Monsieur can do better?"

Simon turned back towards the stage, raised one eyebrow. He cast his gaze over the audience, saw an old couple at one of the tables on the top level. The right corner of the man's mouth drooped and he had a cane with a three-toed end.

Simon rose and approached the couple. He asked the man, "What happened to you?"

The man replied, but it was difficult to make out the words, his speech was so slurred.

His wife said, "Stroke." Chesney couldn't imagine a sadder word more sadly said.

Simon nodded. "Stand up.".

It took a few seconds, even with the cane, for the old man to get to his feet. Simon looked him up and down, then reached out and touched the short gray hair on the left side of the man's head. "Done," he said.

The old man's eyes widened. The slack corner of his mouth drew up to where it ought to be. He stood straighter, firmer. "What did you do?" he said, his voice clear.

Simon looked over at Darnay as he answered. "Magic."

The man on the stage had gone pale with anger. "Bullshit!" he said, all traces of a French accent having fled. "A cheap publicity stunt! Who's the old coot, your daddy?"

Simon's attention was drawn back to the elderly couple, because the old woman had seized his hand and was kissing it. And now her husband leaned in and whispered something to the magician. Simon listened, shrugged, then briefly touched his hand to the crotch of the old man's trousers.

The old fellow's eyes went wide again for a moment. Then he seized his wife's hand and said, "Come on, Betsy! Back to the room!" Pulling her behind him, he went out the doorway to the concourse at a flat run. The three-toed cane remained teetering behind.

The audience couldn't settle on a common response. Some applauded, some muttered to each other, some watched to see what Darnay would do.

The stage magician opted for all-out war. "You son of a bitch!" he said, in what sounded to Chesney like a distinctly Texas accent. He stepped down from the stage and came up through the terraces toward Simon, his fists balled. The magician regarded him coolly and said, "The trick with the fire in the hand, can you do it with your head?"

"I'll show you some fucking tricks!" said Darnay, pushing aside a chair and preparing to jump up onto the terrace where Simon waited.

"Because," said Simon, "I can."

He gestured with one hand and Charles Darnay's shining dark hair burst into flame. The stage magician howled in pain. He unballed his fists and beat at the flames with both palms, but without noticeable result, except to set the cuffs of his sequined jacket on fire. Meanwhile, the audience decided on a collective response built around screaming and rushing for the exit.

Darnay was making a hoarse sound and continuing to slap his head. Chesney concluded that magic fire was more difficult to extinguish than the regular variety.

"Xaphan!" he said. "Put the fire out and get us back to the room! Now!"

An instant later, Chesney and Simon were back in the suite. Xaphan arrived a moment later. The rules of demonic interaction with Creation did not allow fiends to move from one place to another on Earth. Xaphan had to route via the toehold in the outer circle of Hell. The demon took the opportunity to acquire a fresh cigar and a tumbler of rum.

"That was fun," it said. "Now what?"

"I'd like some more of that," Simon said, indicating the liquor. "The bourbon kind. And maybe I'll try the burning stick."

In preparation for steering W.T. Paxton toward the

governorship, Blowdell had leased office space and hired staff. Once he disappeared and the staff found no one to sign their paychecks, the place emptied out. The furnishings were still there, as well as some of the equipment, though the departing employees had helped themselves to computers and other resellables in lieu of wages. Blowdell's private lair, secure behind heavy locks, had remained inviolate.

His office contained a couch and its own washroom. The break room kettle, coffeemaker, and miniature fridge were still there, though someone had appropriated the microwave. Blowdell got one at a discount store, along with boxes of packaged food whose preparation required only boiling water. He had used to enjoy eating. Now, even though his digestive system had been returned to service, he had no interest in how food tasted. It was only fuel. Sometimes he didn't bother to soak the pressed dried noodles in water, but chewed them dry while he sat at his empty desk with its speakerphone.

To begin with, he had altered the part of the spy program that would send him a nightly package. Instead, he had reprogrammed the listener to contact him the moment it heard one of the keywords. But after a few hours of sitting and waiting for a call, he had again revised the system so that, unbeknownst to the Paxton household, the line was always open. Blowdell now spent eighteen hours of every day sitting and listening to the audio feed that captured the life of Poppy Paxton. During his brief intervals of fitful sleep on the couch – never more than twenty minutes – the computer listened for him.

Poppy's was now a sadly diminished life, a routine of feedings and cleanings, of being woken and put to bed –

all of which, added together, took up less than an hour a day. The rest of the time was spent in silence, the young woman sitting and staring. Her father had engaged a physical therapist who came in three times a week to try to help her keep some muscle tone, but the effort was not being rewarded. Blowdell could sometimes hear the physio swearing under her breath as she struggled against her patient's passive resistance. Once he heard the therapist whisper to herself, "God, how I hate working with catatonics!"

When the Paxtons were all tucked in for the night, Blowdell rose from the chair. He hadn't slept at all in Hell – who could? – and the experience had done something to his brain. He believed he now often slept, if it could be called sleep, with his eyes open and even with his body active. After months in the underworld, the reality he had returned to was much like a dream. Now he wandered the night streets, sometimes encountering others who preferred to live their lives in darkness. Some of them thought they were predators and Blowdell their prey. He taught them otherwise. It was invariably a final lesson; he still retained the strength and speed that Melech had given him.

Often, he would walk over to the Paxton mansion and loiter there, on the off chance that his nemesis might also be drawn to the place. So far, that hadn't happened, but Nat Blowdell had always cultivated the political virtue of patience, and a season in Hell had refined that quality to its essence.

"So here's the deal," Chesney said. "We'll take you out of here," – he gestured to Simon's marble-floored room and ancient Rome out the window – "and we'll set you up in our world so you can live decently. In return, you will heal a young woman whose memories had to be edited."

"Why did they have to be edited?" Simon asked.

"She saw things, terrible things, that she shouldn't have had to see."

"Who did the editing?" Simon looked to where the demon hovered to one side of where Chesney sat on one of the couches. "That?"

Xaphan inclined its head.

"Huh," said the magician. Then, "What else?"

"Nothing else," said Chesney.

Xaphan leaned down toward Chesney's ear and said, "Uh, boss?"

"What?"

"I don't wanna be a kibitzer, but you ain't doin' this right."

"What do you mean?"

"I mean, look at him." Chesney did. The demon had stopped time so he could intervene. Simon's face had frozen just as a micro-expression of deep distrust had flashed across it. "He thinks you're tryin' to pull somethin'. You ask for a little, then when he bites you gazump him."

"Gazump?"

"Once he's in, the price goes up."

"I see. What do you suggest?"

The demon said, "This kinda thing, the traditional set-up is three wishes."

Chesney thought about it. It rang true. He turned back to Simon and time started up again. "I can see it's no good trying to fool you," he said. "The fact is, we're going to want you to perform three acts of magic. The first one is healing the young woman."

Simon looked at him sideways. "And the other two?"

"We're not sure, yet."

"Will they just involve healing damaged minds?"

Chesney shrugged. "Probably. My assistant can do just about anything else I need doing."

"Will you require a contract? Satan wanted a document."

The statement took the young man by surprise. "You did a deal with Hell?"

Simon snorted. "Not likely! Would you?"

"Not the kind Satan likes," Chesney said. "But he offered?"

The magician glanced at the demon then appeared to make up his mind about something. "My sense of you is that you have been telling me the truth, your choice of assistant notwithstanding. So I will reciprocate."

He raised his hands to clap for the slave, then thought better of it. "Could we have some of that strong drink?" he said.

Chesney said, "Xaphan." A glass of whiskey appeared on the couch beside the magician. As the man reached for it, Chesney said, "Make it on the rocks." His comix hero, Malc Turner aka The Driver, liked bourbon on the rocks.

Simon poked at the floating cubes. "It's ice, isn't it? I saw some once at a Poppea's house in Pompeii. It had been brought down from Vesuvius packed in sawdust." He sipped the whiskey and his lean face registered pleasure. "A very fine effect."

He sipped some more, then said, "Where was I? Ah, yes, the offer. Well, there's not much to tell. He went to each of us – me, your friend from Nazareth, and the other one – and offered us the world. I could be emperor, he said. And I suppose I would have been, except that I would have been beholden to him – and what good would that have been? Even Yeshua was not too naive to turn him down."

He sipped some more of his whiskey, reflecting. "I see it now, of course. The great book, the story. It all makes sense." His head nodded upwards. "He had come to a point where the story could go one way or another. He tried out different characters: Yeshua, me…"

He noticed that Chesney was leaning forward, listening intently. Simon's expression had been that of a man recollecting past events; now it sharpened and he became very much in the here and now.

"You're waiting for me to say the name, aren't you?" he said.

Chesney had never been good at disguising his feelings. "You said, 'the other one.' Who were you talking about?"

Simon's eyes narrowed as he assessed the young man. "Why don't you ask your demon?"

"Xaphan, do you know who he's talking about?"

The fiend consulted its store of knowledge. "No," it said, "I don't."

"Is it another 'wild card'?"

"Could be. Or it could be I don't know cause the Boss don't want me to. Or…" Xaphan's weasel brows drew down with the unaccustomed effort of thinking. The fiend indicated the magician. "He's sayin' the Boss was makin' offers that him and your buddy turned down. If there was another wild card at the same time, and that guy took the offer, that would make it a personal contract between the mug and the Boss. For sure I wouldn't know nuttin about it."

Simon had heard none of their exchange. Chesney told him the demon didn't know.

"Hell keeps secrets from itself?" the magician said.

"They don't do a lot of trusting," Chesney said. "So who was the other wild card?" Then he had to have Xaphan put an understanding of playing cards in Simon's head.

"Interesting," the other man said. "I want to try some of those games."

"They're less fun if you cheat," Chesney said. "Now what about the wild card?"

Simon regarded him speculatively for a long moment. Then he said, "Do you know, I believe I will keep that information to myself for the time being."

"Why?"

"Because it may be useful to me to know something that you don't. Just in case it turns out that you want something more than three healings."

"I assure you–"

"No, you do not," said the magician. "At least, not yet." He drank some more of the iced bourbon. "But I think we have enough common ground to get started, don't we?"

Chesney looked at his demon. The pinstriped shoulders went up and down. "It ain't a perfect deal," it said. "But what deal is?"

SEVEN

Even though Simon had had a good taste of the life he might soon be living, and even though the alternative to making a deal would be to return to the filthy Roman street and be murdered over and over again forever by assassins sent by Yeshua's follower Peter, he remained a hard bargainer. He wanted wealth. He wanted security. He wanted prestige. And, offered all of them, he wanted more of each.

Chesney had started out by offering the man a million dollars.

"Is that a lot?" Simon had said.

"Yes."

"Will it buy a house with slaves in a good district?"

"We don't allow slaves."

"Who will cook, clean, take care of my needs?"

"You can hire servants."

Simon looked askance. "Freedmen? They always steal and they only stay as long as it takes to steal enough to set up on their own."

"A lot of what slaves do for you in your world is done

by machines in ours," Chesney said.

"You have machines for…" Simon made a rude motion with his pelvis, his hands outstretched as if holding something in front of him.

"No," said Chesney, then reconsidered. He'd seen ads in porn magazines. "Maybe. Or you can hire women."

Simon's mouth turned down at the corners. "It's all sounding quite expensive."

"All right, two million."

"Better make it four." The magician stroked his chin. "I'll want to travel. So a stable of horses. And a galley. Do you have machines that row?"

"We have machines that fly."

Simon made a dismissive gesture. "I can do that myself."

Chesney was becoming irritated. "Then why didn't you save yourself when those men threw you off the roof?"

For the first time, he saw the magician discomfited. "I don't want to discuss it," the other man said.

The old Chesney might not have noticed the shift in mood, but the healed Chesney did. And he was annoyed enough by the man's overbearing attitude to want to stick a pin in Simon's inflated sense of self-worth. "Come on," he said, "what's the story? You forgot how to fly all of a sudden?"

Simon's lean face flushed red. He rose from his couch and made a dramatic gesture. Immediately, his feet left the marble floor and he rose until he hovered with his head just below the high ceiling. Then he gently lowered himself to the floor. "There," he said.

"But…" Chesney said, "why did you fall?"

Xaphan spoke in the young man's ear. "Ask him does he want me to take him out on the balcony and drop him."

Chesney relayed the request.

"No," said Simon.

"Ask him," said the demon, "if it's on account of he can't go no higher than he just did."

"Yes," was the magician's reluctant reply.

"So you can't really fly," said Chesney. "You just hover a couple of feet in the air."

"I did not ask for the power," said Simon. "When I became a man, I just found I could do it. I can also make fire." He gestured with one hand and a flaming ball appeared in it. He cupped the other hand over it and when he opened them, the fire was gone. "I can also create illusions."

"But none of these powers came from Satan?" Chesney said.

"I didn't meet him until I had already begun to heal people and attract a following."

"So they came from God?"

"If they did, He never showed up to take credit. I was left to work it out on my own." Simon made a brushing-away gesture. "Let us get back to our negotiation."

Chesney tried to bargain, but Simon just kept raising the stakes. The young man tried to turn the business over to his assistant, but the magician refused to deal with a demon. Chesney felt himself outmatched. The sensation reminded him of how he used to feel in the times before casual contact with Joshua Josephson had cured him of his autism. Back then, so much of his everyday life was steeped in darkness and his pools of light were few and precious. Thinking of what was precious brought him around to the most precious thing in his new life. And there he found an answer.

"I'm not good at this kind of thing," he said. "I'm going to take you to someone who is."

He gave an order to the demon and an instant later the three of them appeared in the foyer of Hardacre's mansion. "Melda!" he called.

"I'm in the study!" came the answer.

"This way," he told Simon.

She was seated at the preacher's desk, spreadsheets and account books before her, as well as a laptop and a calculator. She looked up and said, "Who's this?"

"The man who's going to fix Poppy."

"That," said Simon, "remains to be seen. First we must come to an agreement."

She switched her attention to Chesney. "What have you offered him?" When Chesney told her, she said, "That seems more than fair, especially if it's coming out of our pockets."

"But he keeps wanting more."

She looked at Simon. "Hard bargainer, huh?" He gave her a look that said he thought highly of his abilities. She turned back to Chesney and said, "Remember how you convinced that con man to give back what he'd stolen?"

Chesney was shocked. "But that man was a criminal!"

"And you don't see this one trying to steal from us with both hands?"

"You just wait a moment–" Simon began.

But she cut him off. "Have Xaphan take him down to Hell for a little while. Wherever you found him, there's worse places he could spend his time. In the meantime," she indicated the material on the desk, "I've got a lot on my plate here."

Chesney had wanted Melda to provide an answer.

Now he'd heard it. He was a little shocked at the hard-nosed way she'd summed up the situation and offered a plan. It occurred to him that maybe the woman was more complex than she had appeared to him when he was his old self. For a moment that made him sad. Then he realized that she was looking at him with an expression that said: *Can we get on with this? I'm busy.*

"Xaphan," he said, "do what Melda suggested. Keep him there until he's ready to bargain seriously."

"Gotcha, boss," said the fiend. It disappeared, and so did Simon. A moment later, they were back, the magician pale and windblown. "He's reconsidered his position," the fiend said.

"Fine," said Chesney. He looked the magician over. The linen suit was streaked with grease and grit from Hell's contaminated air. His hair was disordered, and his eyes were wide. "We'd better get you a drink. Come to the den."

Simon followed him out of the study. Melda went back to work.

Seth Baccala waited in the underground parking garage beneath the offices of Baiche, Lobeer, Tressider. It was an uncomfortable wait, his position behind a concrete pillar gave him not only a view of Tressider's Lexus but of the freight elevator in which, years before, he had helped carry the body of Cathy Bannister before it was taken out into the woods and buried. Baccala knew why that memory disturbed him: partly because it was a shame the young woman had died the way she did; but mostly it was because that incident was the first time he had ever let passion overrule his better judgment. It was also – and would always be, as far as he was concerned – the only time he would be that weak-minded.

He crossed his arms and leaned back against the rough gray wall, drove the memory from his thoughts. He watched the Lexus and emptied his mind of all but the business of the moment. Time stretched on, then suddenly the car's parking lights flashed twice and something beeped under the hood. Baccala stepped farther back into the shadows. A moment later, Tressider arrived, briefcase in hand, got into the vehicle and drove away.

Baccala waited until he heard the exit door go up and down. Then he made his way to the passenger elevator, entered the code he remembered from all those years ago, and found it still worked. He rode up to the floor the lawyer had come from. The main doors to the firm's premises were locked, but the young man went around the corner to a small door marked *Private*, with an electronic keypad on the wall. He entered a five-digit code and was not surprised to see that it, too, had not been changed since the days of Cathy Bannister. The door clicked and he pushed it open.

He saw lights on in a couple of individual offices, but the back area of the suite of rooms was dark. He went down a short corridor and keyed in a different code to a different keypad. The door opened and he went in. The memories hit him hard now. This was the file room where he'd brought her, there was the actual table where she'd sat and let him enter her, the same table where she'd struck her head while he was wresting from her the file she'd tried to photograph. Taking pictures hadn't been part of their deal.

He pushed the image out of his mind, went to the heavy

steel filing cabinet against the back wall of the room, the one with the double locks. He still had the keys from all those years ago – copies he'd had made in order to be able to meet the reporter's terms. He opened the top drawer and pulled it all the way out. The files hung in plastic folders. He took out the first one, carried it over to the table, and used his phone to take a picture and transmit it over the internet.

He turned pages and took pictures until he'd gone through the whole file. Then he returned it to the cabinet, got another, and repeated the process. He resolutely did not look at the corner of the table, did not think about what kind of person Tressider must be, to have kept the damn thing after washing off the blood and hair with soapy water.

He kept no track of time, but it was at least two hours before he had all the material copied – the ledgers, the secret reports, the agreements signed but never notarized, the minutes of meetings of the Twenty, starting during the years of Prohibition and continuing right up until last week. Every page of it was now stored on the hard drive of the notebook computer that sat on Chief Denby's desk.

The job done, Baccala locked up the cabinet, turned off the light, and eased open the door. The office suite was completely dark. The last of the late-working lawyers had left, and the cleaning service would not arrive until six in the morning. Still, Baccala did not exit the file room. Something was faintly tugging at his senses, below the level of consciousness. He stood in the doorway, darkness behind and darkness before, and realized that the hairs on his arms and the back of his head were standing on end.

He listened, ears straining. Not a sound. Nothing stirred the air. He slipped through the door, closed it softly behind him, the click of its lock strikingly loud in the silence. He stood still again, listening. If anyone was there, the sound of the lock should bring them, and he should hear them coming.

But there was nothing. He felt his way along the wall of the short corridor, out into the administrative section. Here there was faint light, from the standby telltales of the electronic equipment. He made his way between desks, heading for the door he had come in by.

But again something teased his awareness. He stopped, listening. Again he heard nothing, not even the swish of traffic outside; the walls were insulated and the windows double-glazed. He was about to take a step when he realized that what had been bothering him was not sound, nor movement of air.

It was an odor, a faint, musty smell that was at odds with the conglomerate smell of an office suite that was regularly cleaned. It was the scent of an ancient tomb, of a moldy old book found covered in mildew on the back shelf of a ruined room in a ghost town.

He drew a long, slow breath, felt his nostrils flare to catch the thin stream of molecules. *What the hell is that?* he thought. He took in another draft of air, and it seemed that the smell grew stronger, ranker. It seemed to surround him, made him cough, then the cough turned into a dry retching.

He made a noise of mingled phlegm and disgust. He had to reorient himself, his eyes swimming from the coughing spasm. There was the door to the outside. He could see a faint light leaking in from under it. The odor was even stronger now. He stepped toward the exit.

Something cold touched the back of his neck. The smell had become a stench. He gasped, then felt himself falling forward. Before he reached the floor the blackness became complete.

"We're here to see Poppy Paxton," Chesney told the butler when he answered the door.

"Miss Paxton is not receiving," the man said, as if from a great height.

"I believe she will be happy to receive us," Chesney said.

"Be that as it may, my instructions are..." The rest of the sentence was lost as the door closed in Chesney's and Simon's faces.

"I'd have that slave whipped," the magician said.

"He's not a... Never mind," Chesney said. "Xaphan, I think we need to do this the quiet way."

"Any way you say, boss."

"Where is she?"

"In the glass room with all the plants."

"Is she alone?"

"Yeah."

"OK," the young man said. He told the demon to have them appear in the room outside Poppy's field of vision, as if they'd just walked in. Then he asked Simon how long a cure would take.

"It never takes long," was the answer.

"Like the old man with the stroke?"

"Yes."

"Then, Xaphan, if anybody else in the house is heading for the conservatory while we're in there, you arrange for them to be distracted."

The demon nodded and took a puff on its cigar. "Distracted they'll be."

Chesney was about to say, "Let's go," but instead he thought for a moment, then added, "When I say 'distracted' I mean that they just thought of something else they needed to do. Not that something jumped out of a closet and scared them half to death."

"Oh," said the fiend. "That kind of distracted."

"Yes, not the kind that will have them waking up screaming for the rest of their lives."

"Gotcha," said the demon. "Now?"

"Now."

The plant-filled room was humid, the air heavy with vegetative odors. Xaphan eased them into the space behind a huge spreading fern near the old French doors. Chesney could see Poppy sitting in a white wicker chair underneath a potted palm. She was looking up into the fronds, vague puzzlement on her face.

"I distracted her, too," the demon said.

"Good," said Chesney, then to Simon, "Come on."

They stepped out from behind the fern and crossed the floor. Poppy's gaze came around and found them. If she was surprised, it didn't show.

"Hello, Poppy," Chesney said.

She cocked her head at him. "Have we met?"

"I used to work for your father."

"Oh."

She looked down at her hands. After a while, Chesney realized that she wasn't going to look up again unless she had a reason. "This is Simon," he said. "He might be able to help you."

She looked up. "To do what?"

"To get better."

"Better than what?"

Chesney had spent almost all of his life without experiencing guilt, even though he was raised to his late teens by one of the world's most skilled practitioners at the inducing of remorse: his mother. Letitia could have conducted master classes in the art of making people feel just awful. His autism had insulated him. Now, for the first time, he was confronted by the evidence of a wrecked life, for which wreckage he was largely responsible.

A bubble rose to burn the back of his throat. He found it hard to speak, and even harder to meet the young woman's wide-eyed gaze. He cleared his throat and looked away. "Just better," he said, his voice hoarse.

Simon had meanwhile been studying her. He turned toward the demon. "You removed the memories?"

Xaphan was paying attention to its drink. It swallowed rum and said, "Uh huh."

"But not the shock?"

"Nah, that was more the general situation."

Chesney weighed in. "There was a fight between demons, and the man who kidnapped her to Hell was treated rather brutally. She saw it all, close up."

"Ah," said Simon, nodding to himself. "So the contamination was spiritual."

"Is that a problem?" Chesney said.

"I worked mostly with disease and injury. One raising from the dead, but he wasn't very dead. Still warm." The magician was stroking his chin and examining Poppy from different angles. Now he stood back and clapped his hands together softly. "Still, I don't feel anything here that resists me."

"What do you mean?" Chesney said.

The man glanced at him with irritation. "I don't know how I do what I do," he said. "I didn't acquire the power to heal. I arrived with it. Do you know how you turn bread into excrement?"

Technically, Chesney did know that, without all the chemical details, but since becoming normal he had learned that some of the questions people asked him did not require an actual answer. "I understand what you're saying," he said.

Which seemed to be the right thing to say because the magician went back to studying Poppy, who had been turning her head towards each one of them as they spoke. She seemed to be growing anxious.

"There, there, young maiden," Simon said. He moved a hand as if smoothing invisible plaster on an invisible wall. "All is calm. Be at your ease."

The rigidity left the young woman's shoulders and the tension around her lips faded away.

"Very good," said Simon. "You're doing wonderfully. Now if I may just touch you?"

Softly, he put his fingers to her ears, to her eyes, to her nostrils, to her mouth, then finally took her hands gently in his. He shuddered slightly, closing his eyes; when he opened them they had, for a moment, the same far-away stare as Poppy's. Then he blinked three times and shook his head.

He released the young woman's hands and looked down at her. "There," he said, "how are you now?"

Nat Blowdell had spent the night walking the streets of the

city, occasionally wandering through parks, sometimes
sauntering down dark alleys. He hadn't been bothered.
Word must have spread among the other night haunters,
the predatory kind, that the tall man with the hunched
shoulders and the hard-drawn face was best avoided. Now
and then, he would go into a bar and order liquor, but
often as not after the first sip he would sit looking into the
mirror behind the array of brightly colored bottles. After
a while he would get up and leave. Only the drunkest of
drunks ever tried to talk to him, and even they would
soon give up, seized by a sudden shudder.

This morning, Blowdell returned to his office just
before nine to find his computer's monitor flashing a
single word at him and its speakers matching the flashes
with a strident tone. The word was *Contact*.

He touched a button on the keyboard. The tone
stopped and the screen cleared. Another clicked open an
audio feed. The computer had isolated key words: *demons,
kidnapped, Hell*.

He checked the time signature and a shot of cold energy
went through him. The words had been spoken only
seconds ago. He touched another key and heard a voice
he did not recognize say, "...turn bread into excrement?"

Then a voice he did recognize said, "I understand what
you're saying."

Blowdell did not wait for more. He addressed the empty
room: "Adramalek!"

The archduke's voice spoke from the air. "I hear."

"He has taken the bait! He is with her now!"

The demon's next words were sharp with frustration.
"I cannot see them! Why are they hidden from me?"

"I don't know, but I know where they are!" said

Blowdell. "Join me and I will lead you there!"

Far off in Hell, Satan's first assistant knew a moment of agony. All of the archduke's powers derived from the only creature in Hell that possessed free will. If it could not see something in the mortal world, it could only be because the Devil did not wish it to be seen. That was one of the cardinal rules, and had been so since the moment Lucifer had declared his rebellion and said to the multitudes of thrones, dominions, powers, archangels and angels, "Who is with me?"

At that time, Adramalek had been a mere archangel – little more than a corporal in the heavenly host. But because it was the first to say, "I am!" to Satan's question, it had been the first to receive high rank in Hell.

It had faced no crisis then, had not had to think. Throwing in its lot with the rebellion had seemed natural, as if that was what it had been created for. But this was different. Adramalek was torn, as demons are rarely torn. Something was going on, something Satan wanted kept to himself. Or maybe, and here the darkness grew even more stygian, the something that was going on was beyond even the Devil's knowledge. And Adramalek couldn't go to its master and say, "What's happening?" because the Boss was out of sight and out of contact.

But *I need to know* the archduke told itself. It wasn't used to introspection – simply wasn't designed to look inward – but when it made the effort, that was the phrase that bubbled up like methane from a marsh bottom: *I need to know*.

Join me and I will lead you there! the mortal Nat Blowdell had said. As if it were that easy. But then it struck

Adramalek like one of those bolts from Heaven that You-know-who used to send smashing down: Blowdell, as a mortal, had free will. He was of Hell, but not dead. And any demon could go into Creation if bidden to do so by a mortal who had mortgaged his soul.

Which Blowdell had done. The contract was still binding. And Adramalek had the administrative power to substitute another servitor for the disgraced Melech – the fine print said so. He called for the contract to be brought to him forthwith. A clerical demon scuttled in, offered the archduke the scroll. A quick unrolling, a flourish of the pen, and now Adramalek was empowered to use the free will of Nat Blowdell to go topside.

The elephant-sized mouse made a mess of Blowdell's office. There just wasn't room for a man and all his furniture as well as an archduke of Hell. The credenza was splintered, the desk pushed against a wall, the couch flattened. The ceiling would need replastering.

"Where?" said Adramalek.

"The house of W.T. Paxton," Blowdell said, from where he was backed against the door. "In the conservatory."

"Who?"

"The Actionary. I know his voice. And another man I don't know who seems to be some kind of faith healer."

The demon's piggy eyes squinted with effort. "I cannot see him."

"And I'm pretty sure," said Blowdell, "that that weasel-headed demon is with them."

The words gave the demon pause. Legally, he was probably all right to be here with Blowdell. But to crash in on the Boss's pet human, the mortal who was part of some plan Satan hadn't wanted his first assistant to know about? That could be tricky. That had the odor of disobedience about it, and though Lucifer was the originator of the concept, he had never shown any inclination to tolerate it in his servants.

"What are they doing?" Adramalek asked Blowdell.

"I can't hear it anymore," the man said. "You smashed the computer."

Adramalek noticed its surroundings for the first time. It exerted itself slightly and became a pig-sized mouse with a crocodile's jaw and teeth. It then exerted itself almost negligibly, and the damage it had done to the office was undone.

Only seconds had passed since Blowdell had called upon the archduke. The speaker on the computer was saying, *"There, how are you now?"*

"Who are you, again?" Poppy Paxton said. She turned to Chesney. "You look familiar."

"We rode up together in the elevator once," he said, "in your father's building."

"Oh," said Poppy. "What are you doing here?"

Simon stepped in. "We heard you were not well. We came to see if we could help."

All vagueness had fled from Poppy's expression. "What business of yours is my health? How did you get in here? Where are the servants?"

She rose from the chair as she spoke. Now she looked around and said, "What am I doing in here? I hate this place! All these stupid plants!" She batted at the palm fronds that, now that she was standing, were brushing against her head.

"I think we should be leaving," Chesney said, putting a hand on Simon's arm. "Our work here is done."

That brought Poppy's attention back to him. "I do remember you!" she said. "The uber-geek with the numbers! Does my father know you're creeping around here? Are you some kind of pervo stalker?"

As she spoke she stepped out from under the hated palm and punctuated her questions with a sharp fingernail to Chesney's chest.

"We'll be leaving," Chesney said. He tugged more forcefully on Simon's arm while calling, in a voice only his demon could hear, for Xaphan's assistance.

But before the fiend could ask for orders, Simon pulled his arm from the young man's grasp. "Ungrateful cow!" he said. "After everything I've done–"

"What have you done?" Poppy said. She looked down at herself and saw for the first time that she was dressed in pajamas and a bathrobe. "How dare you come into my house when I'm not dressed?"

She shouted a name, repeating it, more loudly with each repetition. Chesney realized she was summoning the butler.

"Xaphan!" he said, "Distract her and get us out of here! Now!"

From behind the wicker chair under the palm tree sprang a long-armed ape with canines to match. It gibbered at Poppy, said, "Booga-booga! Ungowa!" and reached for her. She fainted and Chesney leaped forward to catch her.

"That usually works," said Xaphan. It gestured and the ape disappeared. "Ready to go?" it asked Chesney.

Nat Blowdell had plenty of will. Adramalek had plenty

of power. The archduke made its decision. They ceased to be in the man's office and appeared in the Paxtons' conservatory. There they found an unconscious young woman stretched on the tiled floor and a demon and two men just fading from sight.

"After them!" Blowdell said, and the fiend acted without thought, as fiends do. Blowdell's will was like a thread it could pull that, being pulled, became a cord then became a cable connecting Adramalek to wherever the trio of demon and men went.

Thus it was that Chesney, Simon, and Xaphan appeared in the foyer of their mansion, and a moment later Nat Blowdell and Satan's first assistant appeared on the other side of the room.

"What is this?" Chesney said.

Adramalek was stuck for an answer. It had followed Blowdell beyond the limits of the demonic conceptual map and was now operating in the fiend's equivalent of one of Chesney's pre-Joshua fields of darkness. Instinctively – or as much as it could be said that fallen angels have instincts – it fell back on arrogance.

"I'll ask the questions here!" it said, and took the opportunity to reinflate itself to an elephant-sized mouse.

"So ask," said Chesney, "then get out of here. We're kind of busy and you're not welcome."

Which tossed the ball back to the archduke again, and again it didn't know what to do with it. Why was it that when it turned its attention to either of these two mortals – the annoying younger one that it remembered as the cause of Hell's going on strike, and the older one who seemed remarkably at ease when confronted by an immense and toothy fiend from the abyss – Adramalek found that its mind presented it with no knowledge.

The obvious answer – that Satan did not want his assistant to have that knowledge – did not satisfy. Somehow the archduke knew there was more to this situation, and it found that it had a desire to know just what the situation was. With all its ramifications, because somehow Adramalek also knew that those ramifications were *important*.

It saw that the weasel-headed demon was eyeing it closely. Another demonic instinct was to sense weakness, and Xaphan now had the aspect of a fiend that scents frailty. A hitch of the pinstriped shoulders, and a shooting of the cuffs, and Xaphan was saying, "You heard what the boss said. Ask your question."

It was a tricky moment. The last time it had asked what was going on, the fanged-weasel demon had suggested referring the question to the supreme ruler of Hell. Such a referral was not on Adramalek's agenda. The archduke had to work around that pool of light and still navigate through the darkness.

It could feel the energy quivering inside the man beside it, the cold flame of hatred that burned at Nat Blowdell's core when he looked at Chesney Arnstruther. Adramalek twitched its massive head at the man whose will had brought it here. "He'll do the asking."

Blowdell registered an instant's surprise. Then his own instincts kicked in. As he saw it, an archduke outranked a rank-and-file demon; and he, Nat Blowdell, was worth ten of any human being on the planet. Which meant his side had the power here, and the purpose of power was to get your way.

"We want to know what you're up to," he said,

addressing himself to Chesney. He flicked a thumb in Simon's direction. "And who's this bozo?"

The gesture made Chesney look in Simon's direction, which was a good thing because he saw the magician's face take on the same expression as when he had been confronted by the unfortunate Charles Darnay in Las Vegas. He also saw Simon's hand beginning to rise in the same way it had just before Darnay's hair had burst into flame.

He reached out and forestalled the magician's motion, though not without effort. Xaphan, unbidden, increased the young man's strength by the usual factor of ten. "We're not telling you anything," Chesney said. "So beat it."

Blowdell took a step forward. Chesney did the same.

"Wait a minute," Xaphan said, its eyes on Adramalek. "This ain't gonna end happy, you know that."

The archduke had to make a decision. If it retreated now, it could never come back to where Blowdell's will had carried it. Xaphan would report its transgressions to Lucifer, and Lucifer would exert his will. And that would be the end of all the powers and privileges of Adramalek's rank. When the fiend reconstituted, after the blasting the Boss would surely give it, it would be shoveling coals somewhere deep in Hell, and every demon that it had ever lorded itself over would drop by to take in the sight.

The only option was to destroy the weasel-headed demon and the witnesses. Adramalek was sure it could overpower Xaphan, reduce the demon to its constituent particles. If it killed the mortals they would surely go to Hell – consorting with demons was a mortal sin – and once it had them there, among the teeming billions, it could lose their paperwork and put them somewhere Satan himself could not easily find them.

That would buy time. And, with time, Adramalek might be able to ride on Blowdell's will to a place where it knew just what the *something* was that was *going on*.

The archduke made its decision. It drew itself together in the way demons do when they're about to exert themselves seriously. It saw Xaphan take note and saw the weasel-headed demon making the same preparation. Maybe it won't be all that easy, Adramalek thought. But there's no way back now. Here it all begins.

To Blowdell, it said, for his ears only, "I'll deal with the demon. You kill them all."

At this moment, the door to the study opened and Melda stepped out. She took in the scene with one glance, got over her shock quite quickly for a mere mortal, and said, "What the hell is going on here? I'm trying to work!"

"Now!" said Adramalek.

But now was not quite soon enough. Xaphan had read the situation correctly and had a plan. The last time he'd tangled with a demon, this Blowdell mug's Melech, the perturbations through the weft and weave of Creation had brought Satan to the scene. That was exactly what was needed now. The thing to do in the meantime was to protect the humans. And that meant putting them where Adramalek could not get at them.

And Xaphan knew, in the way that demons know things, just the place. It gathered up Chesney, the magician, and Melda, and sent them into hiding. Maybe not the safest place to hide, but one where Hell couldn't find them. As a parting thought he threw ten-ten after Chesney.

The three humans winked out of existence just as Blowdell leapt at them, full of his infernally granted powers. Adramalek saw them go, knew that it did not know where they were bound, but it found that it did not need to know. Blowdell's will was all it needed. As the archduke prepared to strike at the lesser demon, it also took the man into its power and flung him blindly after Chesney, Simon, and Melda.

Then the two demons began their battle in a blinding flash of conflicting energies that immediately hurled them out of the mortal world and down into the infernal realm.

Police Chief Denby came in at 6am, found the usual stack of documents in his in-tray that needed his initials. By 6.30, they were in his out-tray and he turned on his laptop. A box popped up in the middle of the screen to tell him that overnight he had received a surprising number of emails, most of them with attachments. He clicked on the first one, saw that it was from Seth Baccala. He opened the attachment. A wide smile spread across his face.

The screen showed a spreadsheet, full of names, dates, dollar amounts, and the numbers of the bank accounts in which the dollars had been deposited. He scanned the document, scrolling down to where fresh morsels of damning evidence waited. Then he opened the next email's attachment and found himself reading a confidential report of a meeting between two people who, he knew for certain, would deny that they had ever been in the same room together – let alone that they had agreed to the actions that the document laid out in fulsome detail and which would put them both in jail.

"Hee-hee," Denby said to the empty office. Then he keyed the old-fashioned intercom and asked the civilian aide who answered his phone if Baccala was in yet.

"No, Chief," the aide said.

Probably sleeping in after a night's good work, Denby thought, then said, "Send him in the moment he shows up. If he calls put him right through. Otherwise, I'm not taking any calls until I say different."

"Yes, sir."

Methodically, Denby went through the emails, saving each one to a file on his laptop. It was all here, everything that the members of the Twenty had agreed to, every scheme they had ever undertaken, with full accounting right back to the days of Prohibition. Land development deals; rigged contracts for every kind of civic service, from the laying of sewer pipes to garbage collection to the collection of nickels and dimes from kids at the municipal swimming pool; construction contracts for libraries, civic plaza, even Police Central itself; schemes for kickbacks and skims that ranged from the basic fifty bucks in an envelope picked up weekly from a beer-and-shot bar to the thousands skimmed from hotels and restaurants.

And that was before the straightforward take from the whorehouses, bookies, loan sharks, after-hours boozers, bootleggers, insurance scammers, dope dealers, fences, and porno film-makers who paid a portion of their earnings for the right to keep on doing business.

Every aspect of the operation, every detail of who got what from whom, was faithfully recorded and filed by the Twenty's bookkeepers. Because that had been the way of it since the very beginning: nobody trusted anybody; it all had to be accounted for, and everybody had to sign his name to the balance sheets.

The signatures were on everything, right back to the original formation of the cabal, when there had actually been twenty members, instead of the forty-seven who now ran the city. Baccala had found, photographed, and transmitted the original agreement – the Twenty's constitution – signed by men who had, for the most part, been dead for fifty years. He saw the name Tressider at the bottom of the page – it would have been the current holder's father or even grandfather. And the others, the old family names, some of them dating back to the days of wagon trains and Indian attacks, who believed they had the right to take every penny the city offered because, *dammit, our forefathers built this place!*

Denby was thinking, and your great-grandsons are going to jail in it. He keyed the intercom. "Has Mr. Baccala come in yet?"

"Not yet, Chief."

He went back to the Twenty's Ur-document, read each one of the signatures. The list of signatories was pretty much interchangeable with the city's social register. When Denby took this trove to the FBI and the US Attorney – there was no way he could handle this with local or even state forces – his home town would have to grow itself a new elite.

He leaned back in his executive chair and smiled at the ceiling. It was the best day of his professional career; hell, it was the best day of his life. He'd never been much for high-fives and victory dances, but he wanted to slap his palm against somebody else's – just once – but the only person he could safely do it with hadn't come in to work yet.

He picked up his desk phone and hit the button for his private line. He punched in Baccala's cell number. It rang once and immediately went to voice mail. "Get in here," Denby said. "We've got a lot to do. Call me as soon as you get this."

He went back to reviewing the material. He realized it needed a team of accountants to put the whole thing into its proper shape for indictments. Definitely the kind of investigation the Feebs specialized in. He picked up the phone again and used his laptop's search engine to find the number for the FBI's local office.

Then he thought better. He closed the laptop, put it in its case, and went out, telling his phone-minder he'd be back later, and that he wanted to hear from Baccala forthwith.

He'd drive out of town, find one of the vanishing remainder of pay phones, and call the FBI from there. As he wheeled the Chief's Lincoln Town Car up and out of the Police Central garage, the smile kept coming back. But he was wishing he had Baccala with him. His arm was itching for the high-five.

Xaphan was not there to fade them gently into the new place so the three of them landed with a certain amount of momentum, tumbling and rolling across a slope of long grass. Chesney saw Simon and Melda pitching forward in slow motion. He quickly recovered his balance, turned, and put out his hands to catch the woman and lower her to the ground. Then he pivoted and did the same for the slowly windmilling magician.

Melda sat up, again very slowly from Chesney's point

of view, and made a peculiar noise. It took a few seconds for her to get the strangely deep sounds out, and before she had finished, the young man understood that he was hearing a heavily slowed down version of, "Where the hell are we?"

"I don't know," he said. She lethargically turned her head toward him. Her mouth leisurely opened and she began to say, "What?"

Before she was halfway through the syllable, he realized that, to her, his answer must have been a high-pitched squeak. He waited, reigning in his impatience, for her to finish the one-word question, then said, as slowly and deeply as he could, "I... doooon't... knooow."

While he was waiting for her to put together a reaction, he summoned Xaphan. Nothing happened. He called again, and again there was no result. Wherever we are, he thought, we're on our own.

Simon was watching the two of them with a curious expression. Now he slowly passed one hand in front of him, a gesture which Chesney interpreted long before it finished as, *Who cares?* and began a glacial-speed rise to his feet.

Melda was still opening her mouth to say something else. Rather than wait, Chesney decided to examine their surroundings. They were about three quarters of the way up a hillside that was covered in long grass, with a forest of thin-trunked, broad-leafed trees farther down the slope. The trees thickened in both girth and numbers as they went down to the bottom of the hill, from which a dense forest rippled into the distance over other hills and declivities, with here and there a bare patch that Chesney thought might have been caused by forest fires in years gone by. As he looked at their closer surroundings, he saw a few blackened stumps. Upslope, at the top of the hill, a blasted fragment of tree bole lifted charred spikes to the sky.

That sky was blue with a few clouds, the sun behind one of them at the moment. It was either late morning or early afternoon. Chesney took another full survey of the landscape, saw no roads, no power lines, no buildings, no jet contrails. He remembered a line from something he'd read: *where the hand of man has never set foot*, and decided that this place fitted the description.

He turned back to Melda as she concluded a 16-rpm version of "What happened?"

Very slowly, he said, "Xaaaphaan se-e-ent us heeeere. Sa-a-a-a-fe-teeee."

Interminably, she said, pointing at him, "Ten-ten?"

He knew about the speed; what about the strength? He saw a rock nearby, the size of his fist. He picked it up and threw it into the trees below. To him, it seemed to go at normal speed, but the trunk it struck burst asunder, throwing splinters in all directions as if it had been hit by an artillery shell.

"Uh," he said, then after a pause, "huh."

Simon had been following their conversation. "Explain," he said, as quickly as he could.

It took Chesney a while to do so, even in shorthand: "Bad man, bad demon. Fight? Xaphan make safe."

"So it will come and get us when it's safe to do so?" Simon said.

The easiest answer for Chesney was a slow-motion shrug.

"We might be here for a while," Melda said, looking slowly around.

"Shelter," Chesney said, when she finally finished, to which she slowly nodded her head. He added gestures to indicate food and water, then had to repeat them more languidly. He was beginning to feel silly, and a little resentful, even though he knew it was not their fault that they took forever to say the simplest things.

He pointed upslope, then to himself. He put his hand like a flat shelf over his eyebrows to mime scanning the terrain. The other two signaled their assent and he waited no longer than politeness required before he ran up to the top of the hill, took a good look at what there was to see – more hills, more forest – then ran back down to where they were perhaps three steps higher than before.

He made a frown and held it until they had registered the expression. Simon said, "Nothing?"

A slow wag of the Chesney head, a long pause to make sure they had understood, and then he pointed downslope and followed the gesture with a cupped palm to the lips. The best place to find water was down in the trees. When he saw them nod their tardy understanding, he turned and strode down the hill and into the forest. At the treeline he looked back and saw them gradually following.

It was darker than he expected in the forest, the canopy soon thickening to exclude the sky, and the sun still behind its cloud. He supposed the sensible thing to do was to listen for water, but realized that, while he was in ten-ten, he wouldn't be able to hear anything quieter than a raging torrent.

From above came solemn hoots and drawn-out rattling sounds that he reasoned must be the chirps and tweets of birds. The trees grew fairly close together, but the dense overhead foliage meant that only a little light reached the leaf-mold-covered ground, so there was not much undergrowth. He peered between the trunks as far as he could see into the gloom, and saw nothing but more trees.

It would be easy to get lost here. He looked and found a rock near a root and used it to gouge a blaze in a nearby trunk. Then he went deeper into the woods, making a new mark every few feet. The ground was still sloping down, so he followed gravity until the footing leveled off. Then he went straight forward, keeping his direction true by lining up the marks he made on the trees.

A few dozen yards brought him to what looked to be a game trail. He stooped and gently poked the ground. It was soft to the touch, which he figured might mean that there was water nearby. There were some bird tracks, pigeon- and turkey-sized. Probably a good sign, he thought. Birds need water.

Most of the tracks went in one direction. He went that way, after first making an arrow of twigs to tell Simon and Melda, if their sluggish pace got them this far before he met them on his way back.

He followed the trail, still making the occasional blaze. It curved down a slope, then through the trees ahead he saw more light, as if the canopy was broken. He went forward and at that moment the sun came out of its cloud and Chesney saw a slow play of light among the trees. It had to be sunlight reflecting off water, and so it proved to be.

There were bushes along the edge of a stream that was perhaps ten feet across, and probably fast-moving if he'd been operating at normal speed. The water looked clean and fresh, even though to Chesney it moved like thick mud. And there was some actual mud at the stream's edge where the trail came down and widened.

There were more bird tracks here. He went down the last incline to get a drink; all this exploring at high speed had left him thirsty. The liquid went down his throat like a thick milkshake, which was a novel experience. He chuckled to himself, feeling good about having succeeded in his quest. Then he looked down at the mud beside the water's edge and froze.

There was a three-toed bird track, mostly filled with water. But he could see the deep impression that the three claws had made in the mud. They were easy to spot because the track itself was twice the size of a manhole cover.

EIGHT

Nat Blowdell arrived in a tumble that only ended when he fetched up against a boulder. Fortunately, he was largely indestructible, so the main effect of his landing was shock. He got over that fast – you don't succeed in politics unless you're fast on your mental feet – and within seconds he was focused on finding out where he was and where the opposition might be.

The first thing he ascertained was that the big piece of stone he had struck was not a boulder – it had been shaped into a cube, and on top of it stood a squared pillar of sandstone maybe three times taller than he was. He stepped back a little and looked up: there was some kind of statue on top of the pillar, its shape vaguely humanoid, but the details worn away by wind and weather.

He looked around. The pillar and its pediment stood at one side of a square platform some fifty feet wide, made of closely fitted slabs of the same sand-colored stone. In the center of the space was a waist-high oblong block whose top was darker than the rest. Blowdell went over to take a look. There were probably a number of explanations for the stained upper surface, but he'd put money on the most obvious: blood, and plenty of it, spilled over and over again.

From his vantage point beside the altar, he could see a fair distance. The platform had been built on top of a hill, with a set of at least a hundred stone steps leading down to a path beaten through the short grass that covered the slope. There were trees down at the bottom, enough to make a forest, but less than half a mile beyond where the trees began was a big clearing. He saw the regular shapes of buildings – more pale stone – and what looked to be a wall with a watchtower built into it.

Blowdell was an educated man. He'd studied history all the way back to Greece and Rome, Persia and Egypt. What he was seeing now was nothing modern; that wall enclosed a civilization illuminated only by sunshine or fire. But it was not a civilization that he recognized at first glance. He sat on the top step and studied the place as closely as he could from this distance.

The architecture was like a blend of Pueblo Indian and Roman military engineering: square shapes piled one on top of each other, with flat roofs supported by rafter beams that poked through the upper walls of the houses. He had a vague memory of an early culture that had built a city called Mohenjo-Daro in northern India; this might be it.

He wished he'd included supervisual powers in his list of demands when he'd originally bargained away his soul. He could see tiny figures walking the distant walls in the manner of sentries. They carried spears and might have been wearing some kind of armor; certainly, the sunlight gleamed on them in a way that suggested smooth, hard surfaces. And they looked to be wearing long-visored helmets.

Thinking of the sun reminded him that he ought to see where it was in the sky. There were some clouds, but they were on the move. Blowdell soon established that it was afternoon; in fact, it wasn't too far from the onset of evening. When the sun broke through a gap in the shifting sky, its rays slanted down. When they struck the sentries on the wall the pacing figures took on a silvery glow.

Definitely some kind of armor, he thought. And the fact that all the worked stone he was seeing was the relatively soft and easily worked sandstone, probably meant that the toughest metal the people over there could work was probably copper. Indeed, he might have arrived in one of the primitive civilizations of the Neolithic, where the first masons used tools of flint and chert to shape softer stone.

This could work out all right, he told himself. He knew how primitive societies worked, had studied anthropology and mythology. He had powers of strength and speed that should establish him as at least a demigod. He would just need to get a good look at how these Mohenjo-Darians, if that's what they turned out to be, conducted themselves; then he would frame a narrative and spring it on them.

Not much difference than a typical American political campaign, he thought. Sell them a myth, but make sure it's the kind of myth they've already bought into.

The bloodstained stone behind him reminded him that he would be playing for keeps. He would probably need to show some brutality right from the start. Again, though, that wasn't too far removed from how he'd made his living before he went to Hell.

He was thinking that he'd better make his way down to the city before dark, so he could find a place to hole up and observe the goings-on. He stood up and saw that his shadow had lengthened. The sun was almost touching the forested hills on the western horizon. He began to descend the steps.

But then he stopped. He saw motion on the path at the edge of the trees. Six figures emerged from the forest, carrying large round objects. They ranged themselves to either side of the path and after some positioning produced white batons – bones? Blowdell wondered – and began to strike what he now saw were kettledrums, setting up a steady, monotonous rhythm.

They continued to beat out the pulse as the sun slid behind the wooded hills. There was no lingering twilight, making Blowdell think he must be fairly close to the equator. So maybe Mexico in the time of the Olmecs? he speculated. He slipped around to the side of the platform and crouched low, keeping an eye on the drummers.

As darkness fell, he saw lights through the foliage. A pair of torchbearers came out of the woods, followed by another pair and then another. Behind came a single figure walking in a stately manner, then two who appeared to be attendants. Then came a column of marchers, some with torches, some with spears, making their way between the three pairs of drummers and beginning to climb the path that led to where Blowdell watched.

He waited until the lead torchbearers were no more than a hundred yards below him before he slipped back along the side of the platform and into the darkness of the now fully arrived night. But he had seen enough to predict what was about to occur. In the middle of the

column, surrounded by a circle of empty space, trudged
a figure bound in coils of rope, head down. Occasionally,
a spear-bearer poked at the sacrifice's back to make him
keep pace with the rest of the procession.

Blowdell withdrew. An audacious plan was forming
in his mind. There would be a ritual, an invocation to
the god – it had to be a god – atop the pillar. Then the
knife would flash and the blood would flow and all the
multitude would shout. That would be the perfect time
for him to leap onto the torchlit platform. His strength
would allow him to jump high over the crowd and come
down in their midst. It would be as if he had come down
through the darkness from Heaven.

Since the features of the weather-worn idol were
indistinct, it shouldn't be too hard to convince them
that their deity had blessed their rite with his incarnate
presence. He'd decide when the moment came whether
he would be a god who was pleased with their worship,
or a vengeful divinity come to deliver a smiting or two.

He fell back across the grass and let the procession
come. The torchbearers, priest-king – so Blowdell guessed
– and spear-carriers mounted the steps and gained the
platform. The sacrificial victim was chivvied up the stairs
and pushed toward the altar, then the rest of the column
arrived. There was not enough room for everyone on the
platform, so most of the crowd spread themselves out on
the slope and stood in a demilune bisecting the stairs. The
drummers had followed the tail of the column and now
came up onto the flat stones and began to beat a different,
faster rhythm.

Blowdell watched. They all wore some sort of scale
armor – leggings, too – and helmets with a conical face

piece, like ones he'd seen in a museum exhibit on late-medieval warfare. Surprisingly, even the victim, as he was lifted and laid on the blood-stained stone, wore the full outfit.

There was guttural chanting, some clacking sounds, then a kind of dance that involved shuffling alternating with jumping in place. The beat of the drums grew faster and faster, the clacking and grunting louder and louder. The priest-king approached the altar at a solemn pace.

The torches were lifted high, all sound and motion abruptly ceased, save for the arm of the officiant bringing down the long stone knife and the strange, bird-like cry of the victim as the point entered his lower torso and the blade sawed its way up to his sternum. The priest laid down the blade, dug into the incision, and raised up a gobbet of dripping flesh.

A soft sound went up from the crowd.

Now! thought Blowdell. He ran forward, gathered his strength and leapt into the air, sailing over the heads of the mob, turning a neat somersault to bring himself to an Olympic-quality landing on his feet on the other side of the altar from the celebrant of the rite, still holding aloft the victim's heart.

"Hah!" cried Nat Blowdell in an amplified voice. Every eye, save that of the dead sacrifice, turned toward him. Every yellow eye with a vertical slit of a pupil, set in a face covered in scales of green and silver, and shaped into a pointed muzzle, now open in surprise to reveal rows of conical teeth in a lipless mouth.

Not men of Mohenjo-Daro in scale armor, Blowdell realized. He was after all, an educated man. Thus he was able to recognize intelligent, fire-using, spear-carrying, god-worshiping dinosaurs when he saw them.

Chief Denby knew of a gas station that still had a pay phone. It was north of town near where the state highway connected with the interstate. He called up the regional FBI office and talked to a Special Agent named Walt Leatherbarrow. He'd met the fed some years back when a gang of traveling bank robbers had hit three banks in the city. With the usual cautiousness of a federal agent, Leatherbarrow agreed, for the time being, to be the contact man between Denby and the Bureau; but he would pass anything the Chief gave him to an anti-racketeering task force that was investigating corruption in a swathe of the country between Chicago and New Orleans.

"This will go to the top of the action list," Denby told him. "We've got everything, chapter and verse, going back to the days of speakeasies and rumrunners."

"Is it kosher?" the FBI man asked. "Or can some smart lawyer magic it all away as fruit of the poisoned tree?"

"It is completely kosher. It comes from an inside man who has volunteered the information."

"Will he testify to that?"

"He will."

"Then we're going to need to talk to him, soonest," Leatherbarrow said.

"No problem," Denby said.

And it would have been no problem, *should* have been, except that Denby still couldn't get in touch with Seth Baccala. After an hour's trying, he called the FBI man back again and asked if he could use the Bureau's resources to trace the location of Baccala's cell phone.

He explained the connection to the Twenty case and his growing concern.

Leatherbarrow took the number and said he'd call back. Denby hung around the gas station for an hour. Finally the pay phone rang. "The phone is turned on," he said. "It hasn't been used since last night, when it sent a lot of data to your department."

"That was the evidence," Denby said.

The Special Agent told him that the phone was still in the same general location that those calls were made from, four square blocks in the city. He named the streets that bounded the area. Denby knew they were downtown streets and that within the target area were the offices of Baiche, Lobeer, Tressider.

He left the gas station and drove back to Police Central, told his aide that he didn't want to be disturbed except by a call from Seth Baccala. He opened his laptop and transmitted all of the Twenty evidence to Leatherbarrow, then made copies of it on two flash drives before erasing it from his computer. The memory sticks went into his pocket. Later on, they would be placed in a safe deposit box he intended to open at a federal bank.

He tried Baccala's phone again. Again it sent the call to voice mail. Denby sat at his empty desk, fingers drumming on the top of his reclosed laptop. Sometimes, all you could do was wait. And try not to worry.

Chesney ran back up the trail. Where he'd left the arrow he went into the trees, following the blazes he had cut in the trunks. His eyes constantly probed the dark forest to either side. Twice he stopped and listened, but again he heard only the crackle and rasp of slowed-down bird calls. Or were they birds, after all? He'd never been fully interested in dinosaurs, but had had more interest in them than in other living organisms. He knew the basics, including that they had been closer to birds than to lizards and alligators. He also knew that paleontologists had mostly come around to the notion that the big, lumbering, scaly beasts of Fifties monster movies had in fact been warm-blooded, quick on their feet, and at least partially covered in feathers.

He stopped and listened a third time, near the edge of the forest. Through the last few trees, he could see Simon and Melda laboriously making their way down the slope to follow him into the woods. From their viewpoint, he had only been gone less than a minute.

Chesney strained his ears. From not too far away, he could hear a low, rumbling sound. It would last for a few seconds, like distant thunder, then cease for several more seconds, then begin again. And was he feeling a vibration through the soles of his feet? It was hard to tell. He could try to deduce what a slowed-down noise might sound like if it were speeded up to normal. But if the ground was shaking from leisurely impacts?

The trail he had followed had wound around quite a bit before turning toward the stream, but he could make a rough guess as to the direction in which the big footprint was to be found. He peered into the gloom of the deeper forest in that direction, put his hands behind his ears, palms forward, to try to focus his hearing more sharply.

It seemed to him that the off-and-on rumblings were coming from that direction. He stared and listened and after a few more episodes of the intermittent sounds, he thought he saw movement between the distant trees.

Slow movement, but only because he was speeded up by a factor of ten.

At first it was hard to make out. The moving thing was dark in color, like everything else in the forest, and its outlines were indistinct. Also, there were plenty of trees in the way and not much light from above, the sun having gone behind clouds again. But whatever it was, it was big, he soon had no doubt of that. He walked toward it, weaving his way between the dark trunks. By the time he had covered half the distance, he knew what he was looking at.

He turned and wove his way back through the trees, fast, and burst out onto the grassy hillside. Simon and Melda were still well up the slope and that was good. He ran up to them, and they were probably startled when he stopped in front of them, because he would have been no more than a blur. He didn't wait for the surprise to show on their faces or to make signs and signals. He picked them up, one under each arm, and ran as fast as he could – which was so fast the soles of his shoes grew hot from friction – up to the top of the hill.

He set them down, took a good look around for other dangers, and when they had recovered from the shock and focused on him, he pointed to the ground and lay down. Slowly, they sank down beside him. He parted the grass in front of his face and watched the treeline below.

Melda was saying something. He turned his head toward her and put a finger to his lips, held it long enough for her to get the meaning. Then he turned back to the view down the hill.

It came out of the trees, slowly knocking the thin trunks aside, leaves raining down on its feather-crested head. It was at least fifteen feet tall, Chesney judged, and probably closer to twenty. Its teeth, visible through its open mouth – the off-and-on rumblings had been its panting breath – were a foot long. He peered closely at its chest, saw the absurdly small front legs, naked and scaly as a chicken's, and the clawed hand.

The tyrannosaur paused at the bottom of the grassy slope, its head moving to scan the area. Chesney was remembering the one from the movie, that couldn't see anything unless it moved because some of its DNA had been borrowed from frogs. This one looked a lot sharper in the vision department.

Worse, he could see its huge nostrils slowly opening and closing. And now it gradually lowered its head toward the ground and the great orifices expanded again. Then the massive, feathered head swung ponderously up again and the improbably small eyes locked on the top of the hill. Where the three humans lay.

The head stretched toward them and the body followed. The tyrannosaur began to run up the hill. Chesney was no expert, but he wouldn't have been surprised to be told by one that the big beast was doing twenty miles an hour. On the flat, it would probably make thirty.

He got to his knees. Melda and Simon had just got themselves down on their bellies. They were still gaping at the on-rushing dinosaur when he scooped them up again, turned, and ran down the other side of the hill.

Tressider came in to work early, as was his habit, his office being pretty much the center of his life. The premises of Baiche, Lobeer, Tressider were empty, the scent of cleaning fluid still hanging in the air. But beneath the piney scent he smelled another odor, and that surprised him. He went into his own office and crossed immediately to the armoire. Its door was open. So was the panel in the back.

The lawyer let out a breath he hadn't noticed he'd been holding. He stepped through onto the staircase and climbed to the landing above. The unmarked door was closed. He knocked. After a moment, it slid open. The room was dim, as usual. He could scarcely make out the shapes of the furnishings. The odor that had been faint in the office, stronger in the stairwell, was rank here.

"Where are you?" he said.

"Here," came the voice from a far corner.

Tressider made his way around the empty chair and its side table in the middle of the room. The voice had sounded stronger, deeper. He knew what that meant, had seen it several times since his father had handed over the responsibility for what went on in this room. His main concern now was that this would not be another case of having to make plausible the disappearance of another employee or someone from the building's maintenance staff – although the lawyer was good at laying false trails that led investigators elsewhere, then nowhere.

Gingerly, he approached the dark shape in the corner. He had never known exactly what the process was that happened here every seven years. His part in the matter had been to find someone suitable – essentially, that meant young and disposable – and deliver them here in no fit state to resist. A day or two later, he would collect the dry, bone-rattling husk and dispose of it.

Looking down now, he couldn't make out any details. He said, "I'll need to know who it is. Was."

"He still is," said the voice from the dimness. "He won't be 'was' until later today."

"Show me the face."

A fold of cloth moved aside. Tressider looked down into the drawn features of Seth Baccala. The young man's eyes were closed, though motion flickered under the lids. The mouth hung slackly open, drool dripping from a corner. The pink flesh inside seemed paler than it should.

Tressider was confused, and not happy. Baccala was playing an important role. Had the young man come looking for him? Perhaps with something vital to report? "He's one of ours," Tressider said. "You shouldn't have–"

"Not one of ours," said the figure hunched over the body. "He was in the file room. For a long time."

"The file room? What did he have on him?"

"One of those things you use these days instead of telephones. It has been lighting up and vibrating."

"Give it to me."

A pale hand pushed a smart phone across the carpet toward Tressider's feet. He stooped and picked it up. Whatever was going on in the corner continued. He heard noises: a discreet gurgling, a faint whimper, a soft scratching that he took to be Baccala's fingernails scraping across the carpet.

He turned and went downstairs, closing the three barriers behind him. He sat at his desk and pressed the screen on the phone, saw that there was a voicemail message from a sender whose identity was blocked. He opened the message and recognized Denby's voice saying, *Get in here. We've got a lot to do. Call me as soon as you get this.*

He played the message again. The words told him nothing except that Denby relied on Baccala, which was precisely the relationship the Twenty wanted the two of them to have.

But what had Baccala been doing in the file room? A shiver went through him. He opened the phone's log and checked the outgoing calls, saw nothing. Then he checked the email outbox, and the shiver became a chill. He opened one of the emails then opened the file attached to it. Icy dread cascaded over him, as if he had been drenched in arctic water. The feeling did not go away as he opened other emails. The disaster was comprehensive.

He pocketed the phone and went back upstairs. In the dark corner of the room he said, "I need to ask him something."

"You cannot," came the answer, the tone firm and commanding. "The higher faculties are the first to go."

Tressider swore. "We may have a problem," he said. "A big problem."

"I've had big problems before," said the voice. "I solved them."

"Not this big."

He heard a sigh, then, "Tell me." In a few words, Tressider explained what Baccala had done, and what it could mean. When he was finished, there was a silence, then the voice said, "This policeman cannot just be removed?"

Tressider did not want to go into the details. "No."

There was a silence, then the voice said, "I will take care of it."

"You?" said the lawyer. "How?"

"Leave it in my hands. And didn't your father tell you not to ask questions in this room?"

"Yes, sir." Tressider's father had told him exactly that,

on the day he had taken his son into what was then his office and escorted him up the stairs.

"Then leave it to me."

"All right." The lawyer turned to leave. But before he could reach the door the voice spoke again.

"I will need to hurry now. Come back tonight for the… leavings."

Tressider suppressed a shudder. "I will."

In the foyer of Billy Lee Hardacre's mansion, having hauled themselves back from the inferno, Adramalek eyed the weasel-headed demon with the sabertooth fangs. Xaphan returned the archduke's gaze with no sign of deference to a superior rank. The elephant-sized mouse clacked its crocodilian jaws together twice. Normally, that would have made a fiend of Xaphan's rank step back. But the junior demon continued to hover. Then it sucked on a cigar and polished off a glass of amber liquid it held in its other hand.

"You'll recall," Adramalek said, "our recent conversation."

"I do."

"I'm going to ask you the same question again, about the Boss's whereabouts. But this time I'm not going to take no for an answer."

"My memory is that I said I'd go ask him if he wanted me to tell you."

"My memory is the same," said the huge mouse. "Except, suppose he was nowhere to be found. Suppose I said, 'Sure, Xaphan, you go and ask him,' but you didn't do that. Suppose you just went off somewhere for a while then came back and told me that he said not to tell me."

"Why would I do that?"

"Good question," said Adramalek. "Let's say that the answer is: because there's something going on."

The weasel-headed demon blew smoke toward the ceiling. "Like what?"

"If I knew that," said the archduke, "we wouldn't be having this conversation."

Xaphan drained its glass, clamped the cigar between its fangs, and said, "We ain't havin' this conversation. I'm gonna go ask the Boss, whether you want me to or not."

"No," said Adramalek, "you're not."

Xaphan exerted itself to depart. The archduke exerted itself to hold the demon here. There was a struggle, but it was unequal. The mouse overpowered the weasel.

"OK," said the latter. "So now what?"

"So now you tell me what's going on."

"The Boss don't want me to."

"So you say."

"Yeah, so I sez."

They looked at each other for a while. Adramalek saw that the junior demon was not going to offer up any information. The archduke said, "There's a way to find out what the Boss wants."

"Yeah. I ask him."

"Another way."

"What's that?"

"I take a good hard poke at you – say for disobedience. If the Boss has got his eye on you, he'll come to straighten me out, right? Because Hell doesn't fight Hell."

"That's right," said Xaphan. "You remember Melech? You want to take that risk?"

"I talked to Melech. I heard about the book. I heard

there might be big changes coming. Maybe one of those big changes is that the Boss doesn't want to be boss anymore."

"That would be a big change, all right. So then you're the new Boss?"

"Maybe."

Xaphan shrugged and straightened its cuffs. "So take your poke," it said. "We'll see what happens."

Chesney had to slow his pace when he was most of the way down the other side of the hill. He had never moved at superspeed over such a distance, and he wasn't wearing his Actionary costume, which was proof against all kinds of forces – including the friction his ten-times normal pace was generating. The soles of his shoes were smoking and the soles of his feet were correspondingly uncomfortable.

The grass continued at the bottom of the hill and up the next one. As he came down onto the flat, Chesney slowed to give his feet some relief. He looked to left and right but saw no reason to go in either direction. He was wondering if, with his augmented speed and strength, he could take on a tyrannosaur. Probably, if he could find some big rocks and get above it; most predators' skulls were not meant to take an artillery barrage.

But he would have to find somewhere safe where he could put Melda and Simon. A cave would be ideal, provided it was untenanted by something with claws, fangs, and an appetite. He'd take a look on the far side of the hill.

Melda was saying something, but he couldn't take the time to listen. She was probably uncomfortable, scrunched up on top of his hip like a tote-sack without handles. He would have to apologize later when he could afford the time.

He was almost to the top of the hill when he looked back and saw the dinosaur cresting the rise they had been on. It was still running and now it was gathering speed as it came down the slope. He watched it for a moment. Its nose was up and its nostrils flared. He'd read somewhere that paleontologists reckoned that a tyrannosaur's huge nasal cavities probably gave it as sharp a sense of smell as a vulture's – able to detect a few molecules of odor from a decomposing carcass miles away.

If that was so, they couldn't just outrun the beast. It would follow their scent until it found them. Unless they happened to come across an easier meal for their pursuer, Chesney would have to find some place that offered rocks, height, and shelter.

And he didn't have forever. When he'd specified the strength of ten men and ten times normal speed as one of his powers, he hadn't added, *for as long as I want*. Nor had he said that the powers should not be a drain on his resources. As he kept to a walking pace on reaching the top of the second hill, he was beginning to feel a little strange. He hadn't gone into detail with Xaphan about ten-ten's effects on blood sugar, aerobic efficiency, the build-up of lactic acid in his muscle cells, and all the other aspects of his metabolism.

He was getting tired. He looked back. The tyrannosaur was coming on, still slow by comparison to a ten-ten Chesney, but showing no signs of fatigue. The young man paused and took a good look around. This hill was higher than the first one, and he had a good view of the landscape. He was now near the edge of what must be a fire-made clearing. Downslope, the forest began again. If there were caves anywhere beneath the trees, he wasn't going to find one unless he stumbled upon it. But some of the trees were ancient giants – a lot taller than a tyrannosaur and too big for it to push over. All he'd need was a few rocks.

When he looked farther afield, something caught his attention: far off, there was another break in the forest. But instead of a patch of grass growing over ashes and charred stumps, this open space showed pale, rectangular shapes. Not natural, Chesney told himself. Man-made. He was struck by an errant thought: Reverend Erwin P. Baumgarten, the preacher to whose church his mother had dragged Chesney through ten years of Sundays, must have been right when he'd preached that mankind and dinosaurs had coexisted. Of course, he'd been right about the Garden of Eden, too, although he'd got some of the details wrong.

He set his sights on a tall tree with a spreading crown not too far into the woods and walked toward it. Melda was really trying to get his attention now. But he couldn't stop to accommodate her. Once under the forest canopy again, he might not be able to make a straight path toward the chosen tree, whereas the dinosaur on their trail would follow their scent like a homing missile.

The new stretch of forest was like the first, but Chesney hit lucky a couple of hundred yards in: a big tree had fallen and torn a hole in the canopy. He got a bearing on the giant he was heading for and pushed on toward it. His arms were getting tired, and his legs were beginning to feel light and at the same time dense. He had no idea what was going on in his cells, but he didn't think it could be in his best interests.

He found the tree and put the two people down. Simon seemed more bemused than alarmed by their situation. Melda's expression was harder to read; Chesney's best estimate was that she was at the same time furious and terrified. There wasn't time to discuss it. He pointed to the tree, ever so slowly, in a two-handed gesture that said, *Get up there*.

Simon began studying the trunk. It was sheer for the first fifty feet or so, before the first branches appeared. But several specimens of creeper had spiraled their way up from the ground, and some of them had been growing on the tree long enough to become as thick as the young man's wrist and covered with a rough bark. Chesney took hold of one and gave it a tug. It came loose from the trunk. He unwound it some more, carefully husbanding his remaining strength of ten, and in not too long a time, he had a climbing rope hanging straight down.

He began the process of signaling to Melda that she should climb, but she already had the idea. He realized that his speed must have slackened, because her movements in taking hold of the vine and beginning to ascend were not as agonizingly slow as he was expecting.

Simon was already tugging at another vine. Chesney took hold of it and added his remaining superstrength. The creeper came loose and he handed it to the magician. But instead of taking hold and putting a foot against the bark, Simon drew his brows together in concentration and slowly rose into the air. When the soles of his shoes reached Chesney's height, the man grabbed the vine and began to climb.

Chesney cocked an ear toward their back trail. He was mostly sure that the tyrannosaur hadn't made it into the woods yet. He turned and watched the two people climb. They were moving slowly, and Melda was having a hard time of it, but they were moving well enough. He made a quick survey of the nearby forest floor, but found no rocks worthy of the name.

He abandoned the plan of pelting the creature from above. He doubted he would have the strength or speed to do anything more than annoy it, and he didn't want to find out if tyrannosaurs held grudges. He unwound another creeper and began to climb. His arms felt odd now, alternately hot and cold.

He gained the lower branches, seated himself, and began to pull on Melda's vine, speeding up her rate of climb. Simon seemed to be doing all right on his own, although the growing speed with which he climbed told Chesney that his superspeed was fading along with his extreme strength.

He got Melda up to the branch and helped her get settled. She was making strange faces. Simon arrived soon after and found a branch of his own. As if on cue, the tyrannosaur came out of the trees and stopped at the base of their haven. It sniffed at the air, then at the creepers. After a while, it looked up at the three humans.

And it kept looking. Clearly, Chesney thought, here was a dinosaur with nothing else on its agenda than finding out if he and his companions tasted as good as they obviously smelled.

"Oh, my god," Melda said. It came out slowly, but not like before. Chesney figured he was running at best on triple speed. His arms and legs were trembling and his back felt as if a cold wind was blowing on it. He swung one leg around and over, so that he was straddling the branch with his back against the trunk. His head lolled forward and, with unbelievable speed, he fell asleep.

Adramalek could not have explained exactly what it did when it gathered its capabilities and exerted them against Xaphan. Demons, whatever their rank, had no understanding of their own internal processes. In the grand narrative of which all creation was the text, they and their counterparts, the angels, were not characters; instead they were like forces of nature or the laws of physics. They did not need to know how they did what they did; they just needed to be able to do it.

Thus Satan's first assistant – it still thought of itself as that – coalesced its energies in some part of its being, and hurled them at the weasel-headed fiend with a specific intent. The intent was to overwhelm the forces that held its opponent together, so that Xaphan would be reduced to its component elements. The result would resemble shadowy dust, drifting away from itself.

Of course, in time, those motes would recompose themselves. What God has put together, no demon can permanently sunder. Depending on the intrinsic fortitude of the disintegrated fiend, the recombining process would be fast or slow. Melech, blasted to bits by Lucifer himself, had taken quite a while to reincorporate.

As the archduke unleashed its blast, it did not know for sure that it would be successful. Disincorporation was a satanic power. Satan was absent, his whereabouts unknown. Adramalek was his authorized factotum in the infernal scheme of things. Therefore the Boss's disciplinary powers should have devolved onto his assistant's mouse-like shoulders.

On the other hand, Xaphan had told the archduke it was reporting directly to Satan now. That made the question of their difference in rank an open one. So Adramalek did not know in advance the outcome of its punitive strike. Not knowing something it needed to know was a troubling matter for a senior demon. Demons, whatever their status, were not used to being troubled, by uncertainty or anything else. The fact that it was troubled was also troubling to the archduke, and the unsettling feeling of being unsettled added a new element to the coalescing of its powers and their subsequent discharge at the half-sized demon in the pinstriped suit.

The concentrated energy left Adramalek and immediately arrived at Xaphan. The effect was brief and constituted a third incidence of troublingness for the archduke. The weasel-headed demon swelled about double in size and became less substantial as its elements were forced apart.

But a second later, it snapped back to its regular size and density. Xaphan looked down at itself, ran a stub-fingered hand over its vested torso. "How bout that?" it said, looking up at the huge mouse. "Looks like we're maybe not so far apart in rank after all."

Adramalek was truly troubled now. Satan had apparently invested a substantial portion of his will in the other demon. The archduke summoned an even greater concentration of its energies, an effect augmented by its being increasingly worried that whatever was going on was not a good thing for Adramalek, and flung them again at Xaphan.

The result was the same: the demon became thinner and larger for a moment, but its particles instantly regrouped and left the archduke looking at a fiend that was brushing nonexistent lint from its sleeves and looking back at Adramalek as if the assault was of no more consequence than a kick from a half-starved gnat.

"If that's all," said Xaphan, "I guess I oughta check in with the Boss, see what he thinks about all this rumpus."

"No!" cried Adramalek. Despite its bulk, its voice resembled the squeak of a normal-sized mouse.

"Yeah," said the other demon. "See you in the funny papers."

Xaphan began to fade. Adramalek, experiencing internal disharmonies such as it had never experienced before, summoned up a strength born of desperation. It hurled its energies at the vanishing fiend with a new intent. Instantly, a shell of adamantine formed around Xaphan, creating an unbreakable cyst. Adramalek waited no longer than it took for it to be sure that the imprisoned demon could not break free. Then it consigned both cyst and Xaphan to a layer of igneous rock ten miles beneath the lowest circle of Hell.

And that, it thought, is that. But as it made its way back to its office in the infernal bureaucracy, it remained troubled. Even with Xaphan out of the way, the fact still remained: *something was going on*, and Adramalek did not know what it was.

Chesney awoke to find himself still straddling the branch, although instead of leaning back against the trunk, he was lying face-down. He put his hands on the wood and carefully pushed himself upright.

"He's back," he heard Melda say. She was sitting near where his head had lain. He realized that she must have been making sure that he did not twitch in his sleep and topple to the ground far below. Unless the tyrannosaur caught him in mid-fall.

That thought made him look down. There was nothing beneath the tree.

"It ran off a couple of hours ago," said Melda. She pointed deeper into the forest. "That way."

"OK," Chesney said. He was still half asleep. His body felt drained and he was ferociously hungry. He blinked and looked around. Simon was seated on a nearby branch, watching him.

"Are you well?" the magician asked.

"I think so. Just tired." It hit him then. "You're not slowed down," he said. "I mean, I'm not speeded up."

"I think you used it all up," Melda said, "getting us up here." She rubbed her side and for a moment her face had an expression that, despite Chesney's childhood training and adulthood, he could not read.

A chill went through Chesney, but he put it down to the realization that he was trapped in dinosaur country without a superpower to his name. "That's not good," he said. "What if we run into another monster?"

"I'll set it on fire," Simon said. He looked thoughtful. "Or I could also make it think we're an even bigger monster."

Chesney remembered something. "You can fly! You can go to that city and get help!"

"I can get no higher than I can stretch my hand above my head," the other man said. "It's only useful for impressing peasants. Oh, and for getting across rivers without soaking my clothes."

"What's the point of that?" Chesney said.

"Don't ask me," Simon said. "I didn't choose my powers, no more than you chose to be the way you were before you met the other Yeshua." He indicated Melda with a nod. "We've been talking while you were snoring."

"Oh," said Chesney.

"In fact," Simon said, "I think now would be a good time for me to climb a little higher." He moved his eyebrows in a meaningful way. "Out of earshot."

"Why?" Chesney said. But the answer came from Melda.

"We have to talk," she said.

"OK. About what?"

She rubbed her side again. "When you picked me up," she said, "you cracked three ribs."

If Chesney had had more experience of conversations that began with "We have to talk," he might have replied with an apology – a really deep and heartfelt apology. Or maybe, "Gosh, that must really hurt." But the extent of his exposure to interpersonal relationships, especially of the intimate kind, was both shallow and recent. So he said, "I had to save you from the tyrannosaurus."

She nodded, as if giving his point full consideration. "Which you wouldn't have had to do if you hadn't got into some kind of argument with that huge mouse demon. In our house."

"I don't know what that was all about," Chesney said. "I didn't have time to ask Xaphan."

"That," she said, "is not the point."

Chesney was confused. "What is the point?"

"That's exactly what I was asking myself," she said,

"while sitting in a tree with cracked ribs, looking down the throat of a dinosaur that was looking at me like I was something tasty at the automat."

"I don't understand," he said.

"I know," she said. "And that used to be cute. The crimefighting thing was also cute." She thought for a moment. "The demon was never cute, but he wasn't around all that much. But now it's monsters trying to kill us in our own foyer or chasing us up trees. And you know what?"

"What?"

"Cute doesn't cover it anymore."

She was looking at him now and he had no trouble reading her expression. He'd seen it on his mother enough times. On Letitia Arnstruther's face, it said, *You're not the son I wanted.* On Melda's, it said, *You're not the boyfriend I want.*

"Oh," he said again. It was as if the air around him had suddenly become cold. "So what do you want to do?"

He would have liked it better if she'd produced a noncommittal answer. But she said, "Get home. Get things settled."

The old Chesney would have asked what she meant by things, and what constituted their being settled. The new, improved Chesney knew exactly what she meant. They were silent for a while, both looking at anything except each other. Chesney said, "Do your ribs hurt a lot?"

"No," she said. "Simon fixed them."

Before he could think that it wasn't the best thing to say under the circumstances, he said, "He fixed Poppy, too."

Now it was Melda's turn to say, "Oh."

The next silence was a lot longer. Chesney gazed out over the forest toward the hill they had come over. The sun was sinking behind it. After a few minutes, Simon called down from above. "I see lights. It looks like there's some kind of city. There are people with torches."

"So?" said Chesney. He would have said something like that no matter what the news might have been.

"So we should go there before the night falls," Simon said.

Melda called up to him. "Can you really protect us?"

"Yes."

She grabbed a vine. "Then let's go." But instead of beginning her descent, she paused then looked up at Simon again. "Would you mind climbing a little higher?" She indicated Chesney and herself. "We haven't finished our talk."

"Has it moved at all?" Chief Denby asked Special Agent Leatherbarrow. He'd called the fed on a disposable cell phone he'd picked up in a 7-11 store a block from Police Central.

"Nope."

"It's got to be trouble."

"Unless he's been playing you and working for them."

"No," said the policeman. "It's trouble."

"Any grounds for calling it a kidnapping?" the FBI man said. "We could put the Bureau right on it."

"Nah." Denby felt sick. He was sitting in an unmarked departmental car a block away from the building where he knew Baccala must be. He could see people coming out the main doors, heading for buses or bars at the end of the working day.

"So what do you want to do?"

Denby tapped the rim of the steering wheel with his fingertips. "I dunno," he said. "Wait, I guess."

"I guess you're right. We'll keep an eye on the signal for–" There was silence from the phone for a few seconds, then Leatherbarrow said, "It's moving!"

Denby started up the car. "Where? What direction?"

South, the special agent told him. The signal was now connecting with a different cell tower. Denby swung out into traffic, drove past the target building and turned south. He was on a wide, one-lane arterial.

"Still heading south," Leatherbarrow said. Denby had put the phone on speaker and laid it on the passenger seat. "It's got to be in a car."

"Keep tracking it." Traffic was heavy, but the city had dedicated curb lanes for buses only during morning and evening rush hours. Denby swung into the left curb lane and accelerated. He honked his horn to clear a pedestrian crossing at an intersection and kept going.

"Between Bleecker and Thurston," the FBI man said. "Wait, now heading west."

There was another arterial one-way street running across the road Denby was on, Chester Avenue. He swung across four lanes of traffic to turn right onto Chester. It was still part of the downtown core, but the old three-story brick commercial buildings that had stood on it since the pre-Depression building boom had been torn down since the turn of the millennium and replaced by high-rise condo towers.

"Not moving anymore," said the voice from the passenger seat.

"Can you run something by your computer nerds

for me?" Denby said. He pulled into a loading zone and stopped.

"Sure."

He asked the fed to crosscheck lawyers who worked at Baiche, Lobeer, Tressider against addresses on Chester Avenue. He wasn't very surprised that he got a match within two minutes. He was even less surprised to hear that the lawyer Tressider had the penthouse in one of the new towers.

NINE

Xaphan was in complete darkness, in a spherical cell no larger than he was, deep in the Earth's crust, and surrounded by an unbreakable, impermeable, impenetrable substance. Adamantine had been created by the Creator, back before He'd made the world, as the perfect metal for making shields, armor, and weapons for the heavenly host. That should have been a clue, the demon thought, that Himself hadn't expected things to go smoothly. After all, why create weapons and an army unless you were also going to create an enemy to use them on?

The thought was unsettling to Xaphan – not because it led to speculation about the deity having had a hidden agenda behind the Creation, but because it was an actual thought. How many times had it told its insignificance that it didn't have the capacity to think but only to know what it needed to know? Actually, the fiend knew exactly how many times it had done that; what it didn't know was why it was asking itself rhetorical questions. Which, it seemed, was part of thinking. Which it wasn't supposed

218

to be doing.

Hmm, Xaphan said to itself, the act another novelty, *something is definitely going on.* It set itself to the unfamiliar task of thinking its way through a situation. First, its assignment was to assist Chesney Arnstruther, who was now trapped in a dead-end world where Xaphan had put him for the time being to prevent Adramalek's mortal from killing him. Hurling the woman and the other wild card into the world of the Chikkichakk along with Chesney had been in tune with the Boss's instructions, which had been to keep his mortal happy.

But Xaphan could not carry out its assignment while immured in a subterranean sphere, so doing its job required it to get out and rejoin Chesney before some rough beast tore him into bite-sized pieces. But the demon could not pass through adamantine, so that was a problem.

Xaphan had never had a problem before. Besides always knowing whatever it needed to know, it had always been able to do whatever it needed to do. It would have liked a smoke and a drink, but neither rum nor Churchills could pass through the substance that enclosed it. Or could they? The demon exerted itself, but nothing appeared.

But the experiment caused another thought to manifest itself: apparently, Xaphan could use trial and error to gain knowledge it didn't have. It could apply effort and win results. So far, the knowledge won had not been useful to the fulfillment of its assignment, but the principle still stood.

Next it tried to determine if adamantine was as unbreakable as it was said to be. It turned out that it was. Next he determined that the stuff had no pores or gaps that a demon, reducing itself to infinitesimal size, could pass through. Indeed, the experiment caused Xaphan to reflect for a moment on the insubstantiality of the mortal world, which was mostly empty space, even the allegedly solid parts being constructed of atoms spaced well apart.

He thought about that now, and it made sense. Maybe the Hardacre mortal was right and the physical universe was, after all, only a working draft. The deity was constantly changing His mind about the story's direction, leaving pieces of it as dangling dead ends, so it was logical that Creation was a sketch. Why put a lot of effort into perfecting something that you might abandon after another chapter, only to start again further back in the narrative?

Now, adamantine, Xaphan pursued the thought, was fully real. It didn't have subatomic gaps because it was made of real stuff, heavenly stuff, which the Creator had fashioned to last forever. *Or did he?* Forever, the fiend thought, runs both ways, forward and back. But there was a time, if you bend the definition of time, when there was no Heaven or Hell. Before there was a Xaphan or an Adramalek or a Lucifer.

The demon was experiencing an odd exhilaration; this thinking business was strangely enjoyable. Heaven and Hell had come along well after the first chapters of the big book, the chapters that had been so completely abandoned that no trace of their characters had ever appeared in what the mortals called Holy Scripture. It was in those long-ago first chapters that the Chikkichakk had appeared.

Xaphan was again startled, as he had been when it first mentioned the Chikkichakk to Chesney. It had said something then about the Boss not wanting the mortals to know about them, but that hadn't been the truth. The truth was, now that Xaphan applied its mind to it, strangely more nebulous. Xaphan had known about the Chikkichakk; but the fiend now found in its mind a new piece of information.

Lucifer didn't know about them.

And now that the demon bent its thoughts in that direction, it realized that it did not know where that knowledge had come from. But it did know that it was the only entity in the present chapter of the big book that had that knowledge. For a moment, the fiend actually shivered. *Somethin'*, it said to itself once more, *is definitely goin' on*.

But now it knew what it needed to know in order to work out a way to escape. It was confined by adamantine, but there had been a time – the time of the Chikkichakk – when adamantine had not existed. If Xaphan could go back to that time, it would be free from its confinement, because it could not be confined by something that did not yet exist.

The question was: could a demon go back to the time before its own creation? The answer: Xaphan did not know. But it had, for the first time in its existence, a suspicion: the knowledge it was finding in itself, and this new propensity for cogitation – though those were not the terms in which the fiend expressed itself to itself – were not coming from the Boss. That left only one other source.

Xaphan did not want to think about the implications of its suspicion, and it was glad to discover that it didn't have to think about things. There was some element of choice. So it decided to think about the practical problem of how to assist its assigned mortal.

It did not know. The only way to know was to find out. The only way to find out was to see if it could go back to the time before its own existence. It exerted itself in the direction of the past. Nothing happened, but the effort did not rebound upon the fiend.

Must be a long way, it thought, and continued to strain.

There was a time to be circumspect, Chief Denby thought, and a time to cut the crap. As he looked across Chester Avenue at the door to Tressider's condo tower, he decided that the hour of the crap-cutting had arrived. He got out of the car and wove his way through the rush-hour traffic.

The place was fancy; it even had a doorman seated at a desk in the lobby. The fellow looked up as Denby approached the glass double doors, holding up his shield, and his hand dropped below the level of the desk. A discreet buzz came from the door and Denby hauled it open. He crossed to the desk and held the badge right in front of the doorman's face.

The man's expression changed from wary to mocking. "Chief of Police?" he said. "Where'd you get that, a joke shop?"

"You like jokes?" Denby said. "Hear the one about the doorman who got his ass slung in jail for obstructing a police officer?"

The doorman's face showed that he had belatedly recognized Denby from the television and that he, too, had just realized that crap-cutting time had come early. "What can I do for you, Chief?"

"Tressider, which one's his?" The doorman named a

floor and number. Denby said, "You got a pass key?"

The man's mouth turned down at the corners. His voice rose in pitch. "Now wait a minute. Don't you gotta have a warrant? Even the Chief of Police?"

"You've been watching too many episodes of *Law and Order*," said the Chief. "I don't need a warrant if I have reasonable cause to believe that a crime is being committed on the premises."

"What crime?"

"Accessory to kidnapping."

The doorman's resolve lasted another two seconds, then he handed over an electronic key card. Denby turned to head for the elevators, stopped, and turned back. "If I find he's expecting me," he said, "that cell is still available."

The doorman showed him both palms. "I'm out of it," he said.

The elevator smelled good and rose silently to the penthouse floor. There were only two units here, and Denby went to the one on the left. He listened at the door but heard nothing. He slid the key card along its slot and gently worked the handle. The door opened on a small foyer exited by a short hallway. He stepped inside and listened, heard nothing.

After a moment, he heard the creak of leather and the soft tinkle of ice in a glass. He went down the carpeted hallway, ignoring closed doors to either side, and came out into a glass-walled living room with a view of the river and its park. Tressider was sitting in a black leather recliner set on a steel ring, looking out over the landscape. His right arm rested on the chair's arm, the hand holding a half-empty glass of liquor.

Denby saw the lawyer's head move as he caught a

reflection in the window. The chair spun and he found himself looking at a haggard version of the man who had been his dinner companion at the steakhouse. Tressider looked to have aged ten years.

The lawyer showed no surprise. Nor did he ask the questions he would have asked if this were a movie: *How did you get in here? What's the meaning of this?* He just waited for the policeman to have his say.

"It's over," Denby said.

"The files?"

"The feds have them."

Tressider puffed out his cheeks and blew a little air into the space between them. "So our deal's off."

"It was never on."

The lawyer drank some more of his whiskey and made a small sound that could have meant anything.

"Where's Baccala?" said Denby.

Now Tressider made a different sound. Then he said, "He's gone."

"Where?" said the Chief. "Where Cathy Bannister went?"

Tressider shook his head, a tiny motion. "No, she was already dead."

"You mean Baccala's alive? Where is he?"

"He's gone." The lawyer looked at his watch. "What's left of him is still breathing, but what's left by now is nothing you'd recognize."

"Cut the crap, Tressider!" Denby said. "I want answers. You've got his phone. You know that makes you an accessory. Where is he?"

The other man sighed. "At the office."

Denby beckoned with one hand. The other was now

holding a pistol. "Then let's get going."

"It won't make any difference," Tressider said.

"It may make the difference between whether you get a cell or the needle," the policeman said.

The lawyer shook his head a fraction of an inch and made another little sound. As Tressider put the now-empty glass on the carpet and rose to his feet, Denby decided that the sound was some kind of laugh, the kind of laugh you make instead of crying.

"What do we need to talk about?" Chesney asked Melda.

"Us."

"What about us?"

Her upper teeth briefly scraped her lower lip, then she said, "There is no us."

"I'm pretty sure there is," Chesney said. He pointed one hand at her then the other at himself. "You. Me." He interlaced his fingers. "Us."

She reached over and gently pried his hands apart. "No," she said.

"What are you saying?"

She took a breath, let it out. "I'm saying this isn't working. It was working, now it isn't."

"What's wrong?" Chesney said. "We're still who we were. I'm a crimefighter. You're…"

"Yeah," Melda said. "That's it? I'm what? Lois Lane, the hero's girlfriend?"

"Well, what's wrong with that? You get to live in a mansion, look after the money, drive a nice car. You don't have to 'do nails' anymore."

Even as he was saying it, Chesney could see that it was the wrong thing to say. Her face was clouding over.

"This is not," she said, "a comic book. I'm at home, I come through a door, there's a mouse the size of a house trying to kill me. Next thing I know, you're cracking my ribs and a dinosaur is chasing us through the jungle. Now we're going to go over there," – she pointed to the distant torches – "and maybe they'll turn out to be cannibals."

"We'll be OK," Chesney said.

"Why? Cause you're the hero of the story?" She spread her hands in exasperation. "Simon was the hero of a story, and look what happened to him! So was Joshua, and he did two thousand years of *Groundhog Day*!"

Chesney could think of a couple of things to say, but neither of them sounded right. Maybe the best thing was to let her get it all out. He wished he'd had more practice at this being normal before he was pushed out of the nest and told to fly.

"I used to have an ordinary life," Melda said. "OK, some of it was lousy, but I could cope. Then I meet this guy, this kinda sweet, kinda strange guy, and then it's not normal, but it's better. But after a while, it all starts to go sideways. Now maybe I'm gonna end up dead."

"We'll be all–"

"Don't!" she said. "Don't tell me we're gonna be all right!" She folded her arms across her chest, looked down toward the ground where the tyrannosaur had left some feathers. "I just want a simple life again. That's all. Just a simple life, like normal people."

"I'm trying to be normal," Chesney said. "I'm still learning how."

"We're in a tree in Jurassic Park," Melda said. "You ain't doing so good." She called up to Simon, "Let's go," and reached for the vine.

Xaphan continued to exert itself. Nothing changed, the adamantine cyst still closely surrounded it, yet there was a sense that it was making some progress. Or *re*gress, since it was straining to move backwards through time. It felt odd to be acting and yet not to know the source of the will that allowed it to act. Another kind of creature might have wondered about that, but demons were immune to wonder. It concentrated instead on what it was doing.

Then, from one moment to the next, the sphere that confined it ceased to exist. Xaphan examined its new surroundings, and found nothing to examine. It was suspended in a featureless void, pale gray in color, with limitless distance on all sides, as well as what would have been up and down if this nonplace had any dimensions at all.

It reached out for Chesney's will, but found nothing. It reached out for Lucifer's, but again there was no return. That should have been an end to the matter. Xaphan had no will of its own, only acquired appetites. It reached for a glass of rum and a Havana cigar. Neither appeared.

To be a demon hanging in a void without access to some source of will was a recipe for inertia. Yet Xaphan became aware of some sensation – not so much an urge as an inclination. In an environment compounded of nothing piled upon nothing, it somehow sensed a tiny difference. Left and down was how it manifested itself, as if there was some faint source of gravity from that direction.

The demon exerted itself to respond to the slight pull. There was no sense of motion. Everything remained exactly nothing. Yet, as it had in the adamantine prison, Xaphan felt itself empowered by a will. To whom the will might belong remained unknown, which was a little unsettling to the demonic mind. But Xaphan was beginning to have a strong suspicion of whose will was powering its ability to operate, and that was more than a little unsettling.

Somethin's goin' on. But at least we're gettin' somewhere, the fiend told itself. It sensed that its referenceless motion might even be picking up speed.

"I said I didn't want to be disturbed!" Adramalek shouted at the clerk that crept through the doorway into the archduke's office.

The lesser demon resembled a centipede with a fox's head and with its arthropodic legs replaced by human feet in hobnail boots. It cringed so that its muzzle touched the floor and said, "Standing orders, sir. Request for service from an alpha-alpha-alpha. His Majesty is not available, therefore the solicitation must be reported to you."

Adramalek's first instinct was to snarl and send the underling scrabbling. But then another strategy presented itself: alpha-alpha-alphas occupied the pinnacle of humans who dealt with Hell; they were the tiny few who had negotiated and signed contracts with Lucifer himself. Those contracts required the ruler of Hell to respond when requested. And a contract was a contract. That was one of the rules.

"How do you know he's not available?" he asked the centipede.

"He's not responding to the request. What other explanation could there be?"

"Perhaps he's not receiving the message," the archduke said. "Try to reach him."

The fox head looked as desperate as any bureaucrat

who was told to violate standard procedures. "We've done so," it protested.

"Then do so again! Harder!"

The fiend skulked out of the chamber. Adramalek folded its giant mouse hands and settled back to see what happened next.

Denby handcuffed Tressider and put him in the back of the unmarked car. He got on the radio and called dispatch. "This is the Chief. Are Webber and Ortiz working this shift?"

"Yes, sir."

Denby knew that George "Tick" Webber and Carmela Ortiz were two seasoned patrol officers who were not part of the threads of corruption that ran through the Department. He told the dispatcher to send the pair to the front door of Tressider's building and wait for him if they got there first. Then he drove the roundabout way that the city core's one-way street grid required and parked in front of the building. A minute after he arrived, he saw Webber and Ortiz's patrol car slip out of traffic and stop behind him.

Denby got out and the two cops came to join him. "What's up, Chief?" Webber said.

"Possible unlawful confinement," Denby said, an index finger pointing up and toward the office tower. "But it's a lawyer's office, so we're going to go in careful and quiet. We don't want to lose the case down the road because we broke some rule."

"You say so," Webber said. "You coming in with us?"

"Yeah."

The two uniforms looked at each other then shrugged

in unison. "We need backup?" Ortiz said.

"You're it," Denby told her. He opened the unmarked car's rear door and helped Tressider out. "Let's go."

They rode up in the elevator. The main doors to the Baiche, Lobeer, Tressider suite were locked, but after Denby took the cuffs off the lawyer he produced a key and let them in. The lights were mostly out, but some of the firm's lawyers were working late in their offices. Denby went with Tressider to each one and had the senior partner order the late-stayers to leave.

When the floor was empty except for Tressider, Denby, and the two police officers, the Chief said, "All right, where is he?"

The lawyer led the way to his private quarters, unlocked the door and led them inside. Denby looked around, saw nothing. "Don't jerk us around," he said.

"Here," Tressider said and went to open the armoire. Denby shouldered him out of the way and looked inside. He could feel anger building in him, but he pushed it down. This was police work, and you did it dispassionately.

"There's a hole, just there," Tressider said, "with a button inside it."

Denby reached and pushed, heard a click, then saw the back of the armoire slide open. A dimly lit flight of stairs led upward. "What's up there?" he said.

"A room," the lawyer said.

"Baccala?"

Tressider nodded.

"Locked?"

Tressider shook his head.

Denby turned toward the two uniforms.

Tressider said, "Better not."

The Chief paused and looked at him. The lawyer had a look on his face that made Denby believe the man had gone through something that had stripped away all the pretense and artifice of his profession. "You and me," he said.

"Yes."

"Then you go first."

Denby told the two cops to wait for him. He drew his pistol and gestured for Tressider to start up. He made sure there was a round in the chamber then stepped through the armoire and began to climb the stairs.

"There's still no answer," the boot-footed centipede said. "If we don't respond quickly to an alpha-alpha-alpha summons, we're in breach."

Adramalek projected an aura of masterful calm, but inside the archduke was anything but. There was only one sin in Hell: to be in breach of a contract. The rules were the rules, and though Lucifer was the original inventor and perfecter of fine print and the ambiguous subclause, if any of his subjects failed outright to meet an agreement's terms, there would be Hell to pay. And the Boss exacted payment to the last painful groat.

For Adramalek, the choice was clear. In Satan's absence, all of his powers and responsibilities devolved onto his first assistant. It had to act. "Bring me the file," it said.

The centipede already had it, and proffered it in a pincer-footed limb that it withdrew from a boot. Adramalek scanned the agreement swiftly. It was a complicated document, with a surprising number of amendments and codicils, but the archduke instantly comprehended all that there was to know about the contract and the unusual mortal who had sold his insignificance for its benefits.

"I'll handle it," the archduke said. It altered its appearance so that it resembled one of the forms that Lucifer favored, then exerted itself. It appeared in a small, windowless room in an office tower. A short, powerfully built man with dark, curly hair and a grim expression, his wide shoulders hunched under a dressing gown, was pacing the rug.

"Where the hell have you been?" the man said.

"I am here now," said the archduke, manufacturing the voice Satan used when he looked like this. "What is your need?"

The man peered closely at the apparition. His coarse-featured face filled with suspicion. "You are not the same," he said.

Adramalek changed his aspect to that which the Boss had worn when first he had negotiated with this mortal. Now he wore gilded sandals and a robe of silk, and his face was a finer version of the man's own features. He used a language that no one but a handful of scholars had spoken since the Arabs had overrun the southern provinces of the Byzantine Empire to say, "Does this satisfy?"

The suspicion remained, but the man waved it aside. "I have a problem for you to solve. Delicately." Quickly, he outlined the situation that Seth Baccala had caused, the evidence he had transmitted to the police.

Adramalek signaled understanding. "The material has already been passed on to others," it said.

"I want it stopped," the man said. "Make the evidence disappear so that it cannot be found again."

"Easily done," said the archduke. "It is nothing but electrical charges recorded on silicon. Written on sand, so to speak." It was the kind of thing Lucifer liked to say. It exerted itself only slightly. "There, it is gone."

"Good."

"Is that all?"

"No." The man gestured to a pile of rubbish in the corner. "Remove that to where it will not be found."

A flick of the archduke's mentation and the dried husk that had been Seth Baccala was relocated to the bottom of a Saharan sand dune. "And now?" it said.

"I have the same complaint as before," said the man.

Adramalek did not know what that grievance might be, but it knew how Satan would have answered. It stared at the mortal without expression until the man swore and turned away.

"Are we finished?" the demon said. It looked toward the door. "You are about to receive visitors."

The man spun around, first to Adramalek, then to the closed door. "Who?"

"One is called Tressider, the other is the policeman to whom the evidence was sent."

The mortal said, "Kill them both." Then he amended the instruction. "No, don't kill Tressider. It would make complications. But kill the policeman."

Adramalek had never done fieldwork. It had always functioned on the administrative side of things. This would be a new experience. Accordingly, it waited until the door opened and the two men came through. Tressider's face registered surprise, then he quickly recovered and looked away. But the policeman flourished his weapon in both hands, aiming it back and forth from the demon to the broad-shouldered man.

"Police! On the floor, now! Both of you!"

The man in the dressing gown looked at the archduke. "What are you waiting for?"

The demon decided that a dramatic gesture would add to the occasion. It pointed a tapered finger at Denby and loosed a stream of coruscating energy. The mortal went rigid, the pistol falling from his hands, his face twisted in a stark rictus. Adramalek cut off the flow of force and the Chief's corpse followed his weapon to the carpet.

The death had been a painful one. The archduke had enjoyed the experience. It said, "There are two more of them downstairs. Shall I kill them, too?"

The room's occupant briefly weighed his answer. "No. Send them away and let them forget they were ever here."

Adramalek was disappointed but didn't show it. "Done," it said after a moment's effort.

The man gestured to Denby's corpse. "Put that somewhere where it will seem he died of an accident." The body disappeared. "And his weapon with him," he said. The pistol vanished.

"Anything more?" said the archduke.

The man in the dressing gown gave Tressider a thoughtful look. The lawyer was trembling. "Perhaps later," he said.

Adramalek inclined its head in the way it had seen Lucifer do and took itself back to Hell.

There was silence in the room. The occupant let it extend. Then he said, "Not one of your better days."

"I am sorry," the lawyer said. "I knew you would be able to deal with it."

"The young one, he was another of your mistakes."

Tressider's face first showed that he was searching for an excuse, then that he had abandoned the effort. "Yes."

"Do you have a son?"

The man saw the fear in the lawyer's face. The answer was a long time coming. "Yes."

"Time to start preparing him."

Tressider swallowed. "He's not interested in the law."

A cold laugh. "And you were?"

The lawyer's eyes were pleading, then Tressider recognized the futility. "No," he said. "I wasn't."

The man looked at the spot where Seth Baccala had eked out the last of his life force. "There are worse things than serving me," he said.

No, Tressider said, within the privacy of his mind, *there aren't.*

Denby was walking through mist. Around him he sensed a stream of other walkers, a flow that he was part of, though he could see no one clearly. It didn't occur to him to do anything else but keep moving. Ahead was a dimly seen archway, very tall and wide, with light behind it. After a while, he reached the opening and passed through.

The stream of people divided as they came into the glow, a few going to the right where the light was brighter, a few to the left where it dimmed and dwindled, each seemingly drawn in one direction by a powerful force. But most of the walkers went straight ahead to where someone was seated on a tall stool at an even taller lectern, head moving back and forth between the stream of people and a massive tome lying open under the figure's gaze.

Denby felt no force. He went with the majority. As he neared the lectern, he saw that the person on the stool was following up each consultation of the book by pointing a finger that directed a walker one way or the other. Until the figure's gaze fell upon the policeman, went to the book, came back to Denby then over to the book again. A finger flipped pages, ran up and down whatever was written there, with increasing vexation.

Finally, the gaze settled on Denby and the figure's voice said in a tone that should have been mellow but came across as strained, "What are you doing here?"

Chesney marched through the trees behind Melda and Simon, unhappy thoughts crowding his mind. He had to admit she had a point: this was not what he had had in mind when he'd seized the chance of a career as a crimefighter. It had all been a lot simpler when he'd first put on his Actionary costume. But, back then, everything had been either simple – in fact, blindingly obvious most of the time – or completely impenetrable. As someone had once said in another context, the old Chesney did not do nuance.

He knew now that for most people life was much more complicated than his pre-Joshua Josephson existence had been. Everything came in shades of gray, never black or white. There wasn't just right or wrong, true or false; instead there was always a spectrum of steps between rightness and wrongness, truth or falsity. It was as if the world had been put together as a complicated maze, with loopbacks and plenty of dead ends, and people had been plopped down into it like so many laboratory rats set to running the twisty corridors.

Chesney had used to be exempt from that rat race. His had been a somewhat bare-bones existence, with few highs or lows. He'd never been as happy as being with Melda had made him, but he'd never been as miserable as he was now. As he marched along behind her, he thought of things he might do, things he might say, to return them to where they had been, as a couple, not that long ago. But as he considered each strategy he was constantly brought to realize that he had no idea whether it would make things any better. Or make them worse, maybe horribly worse.

I'm not good at being normal, he thought. And I don't know if I will ever be.

He heard a crashing in the bushes, not far away. Something big was coming toward them. They all stopped, then Simon held up a hand and spoke a string of syllables. The crashing stopped and they heard a startled squawk. Whatever had been heading their way was now smashing through the undergrowth in the opposite direction at an even greater speed.

"I'm glad that worked," Simon said.

"You weren't sure?" Melda said.

"I've only done it before on Romans and watchdogs."

They walked on, Melda muttering something that Chesney could not catch. After a mile or so, they encountered a creature that seemed mostly composed of spikes and bony plates of armor, with a purposeful-looking bone-headed mace where a tail should have been. It didn't look as if it wanted to eat them, but it also didn't look as if it wanted to share the trail. Simon gestured and spoke again, at which the dinosaur turned sideways and lowered its head, while the blunt instrument at its other end began to sweep from side to side.

"This one," the magician said, "may be too stupid to be frightened. I showed it the thing with teeth that chased us."

"Can you make it see one of its own kind," Melda said, "only a lot bigger?"

"Let's see." The man repeated the mantra, then tried it again with larger motions of his hand. The beast rumbled something in its chest then abruptly battered its way through the undergrowth and out of sight.

"Good thinking," he said to Melda.

She did not take the compliment well. As they moved on, the muttering broke out again and Chesney heard the words, "Thinking. Yeah, right. What *was* I thinking?"

Abruptly, they came out of the trees at the bottom of a conical hill. Light was fading, but they could clearly see, a little way around the elevation, a long flight of stone steps that led up to a platform on the top. The stairs were lined on either side by people holding stone-tipped spears and blazing torches and there was a crowd of them up top making a fuss about something the three of them couldn't see.

Except, as Melda pointed out, "Those aren't people!"

"They've seen us," Chesney said. He thought quickly. They looked like lizardmen from an old Tarzan comic, with long legs that showed plenty of muscle. "We can't outrun them. My powers are gone. It's up to you, Simon."

"I'll try to make a good first impression," the magician said. "Follow me and stay close."

He levitated into the air and glided toward the bottom of the steps. He moved one hand and a ball of flame sprang into the air. He repeated the gesture twice more, and now he was juggling three blazing orbs in a circle.

"Three's all I can do," he said. "Come on."

The lizardmen were making hisses and clicks, but as the three humans reached the bottom of the steps, they fell back and gave the trio room. "Tricky," said Simon as he began to glide upwards along the incline of the stairs. "I've only ever done this on the level."

Melda and Chesney followed close behind. Melda reached out and took Chesney's hand. Her palm was sweaty and she was squeezing hard enough to hurt, but he was almost completely sure it would not be a good idea to mention it.

When they reached the top of the hill, they saw only a mass of scaly backs turned toward them. The lizardmen on the leveled top were so completely focused on whatever was happening in front of them that they hadn't even noticed the arrival of the flying flame juggler.

Chesney, stopped on the first step down from the level of the big stone platform, could see nothing but backs and tails. "What's going on?" he stage-whispered to the magician.

"There's a crowd of them," Simon said, still juggling. "An altar with a dead one on it, cut open. And a pillar with something happening on top. Can't see. Need more light."

The three balls of flame brightened and the magician began to toss them higher in the air. "There," he said. "That's better."

Then he spat out a rapid string of words that included *mother*, *whore*, some references to genitalia and the excrement of two different kinds of animals, and ended with an invitation to an unspecified individual to perform intimate but distasteful acts on his person.

Nat Blowdell's somersault into the Chikkichakk's lunar sacrifice – which they conducted every twenty-eight days during the dark of the moon to engineer the great pale orb's return – was a sensation. The first response was a general hiss that sounded like a thousand tires being let down at once, followed by a cacophony of clacking vocalizations that resembled no sound the man had ever heard.

Then had come the leveled spears.

But Blowdell had not risen to the top echelons of the political consulting business without acquiring the knack of showing fancy footwork in a crisis. He sized up the situation in an instant, homed in immediately on the key symbolic elements – politics is largely about symbols – and took forthright action.

He stepped forward, seized the dripping heart of the sacrifice from the priest-king's three-clawed hand and, after holding it aloft, threw it disdainfully to the stone floor. This action attracted an even greater hiss, followed by clackings and spear-levelings whose intent was unmistakable.

Blowdell showed no fear – *never let them see you sweat* was as firm a rule in politics as in stand-up comedy, two fields that have a surprising number of similarities. He bent his knees and leapt straight up to the top of the pillar on which rested the weatherworn statue. He waited just the right number of heartbeats – timing is also of the essence in politics and stand-up – then he seized the idol in both hands, lifted it over his head, and cast it down onto the platform in front of the altar.

The carving shattered into several pieces, one of which fortuitously struck the priest just below his convex breastbone – Blowdell, besides being skillful, had also always been lucky – and as the dinosaurian sank to his knees, gasping for breath, the spears were lowered. A great sigh went up from the assembled congregation.

Blowdell, atop the pillar, struck a dramatic pose, hands on hips, chin thrust into the air. It had worked fine in Mussolini's Italy, and it worked now in the late Cretaceous. When he finally deigned to look down upon the multitude, where the priest-king was struggling to rise, every eye that had been turned his way now dropped, and every head was lowered.

"That's better," he said, and if the words carried no meaning to his new followers, the tone did. They looked up at him now, although the priest-king was a little shaky in the knees. "Now let's get things organized."

He decided he would start with sign language. He held up his hands, arms spread, then slowly brought them down. The dinosaurs looked at him with reptilian puzzlement. Blowdell let loose a roar of anger and they all went back to the lowered heads and eyes.

He cleared his throat to make them look up again. Now he repeated the arms out and down gesture and fixed the priest-king with a glare. The creature cast its gaze in all directions for a moment, then performed a respectable bow, tail rising in counterpoint.

"Ah!" cried the man on the pedestal. The crowd took the meaning. They all bowed.

"Good start," said Blowdell. "Now what else can I teach you?"

He thought for a moment, then slapped his chest. Every

eye was on him. He pointed to the sky, then slapped his chest again. Another great sigh went up. The dinosaurs all looked to the sky, then to Blowdell.

"Ah!" he said again.

"Ah!" said the priest-king, or at least he managed a reasonable approximation.

"Ah!" said Blowdell again.

"Ah!" sighed the multitude.

Over to the east, where the sky was darkest, a glow appeared above the farthest tree-topped hills. Blowdell, who had studied anthropology the way an electrician would study wiring diagrams, put the elements of the scene together. He pointed at the first sliver of moon that was just appearing above the horizon then slapped his chest again.

The dinosaurians turned and looked at the rising orb then back at the man on the pillar. "Ah," they said, in comprehension.

"Ah," Blowdell confirmed.

He held out his arms to them in a wide, inclusive gesture, then brought both hands together, palms cupped. Next he brought the cupped hands tenderly to his chest – he was guessing that intelligent dinosaurs with hands probably held their offspring in such a manner. The gesture earned him another *Ah*, and he let the crowd know the sentiment was appreciated.

I always wanted to rule the world, he thought, and now I'm a god. Not bad.

The priest-king was eyeing him in a speculative way. There's always one, Blowdell told himself. He pointed a finger at the dinosaurian and cocked his head in a way he'd seen birds do when they were looking at worms.

The priest-king put out both his clawed hands and bowed again.

"And don't you forget it," Blowdell said, mostly to himself.

He rubbed his palms together and turned his supple mind to deciding the next item that ought to be on his agenda. As he did so, he saw a new source of light emanating from over the rear heads of the crowd atop the platform. Something bright was coming up the steps. Moments later, three spinning balls of flame rose above the dinosaurians, followed by a man floating in the air.

"Ah!" said Blowdell, one finger raised to command the dinosaurians' attention. When he saw it, he pointed the digit at the hovering juggler in an imperative mode, then mimed two hands seizing and holding.

The message got across. The dinosaurians spun around, and those within closest reach took hold of the flying man's ankles and hauled him down. The balls of flame continued to spin for a few seconds then went out.

Blowdell leaped down from the pillar onto the gore-streaked altar. "Ah!" he said, finger raised. When he had the creatures' attention, he signaled that the crowd should part for him. They did so and he passed through to the top of the steps. There he saw that his devotees had seized not only the floating man, but the other two he had last seen in the foyer of the big house. The three were struggling, but the dinosaurians were strong and numerous.

"Excellent," he said, nodding to those on either side. His tone and body language conveyed his pleasure, and he received another sigh of happiness from the congregation.

Blowdell pointed down the steps. Without looking to see if he was being followed – one of the marks of a true leader – he started down between the two ranks of spear-carriers and torch-bearers. He heard the sounds of his prisoners being hustled along behind him.

He smiled.

TEN

Xaphan continued to move through the void, drawing energy from the unknown source of will that had allowed the demon to outlast – although in reverse – the sphere of adamantine in which Adramalek had confined it.

The fiend still did not have the capacity to wonder where that will originated. It had called out again to Lucifer and received no response, so it was sure the Boss wasn't providing it with what it thought of as "the moxie" to cross the gray gulf. It had tried to reach out to Chesney Arnstruther, again without success – although the demon had a faint inkling that somehow it was moving toward its assigned mortal.

But though Xaphan lacked any vestige of a capacity to wonder – it either knew or it didn't know – its being was fully stocked with the ability to accept things as they were. Things as they were at this moment were the vast empty immensity, the faint sense of motion, and sufficient will to keep going. A smoke and a glass of rum would have helped, but no demon had ever shed a tear over spilled milk – or anything else, for that matter. Tear ducts had not been part of their design schematics.

But now came something besides space, will, and motion. In the fiend's direction of travel a tiny mote of light appeared. Or it might have been larger, but at a distance. Xaphan watched it for a while. It definitely grew larger, although that happened very slowly. When it was the size of a pea held at arm's length, it occurred to the fiend to ask the void a question. Perhaps whoever was providing the will might also provide knowledge.

"What is that?" it said. And immediately, it knew the answer. That far-off, tiny orb, glowing with white light, was the universe. But not, Xaphan also now understood, the one it was used to.

More knowledge accompanied the revelation: somewhere in that cosmos was the demon's mortal, in dire peril, and the fiend needed to find Chesney in the nick of time.

"Sure," Xaphan told the void. "What else have I gotta do?"

Denby had been plucked from the mist and the stream of newly arriving dead. He wasn't sure how that had happened – everything here had a kind of dreamlike quality – but one moment the old man at the lectern had been giving him a puzzled look, the next he was in a kind of office where the walls, floor, ceiling, and furnishings were of a uniform luminous white. A being with a face of unearthly androgynous beauty and wearing something like a white Nehru jacket was regarding him from the other side of the desk, not with puzzlement but with concern.

Denby had asked the being if it was an angel. No

change of expression had animated the sublime features, but the voice had held a tinge of some emotion when it said, "I am a dominion."

"A dominion? You look like an angel to me."

"A dominion is to an angel as a general is to a private soldier." When Denby nodded, it said, "Now, tell me again."

Denby repeated his story. The dominion stopped him when he got to the point where the tall, shadowy being had pointed a finger at him and a sensation like cold electrical fire had exploded through him.

"And you say that it was the Devil who did that?"

Denby considered the question. He might be dead, but he was still a cop. He'd interviewed enough witnesses to know that the human mind, especially in times of great stress, filled in perceptual gaps. People believed they had seen this or that because their minds insisted that this or that must have been part of the picture, even if they hadn't been.

"He was tall, elegant," he said, "with a long, lean face, a small pointed beard, and an aura of darkness."

The being tapped fingers on the desk. "Did he identify himself?"

"No. Neither did the man in the dressing gown."

"Oh, we know who *he* is."

Denby waited a moment, but no further information was forthcoming. "So, who was he?"

A pale white hand brushed the issue aside. "The real point is that you're not supposed to be here. Not yet. And demons, notwithstanding their rank, are not allowed to kill mortals. That's another point."

It tapped the desk again. "Added to that, Lucifer is right

now in the Garden of Eden, attempting to write a new set
of rules with another pivot."

"Pivot?" said Denby.

The dominion said nothing, just looked at Denby with
a neutral expression. But the policeman suspected there
was something going on behind the bland beauty. It
didn't so much seem as if the being was trying to decide
what to do; it was as if it was waiting for instructions.
After a little while longer, the being said, "Occasionally,
God chooses to invest one of your kind with... special
qualities. It happens when He wants to, shall we say,
change the direction of the... overall flow. We call those
individuals pivots."

"You said 'another' pivot. Was the man in the dressing
gown one of those?"

The heavenly being said nothing again. It seemed to be
waiting again. Then it spoke again. "Yes. He was one of
three mortals created at the same time: two Yeshuas and
a Shmoon. You would say, two Jesuses and a Simon."

"There were two Jesuses?"

"Yeshua was a common cognomen back then. But
one never used that name. He was a revolutionary and
adopted a cover name. Your language doesn't have a
word for it. You use a term borrowed from the French:
nom de guerre. His *nom de guerre* was Son of the Father."

"Doesn't ring a bell," Denby said.

"In Aramaic, it was Bar Abbas."

Denby blinked. "Bar Abbas? Like in Barabbas, the
murderer who was sprung by Pilate?"

The dominion quibbled. "The Romans called him a
murderer. He called himself an insurgent against their
oppressive rule. They wanted to set up a statue of the

Emperor Tiberius within sight of the Temple at Jerusalem. It offended the religious sensibilities of the people. In those days, they took the second commandment quite seriously. Bar Abbas was not particularly offended – he was no prating Pharisee – but he saw in the popular outrage an opportunity."

"To do what?"

"To gain power, to become king of Judaea."

Denby was just catching up. "Wait a minute," he said. "That was all of two thousand years ago. How is Barabbas still alive? And what's he doing in the headquarters of the Twenty?"

"That," said the dominion, "is a long story." It waited a moment, then Denby thought it must have got the authority to tell the tale.

"Let's start at the beginning," it said. "All of Creation is in the nature of an experimental process – a way of working out a problem."

"What kind of problem?"

The dominion made a circular motion with one perfect hand. "The problem of morality, of what's right and what's wrong."

Denby blinked again. "You're saying God doesn't know the difference?"

"From His perspective, it's a work in progress. He now has the broad strokes established but some of the fine details remain to be worked out. That's where you come in."

"Me?"

"All of you." Denby wanted to ask another question, but the dominion forestalled him with a raised palm. "He set up the universe and started it running. He watches it, closely and constantly. From time to time, events reach a point where they no longer make progress."

"We're going round in circles?" Denby said.

"Repeating the same behaviors without productive result is how He'd put it. When that happens, He intervenes, sometimes by vesting one or more of you with extra abilities."

Denby asked for an example. "There are hundreds," the dominion said. "Moses, Alexander the Great, Leonardo da Vinci, Napoleon Bonaparte, Oglog."

"Oglog?"

"He discovered how to make fire instead of having to go looking for it. It made you more sociable. Before that you only used to gather around food sources, and that often led to squabbles."

"But at one time He made three of these pivots."

The heavenly shoulders shrugged. "That was a special case. People were expecting a messiah, but nobody could agree on what he'd be like and what he would do. So He gave them three to choose from. One offered love and charity, the other offered rage and conquest, and the third was kind of a middling mush of the two. What you might call the control part of the experiment."

"So what happened to them?"

"The first Yeshua went out preaching, got in trouble with the authorities, and was put to death. But God didn't want it to end in failure, so He brought him back and that kept the story evolving. But then the next thing you know, Yeshua's followers turned him into a god – in fact, into God Himself – and that made more complications. So God kept the god part of the story, but discarded that storyline, along with the resurrected Yeshua.

"He put Yeshua in a closed loop, where he stayed until your pivot friend, Chesney Arnstruther, came along and rescued him. Now he's in the Garden of Eden seeing if he can work out a modus operandi with Lucifer. God's interested but not optimistic about the outcome."

"Jesus and the Devil are collaborating?"

"Not very well, from what I hear," said the dominion. "They didn't get along back when Yeshua was preaching."

Denby remembered the story. "Satan tempted Jesus, and Jesus told him to get lost."

"Yes. It pleases Lucifer to interfere, but then that's what he was created for. He tempted all three. Shmoon was not interested, either. He could heal the sick, fly a little, do a little fire magic, and make people think they were seeing things that weren't there. But what he valued most was his independence. When the Adversary offered him whatever he wanted in return for bowing down to him, Shmoon preferred to be free."

"And Barabbas?"

Another heavenly shrug. "He took the bait. He hated the idea of gaining power only to lose it to old age and eventual death. He told Lucifer he would bow to him but in return he wanted eternal life and indestructibility. He was smart enough to know that the Devil's deals were like scorpions – a sting in the tail. He could envision himself growing older and older, and feebler and feebler. So he had the Devil build into the deal a means to renew his strength and youth. Lucifer arranged it so that Barabbas can draw the life out of the young and healthy. Every couple of decades, he does so."

Denby thought of Seth Baccala and asked what had happened to him. The dominion said the young man's soul had been processed in the usual way and, since he wasn't good enough for Heaven or bad enough for Hell, he was now being recycled.

"But it hasn't worked out for Barabbas, has it? He's holed up in a room."

"He was already well into his maturity when he made his bargain with the Devil," said the dominion. "He wanted to be young again. So one of the first things he did was to steal the life from a boy who was the son of one of his closest followers. But the victim's father discovered the corpse and when he saw his rejuvenated leader, he understood what had been done. He and his brothers seized Barabbas and tried to kill him. When they discovered that he could not die and that his injuries always healed, they bound him and carried him into a wilderness, where they put him in a hole and covered it with stones."

"But he didn't stay there."

"No, after a few years of living on dew and insects that crawled into his prison, Yeshua called for the Devil to come and help him. But, of course, that meant making a new deal."

"Probably not a good one."

"It could have been worse. Lucifer agreed to protect him from ever being seized and locked away again. But in return, Barabbas had to give up one of the original boons – either worldly power or immortality. There was no question which one the pivot would want to keep. So he has lived on. But he can never be a king. Any power he acquires must be wielded from the shadows. At times he has been an advisor to the mighty, but eventually they come to fear him. Or they look into his eyes and see the depths of depravity to which they themselves might sink. Then they drive him away."

"So he migrated to my city and founded the Twenty," Denby said.

"He found a better home among criminals, hiding away, occasionally drawing life from a young victim."

"And when I came to arrest him, he sicced the Devil on me."

The angelic brows drew down. "That's the difficult part," the dominion said. "He called upon Satan, but Satan did not respond. One of his underlings must have."

"Which is logical," said Denby.

"But the contract states clearly that Lucifer himself must respond to Barabbas's summons. By not doing so, he broke the contract."

"And that's serious?"

"It's never happened before. It's not supposed to be possible. It's one of the cardinal rules."

"Like demons not killing people," Denby said.

The dominion's face was not designed to show worry. But it managed to do so anyway. "I think it means we're entering another one of those... episodes."

"What kind of episodes?"

"The ones where He decides it's all going in the wrong direction."

"What happens then?" said Denby.

"It's always something new," said the dominion. "Once, it was a worldwide flood. Sometimes it's a general collapse of civilization, sometimes just fire and brimstone on a couple of cities."

"None of that sounds good," said Denby.

"Or if He's really unsatisfied," said the heavenly being,

"He wipes the slate clean and starts all over again."

"The whole slate?"

"Heaven, Hell, Creation, you, me," the dominion said. "The whole megillah."

Adramalek had overcome being unsettled. Demons were designed to live only in the moment. The past was irrelevant. So it had filled in when the Boss didn't honor one of his personal contracts. It had killed a mortal directly. So what? Both of those were breaches of the code, but nothing had come of it. Nothing bad was happening to the archduke now, and that was all that mattered.

Up there in the mortal world, humanity went on sinning and falling into the abyss. Down here in the shadows, the infernal bureaucracy was doing its jobs: the Corps of Tempters went on tempting, the Punishment Battalions went on punishing the damned, and for a particular archduke of Hell, existence continued as it always had.

Adramalek remembered Xaphan. It extended its awareness down into the depths beneath the infernal kingdom and found the sphere of adamantine exactly where it had left it. The archduke could not, of course, see into the impenetrable cyst, but it could determine that it was whole and unbreached. Which meant that Xaphan must be still sealed within it.

Adramalek turned its attention to the latest productivity reports. The figures were within the normal range. All was well in Hell.

The Chikkichakk's prison was a hole in the ground, about ten feet square, its walls and floor lined with massive blocks of stone and its roof made of heavy timbers that supported more slabs of roughly hewn rock. The three humans were unceremoniously dropped into it through a hole in the roof, across which the dinosaurians dragged another flat boulder.

Darkness was then absolute, until Simon conjured a small flame. The light did them little good, except to let them know which corner the previous occupants of the prison had designated as their toilet. They sat in a row against one cold, damp wall. The magician extinguished the light, which drew a half-sob from Melda.

"Shall I bring it back?" he said.

"It doesn't matter," she said.

Chesney tried calling Xaphan, but still his assistant did not answer the summons. They sat in silence for a while, then Melda said, "That was him, wasn't it? The guy who kidnapped Poppy Paxton?"

"Yes," said Chesney.

Silence resumed, then Melda said, "I think I hate Poppy Paxton."

"That's not fair," said Chesney. "It's not her fault."

"You're right," said Melda, "it's not her fault. It's yours."

"I didn't mean for any of this to happen."

"Oh, well that's all right, then."

The old Chesney would have wondered if there was anything to say in a situation like this that would have made things better. The new Chesney knew that there wasn't. All in all, right now, he would have preferred to be the old him. Then he would have been just confused, instead of miserable.

Sitting here in the dark offered him an opportunity to look back on recent events and try to determine where things went wrong. At first, as a crimefighter, he had been happy. So had Melda. He remembered a day they had spent together before she had moved in with him. They'd met in the park. She'd packed a picnic basket. They'd sat beside the river, eating ham and cheese sandwiches and pickled eggs washed down with a Mexican beer she liked – Chesney had tried it and decided he liked it, too. Then they'd gone back to his apartment and made love three times. By then it was dinner time so they'd ordered in a pizza and he'd been delighted to find that she liked the same toppings as he did. She'd brought a movie for them to watch. He didn't understand a lot of it – it was about relationships – but he'd liked the way Melda had curled up beside him on the couch, pulling his arm around her shoulders so she could hold his hand.

When it was over, she made cocoa and they drank it looking out over the lights of the city. Then they'd gone to bed and he had fallen asleep spooned against her. The beer and pickled eggs made her fart in her sleep, but he hadn't minded at all.

It had been a perfect day. Then had come the whole business of Billy Lee Hardacre and his mother wanting him to be a prophet. He wouldn't do it, but he'd gone with Xaphan to the discarded draft of God's book where Joshua Josephson was marooned and brought him back to take the job. He didn't blame Joshua for the change that had happened in him: if people were around him they got healed of whatever was wrong with them. After a spending a couple of days in the vicinity of the wild card from Nazareth, Chesney had become normal.

"That's where the trouble started," he said.

"What?" Melda said. It sounded as if she had begun to doze off and his utterance had awakened her.

"Never mind," he said. He decided that mulling over the past was not useful under the present circumstances. But when he turned his mind to their situation and what they could do about it, it turned out that that wasn't useful either.

The pea hanging in the void had grown to the size of a basketball, still bright with white light. Xaphan continued to move toward it at what seemed to be an increasing speed. When the object had first appeared, the demon had exerted itself in an effort to be there. That was the way demons usually traveled within Creation: they didn't actually traverse distances; using the available will, they were "here" now, then they were instantly "there," with no interlude in between. This business of actually going somewhere was novel to Xaphan, although the experience of passing through a featureless void was not particularly engaging.

The glowing sphere was growing larger now, at an exponential rate. In little time, it swelled to the size of a small moon, then a planet, then a vast sun. As Xaphan streaked toward it, the sense of curvature disappeared altogether and the fiend was confronted by a wall of light that stretched up, down, and to either side as far as its eyes could see.

Abruptly the demon was at the boundary, and immediately it was through. Now it was in space and time, surrounded by stars and by the smudges that were distant galaxies. It saw no sign of the edge of the universe through which it had just passed, and no source of the white light that had shone through the void. Another kind of being would have wondered at that; Xaphan turned its attention to the question of finding its assigned mortal.

The question was answered as soon as it was asked. The demon took a moment to acknowledge that things were back to normal. Then it regarded Chesney Arnstruther as he sat with his back against a cold stone wall and his buttocks against a cold stone floor, deep in a hole where the Chikkichakk had put him. The other wild card and the woman were there, too.

The demon extended its awareness to take in the surrounding scene. It noticed the man Blowdell, who had been trouble before and was trouble again. There was no sign of Adramalek, and that was good; Xaphan did not want to have to fight the archduke. In fact, what he wanted to do was to report the whole Hell-fighting-Hell business to the Boss and let him take care of it.

But when he sent out his awareness to locate Lucifer, he got a blank return. Satan was not in this universe. Neither, Xaphan discovered when he took note of the wider situation, were any other demons nor any angels. And now that the fiend focused on the matter, it saw that this entire cosmos contained only four of what mortals called souls. The only insignificances were the ones that belonged to Chesney, Melda, Simon, and, in a deeply tarnished state, Nat Blowdell.

Around the four humans nearly a thousand Chikkichakks were going about their business: mostly hunting and gathering, along with some egg-tending in the birthing grounds, a fair amount of feather-preening, and amongst all of them a constant preoccupation with each one's relative status within the collective community. A small core of high-status dinosaurians were keeping an eye on the man they thought was an incarnation of the moon god, waiting to see what he would do next.

Xaphan was not surprised – demons were not capable of being surprised – to note that not a single Chikkichakk possessed an insignificance. Somehow, that seemed consistent with the absence of Heaven and Hell and all of their teeming multitudes. But why that should be the state of affairs here, wherever here was, was not a demon's concern.

The fiend ceased to be hanging in space and took up a position in a corner of the dark hole where the three prisoners were languishing. It would be ready when summoned. In the meantime, it made a search for rum and cigars and found the exercise futile in this soulless cosmos. It resigned itself to waiting. Demons were very good at waiting.

Adramalek had exerted itself to the maximum to locate Lucifer. The Devil was not to be found anywhere within Creation. He had left Hell without giving any explanation for his absence, though there was nothing unusual about that: Satan was a monarch of the oldest school, who gave his subjects orders, not rationales. He had learned the craft of autocratic rulership from the Originator.

The archduke had made the effort to find his superior not out of concern but from calculation. That the Boss might be gone on some extended jaunt was not unheard of; he was known to like walking to and fro in the world, and because he had free will he could do it. But an extended absence coupled with the remarkable fact that he had failed to answer a summons that was part of a personal contract? That was a new one.

Adramalek's office was next to Satan's chamber, separated by a wide door of black iron. The archduke now rose from behind its huge desk and moved its bulk to the portal. It rapped with oversized mouse knuckles on the metal – just in case Lucifer was actually sitting on his throne of iron snakes, brooding as he often did upon the insufferable slights that circumstances had unjustly dealt him.

Hearing no answer, the demon pushed the door open and surveyed the chamber. It was empty. The throne stood on its dais – expectantly, it seemed to Adramalek. The archduke approached the seat and mounted the seven steps that led up to the seat of power. The cushion on which the Devil's narrow buttocks had so often rested was too small to accommodate a mouse of elephantine proportions. Adramalek moderated its own size, turned, and sat.

It was an unpremeditated act. Demons were not made to be forward thinkers. But they were excellent at providing themselves with reasons and excuses for anything they happened to do. As Adramalek looked out across the shadowy throne room of Hell, a scenario picture presented itself: Lucifer was not to be found anywhere in Creation, nor in Heaven or Hell, and he had failed to honor a contract that bound him personally to the service of a mortal. There could be only one explanation: Satan was no more.

Which meant there was a vacuum at the top of Hell's hierarchy. Or, rather, the archduke concluded, there had been a temporary vacancy, but it was now filled. It considered the situation and found it satisfactory, except for one complication: Adramalek lacked the free will that emanated from the chief fallen angel to power the infernal kingdom. The demon's present actions derived from the will of Nat Blowdell, whom it had flung after that errant fiend Xaphan's insignificance. It would have to find Blowdell and bring him back to Hell, where the mortal could act as a kind of emergency backup battery to keep the system running until Adramalek could find a new font of power.

In the meantime, things were as they should be. The archduke leaned back in the throne of iron snakes and stroked the head of one of the reptiles whose body made up an arm rest. The iron serpent moved under the demon's touch but did not bite the hand that stroked it. Then the archduke heard a gasp of surprise and turned to the door through which it had entered. The boot-footed centipede with the fox head stood in the doorway, its eyes wide.

"What?" the archduke said.

"Another summons for the Boss," said the demon. Its eyes darted about the chamber. "He still doesn't answer."

The archduke grunted an acknowledgment. "I'll take care of it," it said.

"As you wish," said the underling. It turned to go, but Adramalek called it back.

"I will be working in here from now on," the archduke said.

"I see," said the centipede.

"Make that 'I see, sire.'"

The fox eyes regarded the somewhat shrunken but still huge mouse with the crocodile jaws. After a moment, it said, "I see, sire."

Adramalek grunted again. This time the sound meant,

Go away. The lesser demon got the message and departed.

The new ruler of Hell made itself at ease on the serpent-wreathed throne. Word would now spread quickly throughout the underworld. There might be some resistance, but Adramalek was confident it had the will to put down any rebellion. Though it would need to find Blowdell and get him back here.

In the meantime, it would go up into the mortal world and deal with the latest demand. After all, a contract was a contract.

"A contract is a contract," said the broad-shouldered man in the secret room. "And Hell has not met its terms."

Adramalek had reviewed the file once more. "We have," it said.

"No," said Barabbas. "The contract specifies that I be served personally by Satan himself while I live."

"As you have been."

"You," said the mortal, "are not he."

"Of course I am," Adramalek lied.

"You are not. You haven't the gravitas. You are a substitute, an impostor, and I declare the agreement breached."

There seemed no point in carrying on the masquerade. Adramalek dropped the semblance of Lucifer in which it had cloaked itself and said, "Be careful what you say, mortal. The contract is all that protects you."

"Don't try to intimidate me, demon," said the man. "I am no ordinary man. And now that my soul is my own again, I will go out into the world and do my will."

"You are confined to these premises," said Adramalek. "That is clearly stated in the fourth clause of the third codicil. Step outside, and you become dust. And your insignificance is ours."

"We differ," said Barabbas, "and I see but one way of testing who is right."

He strode to the door, pulled it open, and began to descend the steps.

"What about me?" Denby asked the dominion. "Do I go to Heaven or Hell? I mean, I didn't get last rites or anything."

"We don't pay much attention to all your rituals," the dominion said.

When the being didn't answer the main part of the policeman's question, Denby said, "Heaven? Or Hell?"

The dominion shuffled some papers on its desk. "We're... working on that."

"What's the problem?"

Again, a face not built for worry showed discomfort. A perfect finger ran down a page on its desk. "You're... It's difficult to say what you are, because it hasn't happened before. You're here too soon and for the wrong reason. You're... out of sequence."

"What does that mean? You're going to send me back?"

"If we did, it would be into another life."

"Not the one I was living?"

"No. And the one you were supposed to enter isn't ready for you yet."

Denby worked it out. "You're talking about reincarnation. Then why is there a Heaven and a Hell?"

The dominion's face showed something almost like irritation. "There have been modifications. Hell was becoming far too overcrowded. Even Heaven was starting to show strains. The problem was, He kept making more and more of you, and you all had to go somewhere.

"So the senior management committee suggested a change: the best of you go to Heaven, the worst to Hell, and the rest get recycled."

"I'm supposed to get recycled?"

"Yes, but not yet. You're... like a hotel guest who shows up before the room is ready."

"So where do I wait? In the bar?"

The heavenly being frowned. "We don't have a bar. I suppose we could send you back to Earth in an insubstantial form."

"You mean like a ghost?"

"There are no such things as ghosts. But if there were, that's what you'd be. You might find it diverting." The angelic face tightened in unaccustomed thought. "Or we could put you in one of the fossilized versions."

Denby remembered the building of the ziggurat. "No, thanks," he said. He did some thinking. "Where's Chesney, the kid who got me into all this?"

Now the dominion wore the expression of someone who can't remember some fact that ought to be readily available. "I don't know," it said after a fruitless effort. "He's not in Heaven, Hell, or on Earth. Nor is he in the Garden of Eden or any of the discarded universes. Isn't that strange?"

"You ought to know," Denby said. "I thought you guys knew everything."

"So," said the heavenly being, "did I." Lines formed on its brow and around the corners of its mouth. "Something is going on," it said.

"More like something is going wrong," said the policeman.

The dominion tapped a perfect fingernail on its desktop. Its frown lines deepened. It didn't disagree.

Chesney was awakened by a heavy scraping sound. The dinosaurians were dragging aside the great slab of rock that sealed them in their prison hole. The young man had been dreaming a happy dream: he and Melda had been… but the sense of contentment evaporated completely as the Chikkichakk lowered a log into which steps had been cut. They made chittering sounds and jerky motions with their toothy snouts.

Simon said, "They want us to go up."

Melda stiffly got to her feet. "We should have made a plan," she said.

She was right, Chesney thought, and wrong. Without Xaphan, nothing they could do would be of much use against Nat Blowdell's Hell-enhanced powers. Still, he ought to have made an effort, instead of sitting in the dungeon and dreaming of better times. As he stood up and moved toward the rough ladder, he was feeling increasingly unhappy with his own failure. But at least he could try to play the part; he put a hand on Simon's arm and said, "I got us into this. I'll go first."

He scaled the ladder and emerged into an open space ringed by scaly creatures bearing spears and stone-headed clubs. He couldn't read their facial expressions – couldn't even be sure they were capable of making them – but he was willing to bet that the exposed conical teeth he saw on all sides were not set in smiles of welcome, preliminary to an invitation to join the tribe.

The crowd waited until Melda and Simon had exited the hole in the ground, then they hustled the three prisoners

away. The procession passed along narrow streets paved
in rubbish – mostly the bones of small animals – with
twists and turns and occasional short flights of steps
where the ground rose or fell. Birdlike faces peered from
doorways and windows, the females somewhat larger
than the males, the half-grown and hatchlings peering
from behind their mothers. Chesney heard clucks and
hisses as they passed, and a few clackings of jaws that he
unhappily interpreted as expressions of appetite.

They came out of the warren of streets into an open
space at the center of town. In the middle of the plaza,
where the ground rose to a low hill, the dinosaurians had
built a wide platform of squared blocks, half of which
was occupied by a two-story stone building. The shape
of a crescent moon was crudely carved above the lintel
of its doorless entrance. The three humans were prodded
toward the base of the rise, where the mob of warriors
stopped and gazed up at the open doorway in silence.

A little time passed. Simon whispered, "He has a grasp
of the showman's art. He lets his audience's expectation
grow." Then the magician swore as one of the dinosaurians
punished his lèse-majesté with a poke from a spearhead.

A moment later, Blowdell appeared in the doorway
and moved to the edge of the platform. He looked down
at the prisoners with a stern face, but Chesney saw a hint
of a smirk touch the man's lips as their gazes met.

A peremptory gesture and a few croaked syllables from
Blowdell told the crowd to hustle the prisoners toward
the base of a stone-paved ramp that switchbacked up
the mound. By the time they reached the top and were
pressed toward the open space beside the building, the
new ruler of the Chikkichakk had ensconced himself

in a tripod-legged chair upholstered in scaly leather. Ranged behind him were the demoted priest-king and his entourage, the former holding a long-bladed stone knife that was stained darkly for half its length.

When the three prisoners were brought before him, Blowdell affected a thoughtful mien, with plenty of head-tilting and chin-stroking. But Chesney could see the fierce glee in the man's eyes, and he didn't wait for the charade to continue. He was more miserable than he'd ever been before, more even than he'd been under his mother's thumb. If it all came to an end here, then so be it.

"I'm the one you want," he said. "Let the others go."

He felt Melda's cold hand slip into his own. It should have been comforting, but instead it made him feel even worse than he had been feeling moments before. He had let her down. He had let everyone down. He couldn't bring himself to turn and look at her; besides, he thought he'd better keep his eyes on Blowdell.

The man in the chair was continuing his show of deep thought. But now he smiled and said, "And just where would I let them go to?" He extended a hand to take in the surrounding forest. "There's nothing out there but teeth and claws. Besides, I might want some…" – he gave a little shrug and showed a little smile – "company."

As he said the last word, his eyes took inventory of Melda then his face formed an expression that said he'd seen better but had also seen worse.

Chesney felt Melda's grip tighten. Anger came up in him, which was much better than despair. He said, "Forget it."

Blowdell smiled as if the young man was a boastful child. He looked at Simon and said, "What have *you* got to offer?"

The magician returned him a cool look. "A few tricks, some entertaining illusions."

"Can you teach me how to fly?"

Simon shrugged. "I don't even know how I do it myself."

"Oh, well," said Blowdell. "Too bad."

"Listen," said Chesney.

But the man in the chair did not. He extended an index finger, bent at the middle knuckle, then flicked the end of the digit up to point at Chesney. The young man felt a blow strike his chest as if someone had thrown a sandbag at him. He staggered backward, the breath knocked out of him, and Melda's hand was torn from his grasp. He fetched up against the spear-carriers who had hustled them up the slope. The dinosaurians used the shafts of their spears to thrust him back.

"You listen," said Blowdell. "You put me through Hell."

"You put yourself–"

This time, the buffet was harder and lower. Chesney bent double as pain shot through his belly. He put his hands on his knees and had to struggle against the urge to vomit.

"Around here," Blowdell said, "we tend to see things from my point of view. I am, after all, the incarnation of Ekkekkikik, the moon god."

He paused as if to savor a transient mood, then his gaze hardened on the prisoners. "This is not," he said, gesturing to take in their surroundings, "quite what I had in mind. But it is definitely a chief executive position, with the benefit of my not being hampered by any annoying constitutional restrictions.

"True, it lacks certain comforts. For one thing, I'm going to have to teach them how to cook." He raised both hands in mock horror. "The meat's either charred on the outside and raw through the middle, or just raw all the way. And they don't know squat from vegetables." He looked down at the semi-cured hide that covered the tripod seat. "And the furniture is crap."

Then he looked at Melda. "But there are plenty of feathers to make a bed. So it will all work out."

"I'll cut your throat while you're sleeping," Melda said. "Then I'll be the moon queen."

"Oh, feisty," Blowdell said. "Even better." He turned and took the stained knife from the priest-king. He drew it along the rim of the scaled hide between his legs, cutting an incision an inch deep. Then he applied the edge to his own throat. A pale line showed where he had pressed the sharp stone hard into his flesh, but the skin remained unbroken.

"That really impressed them last night," he said. "The same goes for bashing my brains in, or setting me on fire, or putting poison in my breakfast cereal."

He gave them the kind of smile you see on a man who has just learned he's won the lottery, then rubbed his hands together and said, "But now we need to get to business. My followers are no doubt anxious to discover what you taste like, and I'm the kind of god who gives his congregation what they want."

He looked at Chesney. "All that time I was in Hell, I kept thinking about what I would do to you, once you were in my hands again." His mouth turned down at the corners in a clown's frown. "A lot of it is now impossible," – he spread his hands – "I just can't get the equipment."

Now he clasped his hands in a gesture of acquiescence. "But I've told myself that watching you being eaten alive will just have to do."

He pointed at the young man and made some throat-clearing noises. The Chikkichakk replied with a collective hiss and clacking of jaws. Then the ones closest to Chesney seized him in their clawed hands, lifted him from his feet, and bore him away from the others.

"No!" Melda cried and tried to pull him loose, but at a gesture from Blowdell two dinosaurians took her by the arms and held her back.

Chesney's clothes were torn away and he was flung to the hard stone of the platform. A ring of Chikkichakk – the priest and his entourage plus a few chosen warriors – surrounded him. They had dropped their weapons and now faced him with just their natural armament. They bared pointed fangs, flexed clawed hands, and scraped at the stone beneath their feet with oversized talons curved like new moons.

Slavering, ropes of drool dripping from their gaping maws, heads bobbing like chickens that have spotted a juicy worm, they closed in.

ELEVEN

Barabbas stepped out of the armoire in Tressider's office. The usual occupant wasn't there, which disappointed the ancient man slightly; he would have liked to have seen the lawyer's face as he crossed to the closed door and opened it. He'd always thought that Tressider was a bloodless specimen, like his preening father before him, although the ancestor who'd founded the law firm four generations ago had been indistinguishable from a pirate only by his table manners.

It was afternoon when he passed through the main offices of Baiche, Lobeer, Tressider. Clerks and paralegals and junior attorneys were being busy among the desks, file cabinets, and workstations, but the hum of their background noise abruptly stopped as they took notice of him. The fact that he had appeared unheralded from the inner sanctum of the senior partner would have been remarkable enough. The state of his attire – pajamas, dressing gown, leather slippers – was pushing beyond the limits.

A middle-aged woman with a severe haircut and a

mouth whose surrounding lines spoke all too clearly of a lifelong nicotine habit, stepped into his path and said, "Excuse me, sir."

Barabbas did not adjust his pace. He merely raised his eyes to hers and let her see in their brown depths what there was to see. The woman's mouth, which had been set in a firm line, began to quiver. She turned away without taking note of her surroundings and collided with a desk, then scrambled across its top, scattering papers and a phone console, anything to put distance between herself and the man in the dressing gown.

Behind Barabbas came Adramalek, though the office staff were spared the sight of the archduke; it had rendered itself invisible to all but the man it was following. When the mortal reached the doors that led to the floor's elevator lobby, he paused for a moment with his hand on the handle.

"Dust," said the demon, "wafting away on the wind."

"There is no wind, you overstuffed thing of Sheol," said the man, deliberately rendering his words in Aramaic. He yanked open the door and stepped outside. "And no dust."

He had only once ever taken an elevator, and hadn't liked it. He recognized the sign above the stairwell, pushed open the fire door and began to descend the concrete stairs, the demon coming behind him. At a landing, he stopped and confronted the archduke.

"Why are you following me? Your master broke the contract. I am free and have no more need of you."

"It is a different world," said Adramalek. "You will not find it so easy to assemble a following."

"We'll see," said Barabbas and continued down to the

ground floor. He stepped into the lobby, saw a man in a uniform behind a counter shaped like a half moon and went to him. He put his eyes on the guard and spoke sharply: "Name and rank!"

The man snapped to attention, stared straight ahead. "Morrison, sir! Shift supervisor!"

Barabbas looked the man up and down, made him wait at attention, then said, "Anything to report?"

"No, sir! All squared away."

"Good. As you were."

The man relaxed, but remained alert. He said, "Thank you, sir."

Barabbas walked toward the doors to the street. Over his shoulder, he said, "Same world. Only the details have changed."

He yanked open one of the doors, saw the bustle of the street outside, the flow of cars and pedestrians. He smiled. It had been a long time.

"They're always waiting for a messiah. And now here he comes."

"He goes through phases, you see," said the dominion. "There was a period when He thought that He'd get the best results by picking out some ordinary fellow and giving him a nudge. Moses for example, or Joseph, or Samuel. He sent a shepherd boy with a sling out to fight one of the toughest characters of the age. I'm not sure what point He was trying to make."

Denby said, "I'm getting the impression from what you're saying that God is making it up as He goes along."

"Good," said the heavenly being. "That's the impression we get, too. Or working something out to its conclusion.

Now, where was I?

"Oh, yes. After the ordinary folk, He decided to try making them deeply charismatic right from the cradle. That gave you Alexander the Great, Siddhartha Gautama, a few other hinges of history. But then He stopped that phase and went back to working with the humbly born, except that although He chose ordinary folk, He gave them special powers. And, one time, just to see the effect, He created three of these common-folk wonderworkers at the same time and in roughly the same place."

"The two Jesuses and the Simon," Denby said.

"Yes."

Denby wanted to ask a question then, but the dominion went on talking, staring blankly. It told him about how more recently, the deity had entered a mass-movement phase, though He had soon tinkered with it to combine it with a few more charismatic individuals. That led, as it turned out, to some absolute disasters: worldwide war, mass murder on an industrial scale, cultural revolutions.

"Lately, it's quieted down," the heavenly being said. "There's only a faint echo of the mass-movement-cum-charismatic-person phase; you call it consumerism and the cult of celebrity."

"So He's not… tinkering anymore?"

The dominion turned its perfect face Denby's way and showed him an expression of amused disbelief. "Is that what you think?" it said. "Goodness, no. His latest interest is in seeding the population with thousands of little 'nodes of the extreme,' as He calls them: autistics and psychopaths, mostly, along with a few determined serial killers. Your associate, Chesney Arnstruther, was one of those experimental nodes."

"How has he turned out?" Denby asked.

"Hard to say," said the dominion. "He's certainly stirred things up. He's brought back two of the three wonderworkers, and now it seems that the third one is coming back into the picture."

"But you still don't know where Chesney is? I mean, if he's not in Heaven, Hell, or Earth, where could he be?"

The angelic brows drew together. "Apparently," it said, "there was at least one Creation before the present one. That is, before even Heaven and Hell were established." The perfect shoulders rose and fell. "Perhaps your friend is there."

"And you can't… reach out to him there?"

The dominion was distantly silent for a moment – focusing its energies, Denby thought – then it came back to him. "Up until now, I didn't even know it had existed. We can know and do only what He wants us to know and do. It seems He doesn't want us to know about the previous version, but doesn't want us to interfere in it. At least, not right now."

Denby had built his career and his personality on getting the job done. It went against the grain to hang around and do nothing when the bad guys were out and busy. "So we just sit here and wait?" he said.

"They also serve, who only sit and wait," said the dominion with a small smile. It sounded like a quote to Denby, but he didn't know where from. Meanwhile, his detective's mind was sorting through what the being had told him. He zeroed in on one remark.

"What's the significance of bringing the three special cases back together?" said Denby.

"I don't know," said the angelic being. "Perhaps He's

going to put them back in play. Or perhaps he's going to clean up loose ends. Are you not familiar with the observation about Himself that He works in a mysterious way?"

"My job," said Denby, "was to solve mysteries."

"Really?" said the dominion. "Well, good luck with this one."

Xaphan had followed as the three mortals were taken from their prison and chivvied up to the platform to meet Blowdell. The fiend had hovered over the scene, watching without much interest as Blowdell had bloviated at them. Human villains always liked to indulge in that sort of ego-preening; demons were far more direct in their revenge-taking. It watched Chesney defy the man on the rudimentary throne and held itself ready to intervene as soon as its mortal summoned it.

Then the young man was cast down and ringed by hungry beasts – Xaphan could see that their upper digestive tracks were empty and ready to get to work – but still Chesney did not call out for his demonic assistant. The fiend peered into his boss's mind and saw there a layer of fear, but also a resignation to the horrid death that was about to descend on him. There was even a strain of happiness, because after the pain would come an end to the misery he'd been drowning in.

It became clear to Xaphan that he was not about to be called. A demon needs will to act, and its usual source of will was determined to end his existence. It seemed a peculiar motivation to the fiend, but then most human motivations were beyond its ken – a demon could know what humans felt, but never really understand it.

As the toothy creatures closed in, the jaws adrip and the razor-clawed toes on their hind feet twitching reflexively, Xaphan understood that it might have to offer its services to one or the other of the two who would still be alive after Chesney was devoured. Simon was probably a nonstarter; Xaphan knew that the magician had been approached by Lucifer himself, way back when, and had turned down the offer.

The demon supposed it would have to be the woman, although female mortals rarely swapped their insignificances for the usual rewards of power, wealth, or carnality; if they truly wanted those things, they usually preferred to get them by their own efforts. Mortal men were always less patient.

The deposed chief of the Chikkichakk still outranked all the others, and thus would have the first taste of Chesney. Xaphan could see that the creature was opting for the shallow belly bite. That would win it a good mouthful of the human's tasty intestines and their contents, but would avoid slicing into the vital organs. Chesney therefore would still be alive and writhing in agony as, before his eyes, the dinosaurian chewed his tripes and gulped them down.

Xaphan felt no sympathy. It wasn't made that way. It did know regret, however, and was contemplating the end of the days of rum and Havana cigars that Chesney's will had made available.

And then it felt a stirring. The possibility of intervening in the imminent execution-by-tooth-and-claw presented itself to the demon. And no sooner was the prospect understood than the inclination to do so followed on its heels and before Xaphan could grasp the implications of what was happening – where was the will coming from? – it had dropped into the circle of ferocity to squat next to its supine charge.

"Boss," it said, "you need any help?"

Chesney knew it was going to hurt, but he didn't much care. At least it would soon be over. He bitterly regretted what would happen to Melda after he was gone, but felt a cowardly pleasure in knowing that he wouldn't have to witness it. *Flacking mungyfungy*, he thought, reverting in his moment of extremis to the habit of his youth, when he had avoided his mother's oral soap therapy by making up his own profanity. This being normal sure brings with it a whole lot of complicated emotions. It's a wonder anybody ever gets anything done.

The biggest Chikkichakk's jaws slowly lowered themselves toward him, its cruel eye locked on his own. He saw that it was going for his abdomen, and steeled himself for the searing agony. He felt a coolness as a rope of drool touched his naked flesh. He gritted his teeth and whispered, to no one and everyone, "I am very sorry."

At that moment, his demon spoke in his ear, asking if he needed any help.

Chesney was sunk so low that, for a moment, he was tempted to say, "No, thanks, I'm good." Then the thought of Melda's fate, and to a lesser extent that of Simon, broke through his despair and lit up the front room of his mind.

"Ten-ten," he said, then added, "and the suit."

Instantly, he was clothed in the Actionary costume, which made him impervious to the bites of dinosaurians ten times the size of the ones now threatening him. He got to his feet in a blur and dealt the deposed priest-

king a further blow to his pride – although the impact of
Chesney's fist against the dinosaurian's muzzle actually
fractured every bone in his cranium, driving a splinter
into the fist-sized brain that did away with not only the
Chikkichakk's pride but his entire grasp upon corporeality.

Blood spraying from his nose and mouth, the creature
flew up and backwards from the circle of would-be al
fresco diners and was already dead before he hit the stone
flooring. Chesney whirled, delivering uppercuts and
roundhouse kicks to the rest of the chosen few, scattering
them into a wide ring of the dead and the dying. Then he
turned to face Nat Blowdell.

The man in the tripod seat was slowly rising to his feet,
his eyes wide and his mouth half-open. Then suddenly he
was moving at the same velocity and Chesney understood
that the enemy had matched his own super speed.

"You certainly waited long enough," said Blowdell.

Chesney saw no reason to explain. "Why not give
them a show?"

The other man indicated the throng surrounding them,
who were still reacting with slow-motion shock to the
explosion of the diners' club. "It's not much of a show for
them."

"We can drop back to normal speed, if you want,"
Chesney said. "It won't make any difference to the
outcome."

Blowdell stuck out his chin. "I can match you for
strength and speed."

"Can you match me for demons?" Chesney said. He
spoke privately to Xaphan, and the weasel-headed fiend
made itself visible, hovering in the air at his side. He saw
the other man take in the situation, quickly drawing the

obvious conclusion, then slide his eyes toward Melda. One of Blowdell's hands twitched.

"Wrap him up tight," Chesney said, and immediately the other man was wrapped from ankles to shoulders in adamantine chains.

"Good stuff, that," said the demon, "the real McCoy."

Blowdell tried to move, even though it was impossible. The only result of his attempt was to cause himself to topple over.

"Now you just look ridiculous," Chesney said.

But, in truth, Blowdell looked determined. The bound man opened his mouth and called out a name.

Barabbas did not know his way around the city, but he did not have to. He was not just a born leader; he was an anointed messiah. Divinely implanted instincts told him where to turn a corner, when to follow a street for a while, where to make the next turning. As he marched steadily toward his goal, he occasionally caught the eye of a passerby, of someone sitting at an outdoor cafe's table, of a passenger looking out the window of a bus that was stopped at a red light. Each time, the other's reaction was the same: the casual meeting of gazes, then the sudden flash of contact. If Barabbas had then said, "Come, follow me," nine out of ten would have fallen in behind him.

But he wasn't trolling for foot soldiers yet. First, he needed a core contingent. So he walked on, enjoying the strength and that indefinable feeling of renewed vitality that he always got when he had drawn the life force out of someone young.

He passed a store with male mannequins in its window, paused to look, then stepped inside. A man came from the back, wearing the timeless face of a merchant with goods to sell. Barabbas caught him in his gaze, exerted a fraction of his full force, and said, "I need clothing."

Ten minutes later, he left the store clad in a suit and tie. The haberdasher hadn't sold shoes but had been glad to offer the charismatic his own. They fitted well enough, and would do until the messiah could find a decent pair of boots. He had always liked a good boot, starting all the way back to when he'd stripped the hob-nailed specimens from the feet of dead Roman legionaries.

He was in a less wealthy part of town now, the tall buildings having given way to low-rise structures that sold mufflers and tires. He turned from an arterial into a side street and saw ahead an establishment with a neon sign in its window that advertised a brand of beer. The glass around the sign and on the entrance door had been blacked out. He strode toward the tavern, remembering the times he'd done this before. He felt the old tingle raise the hair on his forearms and the slight shiver between his shoulder blades. He pulled open the door and stepped inside.

The place was dark. It smelled of spilled beer and old sweat. Men were standing at a long bar on one side, drinking beer and hard liquor, some of them both together. There were some booths and a couple of round tables, maybe half of them with patrons. A shaven-headed man with tattoos stood behind the bar. When Barabbas entered, he looked his way. So did most of his customers.

The man in the suit let the door close behind him. He let his gaze travel the room, meeting the eyes of the men, taking in the poster on the back wall. It showed a flag with a blue shield against a red background, on the shield a white cross whose point was that of a sword.

To himself, he thought, *This will do for a start.* To the men who were now staring at him, he said, "Brothers, the waiting is over."

Adramalek, being a demon, had never been worried about anything. Until now. As the archduke had followed Barabbas through the city and finally into the tavern, it had experienced a growing sense that events were moving beyond its control. Never before had Hell broken a contract. The territory beyond that doorway was completely unknown.

Certainly, it could be argued that Adramalek itself had not been the one to violate the terms of the agreement between Barabbas and Lucifer: the Boss had done that himself when he had failed to answer a summons. But as the Devil's first assistant wrung its huge mouse paws in unaccustomed angst, it realized that splitting hairs over who did what would not insulate it for one moment against Satan's wrath. Hell did not do fairness. It existed for retribution.

Adramalek called up the file and reviewed it once more. Some two thousand years ago, Barabbas – already equipped from birth with overwhelming charisma and a knack for violence – had accepted an offer from the Devil. In return for bowing to Satan, he had been granted immortality. The man had been intelligent enough to add that he was also to be maintained in robust good health. Which he was, Hell meeting its obligations to the letter. But he had not specified that he should not grow old, and eventually he discovered that a robust sixty year-old is not in quite the same situation as a healthy man of thirty.

So he'd had to ask for a renegotiation. Normally, such a request would be met with cold derision, but Lucifer had always taken a special interest in this contract. He had added a codicil, granting not eternal youth but a mechanism by which the party of the first part could rejuvenate himself every few years. The process involved some alterations to the man's anatomy, specifically the hands, resulting in a system that was similar to the arrangements by which insects with sucking mouth parts got their breakfasts. Although, in this case, it was life force that drained from Barabbas's victims through his fingers and into his own being.

But, as always, as one loophole closed, another opened. Satan didn't commit to protect Barabbas from having his feeding habits become known to those around him. Difficulties naturally ensued, which sometimes made it hard for the charismatic leader to maintain the loyalty of his inner circle. Thus a new codicil was negotiated and added to the lengthening contract; it alleviated some of the problem but, as was usually the case with an infernal agreement, it opened the doors to further complications.

More negotiations followed, and over the centuries, several new codicils were added to the original pact. Eventually, Barabbas found himself healthy, of sound mind, immortal, and invulnerable, but confined to limited space: a room and the adjacent floor of a building. From there he spun a web of intrigue that granted him executive power but denied him the fame and public adoration he hungered for and which had motivated him to make his deal with the Devil in the first place.

But now the whole legalistic edifice had come crashing down. By the terms of the codicils, Barabbas was entitled to all his benefits and was bound by none of the restrictions Lucifer had gleefully woven about him over the twenty centuries of their association. The Messiah was once again loose in the world, and this time there was nothing to hold him back.

Adramalek watched as he cast his net out to the men in the tavern, saw their already darkened insignificances begin to glow with the fierce heat of hatred. Ordinarily, the archduke would have approved, but this certainly could not be what the Boss had had in mind when he'd confined Barabbas to a single room.

The demon asked itself if it had sufficient will to take action on its own account. Again, the answer was in doubt. Lucifer had always been its source of that crucial energy, but the Devil was still out of reach. The only other source of that essential material had disappeared from Creation when Adramalek had blindly flung the mortal after the troublesome humans. It did not understand how Blowdell could have left what it knew to be all that existed. Now that Adramalek focused on the question of where the man had gone – and found no answer – it found its worries multiplying.

Demons had no internal mechanisms for dealing with emotions they weren't supposed to feel. Adramalek's anxiety, once internally acknowledged, began to rise to the level of panic. Once more, the archduke cast its awareness out into the world, seeking the man. It did not find him, but somehow it heard its name being called.

And that was enough. Though it did not know how, the archduke saw that it could follow the thread of the summons to wherever Blowdell, and his all-important will, lay waiting for Adramalek.

It prepared to exert itself and answer the call. At the last moment, in desperation that stirred up an instinct for self-preservation, it scooped up Barabbas and carried him along.

"Something is definitely going on," the dominion said to Denby.

"Why do you say that?" As far as the Chief of Police knew, nothing had happened. They'd been sitting in the dominion's all-white office doing nothing when the angel had raised his head as if he'd heard a voice and was listening. Denby had heard nothing.

"I've just had orders," the dominion said.

"To do what?"

"I am not instructed to tell you." The heavenly being stood up. "But I do have orders to take you along."

Denby was still rising to his feet when the room disappeared. He was briefly in darkness with a sense of space rushing past him, a little like looking out the window of a night train at unlit scenery flashing by, then he was in warm, mellow sunlight, walking with the dominion along a path between waist-high bushes beneath a canopy of tall trees. Every plant within sight was either ablossom with scented flowers, or adroop with fruit in a perfection of ripeness.

"Where are we?" he asked the glowing figure beside him, reaching for a juicy red berry. "And are these edible?"

"Eden." it said. "You can pick the fruit and taste it, but you'll find it hard to swallow. You're not anatomically correct anymore."

It was true. Denby could taste the sweetness of the berry, but couldn't swallow the chewed pulp. There was no hole at the back of his throat. He spat the mush out onto the path and saw it disappear into the soil. The dominion walked on, but the man hung back a moment and reached to see if not being "anatomically correct" meant in his case what it meant when applied to dolls. He found that it did, and that he was as smooth and featureless as Barbie's boyfriend. He was still trying to decide how he felt about that when they turned a bend in the path and came out onto a meadow in the center of which was a vast, spreading shade tree.

Beneath the tree were four persons, three of them seated around a table and deeply engaged in a heated discussion over something they were looking at on the screen of a laptop computer. The fourth, a woman past her fertile years, was lying on her stomach in the shade, propped up on her elbows and making a daisy chain. Denby recognized one of the trio as the Reverend Billy Lee Hardacre and the woman as Letitia Arnstruther, the mother of Chesney.

As the policeman and the dominion came across the meadow, he could hear the older man seated between the two main disputants say, "We keep going around and around on the same issue: the point of the exercise has to be to achieve a balance – a draw, if you will. But you keep trying to win."

The person he was addressing, Denby now saw, was a lean-faced patrician with a nose like a Saracen's blade and a small, pointed beard. His complexion was darkened even more than was natural to him by anger.

The other fellow, curly-haired and bearded, gestured with work-roughened hands. "The idea has to be that neither of us gets everything he wants, but–"

The glowering figure cut him off with a curt gesture. "I don't have to endure this!" he said. "And from a couple of mortals! Must I remind you that I was a prince in Heaven when both of you were not yet even a gleam in–"

The dominion interrupted. "Still working the vanity, Lucifer? Can you never learn?"

The Devil regarded the emissary of Heaven as if it were a tiresome child. "And are you still toadying?" he said. "You're lucky your master has never developed a taste for intimate contact. You'd spend your days bent over–" He broke off, noticing Denby for the first time, and made an off-hand gesture toward the policeman. "What's this?"

"Good of you to notice," said the heavenly being. "He's one of your mistakes."

"I don't make–"

The dominion spoke over him. "Of course you do. You just don't acknowledge them." As the Devil roused himself to deliver a devastating rejoinder, the figure in white went on. "He recently arrived at the gates, ahead of schedule. The buffoon you left in charge – Adramalek, is it? – personally deprived him of life."

"Nev–"

"Put away the bluster," said the dominion. "There's worse."

Lucifer's eyes narrowed and his thin lips formed the perfect arc of a frown. He looked from the dominion to Denby and back again. "What?" he said.

"You're in breach of contract."

Satan began another "Never!" but this time he interrupted himself. He looked off into the distance, but Denby had the impression he was really focusing on something within. After a moment, the Devil's eyes widened and he whispered one word.

"Barabbas."

"Indeed," said the dominion. "While you've been indulging yourself here, you've allowed, if you'll pardon the expression, all Hell to break loose."

Lucifer recovered his aplomb. "It's not my creation," he said. "I didn't make the rules."

"No, but you broke one."

The Devil thrust out a meager lower lip and shrugged. "Not for the first time," he said. "Perhaps I'll make a habit of it."

"You don't understand," said the dominion. "Things have begun to unravel."

Another shrug. Satan examined his long, pointed fingernails.

"I also didn't understand," said the heavenly being, "until a little while ago. He's thinking of doing what He did with the Chikkichakk."

Lucifer's brows drew together. "What are the Chikkichakk?" he said.

"That's what I'm here to tell you," said the dominion. "And then we're going to have to figure out a way to fix things."

"Or?" said the Devil.

"Or we all go back in the pot, and He starts again. From scratch."

Adramalek was passing through a gray void. It did not know how it knew that it was moving, and it did not care. Its whole being was concentrated into a knot of panic, an emotion it had never before experienced and which it did not now wish to examine. It just wanted the hideous feeling to end.

Looking down – direction in this nonplace was entirely relative – it saw between its mouse-paw feet a tiny dot of brightness that rapidly expanded. In moments, the demon was falling – again the angle of attack was relative – toward a small globe that soon became a big one, then swelled into a vast expanse of light. In an instant, Adramalek had broken through into space-time, where it hung in the immensity, surrounded by stars and galaxies.

Barabbas was plainly in difficulties, being unable to die, even though he was instantly freeze-dried by the near-absolute zero temperature and interstellar space's intolerance for moisture. The demon considered letting him suffer, but then it considered the possibility that the mortal might come in useful. It built an insulating shell filled with warmth and air around the man, and repaired his tissues.

The archduke found that Blowdell's call still echoed in its mind, and when it turned its attention to the summons, it felt a sharp tug from the mortal's will. It exerted itself and instantly it was where it needed to be, Barabbas arriving with it.

They materialized on a stone platform at the top of a rise, in the middle of a town also built of stone. Blowdell was lying wrapped in adamantine chains, his rage risen to psychotic levels. Xaphan was hovering nearby, and with it were the three mortals from their previous confrontation. A crowd of soulless beasts armed with spears and clubs were fleeing the scene, squawking and tumbling over each other. A few others, battered and wounded, were crawling toward the stairs as if they hoped not to be noticed. Others were dead.

"Free me!" cried the bound man. Adramalek needed the mortal's will and he reached to take hold of the visible end of the unbreakable chain.

"Do not!" said Xaphan.

The words rang in Adramalek's head with an unusual power. He looked at the weasel-headed demon. "You order me!"

"I warn you," said the fiend.

There was an unfamiliar ring of authority to the voice, as if the lesser-ranked demon had somehow connected itself to a will that could not be withstood. Adramalek speculated that this heretofore unknown Creation might be where the monarch of Hell had taken himself and thus become out of reach. It cast about for Lucifer, for where else could the Devil have gone and his first assistant not know about it?

But the old, familiar connection could not be made. Puzzled, the archduke eyed the hovering fiend and used other demonic senses to feel around Xaphan's presence. It found nothing. The only source of will available to the small fiend ought to have emanated from its mortal. But though that will was palpable to the archduke, it registered as even weaker than normal, and Adramalek caught off Chesney Arnstruther a lingering whiff of an emotion common in the infernal realm: despair.

It examined Xaphan again. Bluff? it thought. The smaller demon showed no sign of distress at facing off against its superior. But neither had it done so at their last encounter. Adramalek concluded that it didn't matter; an archduke could not lose face against a demon that had never risen above the rank of foreman. It took hold of the end of the chain and said, "No, I warn *you*."

The lesser demon let its pinstriped shoulders rise and fall. Adramalek watched to see what Xaphan would do. The answer was: nothing. The fiend merely hung in the air, its fanged countenance without expression. The archduke tightened its grasp on the end of the chain and made as to unwind the first coil from around Blowdell's upper body.

A flood of cold energy entered its mouse-paw hand and traveled at a steady rate up its huge furred arm. The limb became numb then completely inert. The fingers opened and the adamantine links fell to the stone flooring with a musical tinkle-tunkle. Adramalek reflexively made to shake life and sensation back into its arm, but the member refused to respond. It hung from the shoulder like a dead sausage.

Now there was an expression on the lesser fiend's face. If a sabertoothed weasel had ever had the occasion to say *I told you so,* it would have looked exactly like Xaphan at this moment. The rank insubordination so enraged Adramalek that it forgot about its numbed arm while it summoned up all of its power to smite the mocking demon into smithereens.

And then it remembered how things had gone the last time it had directed a disincorporating blast at Xaphan. Hard on the memory came another thought: the other demon's ability to resist the archduke's assault, coupled with the evidence of its power to paralyze a superior's limb, might just mean that Xaphan could and would deliver a counterstroke that would render Adramalek as a cloud of floating dust.

The archduke checked itself. But the energies it had summoned, once assembled, had to go somewhere. It had no experience with the art of dissipating such power, and had no idea how to do so. It was even possible – here Adramalek was forced to embrace another novel possibility – that in trying to defuse the powers back into wherever they came from, it might blow off its own hindquarters.

Yet the blast had to go somewhere. The huge demon's eye fell upon the mortals present, particularly upon the one who had caused all of the recent disruptions by rudely refusing to turn over his insignificance after calling up a demon. The man was dressed in his costume, supposedly proof against any attack. Well, thought the archduke, let us see if it can withstand a blast from Hell. It was a rule-breaker, as had been the destruction of the policeman Denby; but, thought the archduke, what the hell.

"No!" said Xaphan, as if it could read Adramalek's mind.

Again the voice reverberated through the archduke's being, and this time the effect was faintly familiar. It almost called up a memory from long, long ago. But the senior demon had more immediate concerns: it was swelled up with undischarged energies that had to go somewhere.

"I forbid it!" said the smaller demon in its strangely vast new voice.

But Adramalek was too far gone. It let fly at Chesney with a blast that would have torn a hard-shelled demon down to motes and speckles.

The young man had been standing not far away. The interval between Adramalek's hurling of the disincorporating discharge and its impact against the mortal ought to have been so slight as to be virtually instantaneous. But, somehow, in that tiny sliver of time, a shield had been erected between the power and its target. The archduke's assembled and focused spite struck an invisible barrier. There was a great flash and a lingering afterglow. And then it was as if the blow had never been struck.

Chesney looked at Adramalek with an expression that said, *Did I miss something?* Xaphan gave the senior demon another *told-you-so*. Adramalek looked from one to the other with the face of a giant, crocodile-toothed mouse that had not the faintest clue as to what was going on.

"What's going on here?" said a new voice – new, that is, to the established complement atop the Chikkichakk royal platform, but familiar to Adramalek through all the eons since Hell's founding.

The archduke turned. Its first reaction was relief. The Boss was here! Then the demon saw the cloud that sat on Lucifer's brow. It saw Satan take in the scene: Blowdell in his chains, Barabbas still in his bubble, the three humans and Xaphan, the dead and wounded beast-men.

Clearly none of what the Devil saw was to his liking, least of all the presence of his first assistant, the demon he had left in charge of his kingdom.

"Who," said Lucifer, in his deceptively mildest tone, "is minding the store?"

TWELVE

For the second time in only a few minutes, Chesney had faced imminent death. And, for the second time, he had almost welcomed it. Indeed, when the torrent of destructive force from the elephant-sized mouse had splashed harmlessly against an unseen barrier, the young man had been almost disappointed.

Dang doodle, he said to himself. And then he was tempted to even stronger language when he saw who had joined them all on the pinnacle of Chikkichakk social prominence. For behind Satan had appeared Joshua Josephson, who was giving Simon Magus a quizzical look. Then came Billy Lee Hardacre, and Chesney's mother, plus a glowing white figure that must be a high-ranking angel, and finally Chief Denby. This last arrival was even more of a surprise to Chesney than the others; he'd never thought of the policeman as being part of the group that occupied the Garden of Eden; besides, Denby looked qualitatively different, as if he'd gone through some scrubbing process that had left him looking cleaner and somehow purer than any mortal the young man had encountered – except, perhaps, the man who had once been Yeshua bar Yussuf.

Lucifer was obviously surprised and displeased to see the gross demon with the crocodile teeth. He demanded an explanation for the fiend's presence. But after hearing the first few words of a reply, the Devil raised a finger and pointed it at the huge mouth. The demon couldn't seem to decide between groveling or defiance, then settled for an understanding that the nature of its response didn't matter. It shrugged its huge rodent's shoulders and looked away.

"Don't," said a voice, and Chesney was surprised that it was Xaphan's. So apparently was Lucifer, because he paused with his destructive digit still aimed and turned toward the young man's assistant.

"What did you say?" the Devil said.

"I said, 'Don't.'" The weasel-headed demon looked as surprised as its master.

Satan's brows drew together, though more in consternation than in condemnation. "You said, 'Don't?'" he said.

"Yes, Boss."

"And you said it to me?"

"Yes, Boss."

There was a pause while Lucifer processed the news. Xaphan, too, seemed to be trying to come to terms with its own behavior. The elephantine mouse looked from one to the other. Finally, the Devil shook his head like a man plagued by gnats, and raised his other hand to point a finger at his first assistant. "I'm beyond caring why," he said, mostly to himself, "or even how."

He drew himself up and the air around him seemed to

crackle with unseen energies.

"Wait," said Chesney.

Satan turned exasperated eyes toward the young man. "I'll deal with you in a moment," he said.

"No," said the angel, "you won't."

Chesney watched as the Devil's exasperation ratcheted up to pure rage. Satan turned and directed both fingers at the figure in white. The heavenly being only sighed and offered a fly-shooing motion with one perfect hand, leaving a glowing trail in the air. "Don't bother," it said.

From the Devil there issued a wordless sound that went on for several seconds, raising both hands until they were pointed at the zenith. Then he turned, seeking a target, and saw the last of the Chikkichakk wounded still scrambling to escape the action atop the platform. With a growl, he let fly from both digits, loosing paired streams of dark fire that struck the rearmost of the fleeing dinosaurians, charring tails and scorching hindquarters. With mournful hoots and agitated clacks, the afflicted creatures leapt bodily over those in front of them. Chesney saw one Chikkichakk, its tail smoking, scamper across the shoulders and heads of the fleeing mob.

In a moment, all had disappeared into the warren of streets that led to the central square. The occupants of the raised platform, mortals and nonmortals alike, had the place to themselves.

Lucifer, though scarcely mollified by having unloaded on the Chikkichakk, had at least recovered his customary composure. He looked at each member of the disparate group, and at Chesney and the angel with particular dislike, and said, "I want to know what this is all about!"

The figure in white opened its mouth to speak, but

again the answer came from an unexpected source.

"It's like this, see. It ain't workin'."

Once again, all eyes turned to the weasel-headed fiend in the wide-lapelled pinstripes and spats. And no one seemed more surprised at the development than Xaphan.

Xaphan had been increasingly conscious that something well out of the ordinary was happening to it – and had been happening for quite a while now. The strangeness had started as far back as when the demon had told Chesney about the Garden of Eden, and had intensified when it had carried the young man out of Creation and into the discarded universe where they had found Joshua Josephson.

As a demon, Xaphan was accustomed to the phenomenon of finding particular items of knowledge in its mind, as when the fiend was required to carry out some function stemming from the will of the Boss or of a mortal whose insignificance had been pledged in return for infernal services. That was just how things worked.

True, Xaphan had a certain baseline understanding of how the universe was arranged, and even had memories acquired during the centuries of its existence. It could even recall the long-ago timeless time when it had been a baritone in one of the multitude of heavenly choirs that sang the praises of the deity without pause or interruption. It also had acquired likes and dislikes, the former including fine cigars and strong rum, the latter including being ordered about by the infernal bureaucracy.

But some of the items it had found in its mind in recent times went well beyond the normal welling up of information. Take the Chikkichakk, for example. It wasn't just that the knowledge of the dinosaurians and their vanished world had come into its mind. Along with the data came a sense that nobody else knew about them – maybe not even the Boss. So where did the information come from?

When Chesney and his friends were about to be blasted out of existence by Adramalek, Xaphan had known that it had to put them somewhere out of reach. It had hurled them to this world, in the universe of the Chikkichakk, even though it had not known where it was or how to get there.

Something was going on, the demon knew, and now it knew that a lot of that something was passing through its own being. As when it opened its mouth and said, "It's like this, see. It ain't workin'."

Where did that come from? And what would come next?

It realized that all eyes were now turned its way, and that the Boss was wearing that look that said someone in the near vicinity was about to get dusted. Xaphan would have preferred to find itself another location: the little room in the outer circle of Hell, with the box of Churchills and the decanter of rich, amber rum, would have been just the ticket.

Instead, it felt as if a strong breeze was passing through its being, and the breeze was causing the demon to say, "I figured I'd better get alla youse someplace where you're out of the neighborhood, so we can work out what to do."

"*You* figured?" said Lucifer.

"No, Boss, not me! It's like this kinda wind is blowin' through me."

At this, the Devil knitted his brows to their tightest and when, after a moment, they flew apart, he said, "I protest!" He pointed at Xaphan, making the demon flinch, and said to the sky, "This thing is mine! You may not use it!"

"Sez who?" said the fiend, then clapped a hand over its fanged muzzle.

"So says," Satan answered, "every rule and convention of our relationship."

Even through its covering fingers, Xaphan's voice was clear. "Like the rule that sez you gotta honor contracts?"

The Devil's face grew grim, but he did not respond. After a moment, Xaphan took its hand from its muzzle and spoke again. "Here's the thing, we ran inta a hitch when the mortal, here," – a stubby thumb indicated Chesney – "set the ball rollin'. Hell goes on strike and everything stops dead."

"I remember," said Lucifer.

"And then this bird," – a short digit made a circular motion while aimed at Billy Lee – "comes up with the idea that this is all a big book and we oughta trust the characters to work a way outta the corner."

"Noted," said the Devil.

"Well, the thing is, see," the wind passing through Xaphan said, "it ain't no book. It ain't a story. It's somethin' else. And now it ain't workin'."

Billy Lee Hardacre spoke up now. "If it's not a book, then what is it?"

The weasel face took on a strained look. "It's in my mind," it said after a struggle, "but I don't got the words. It's like it's this machine, with lots and lotsa parts, and they fit together. Except it ain't a machine, and the parts ain't real – I mean, you can't touch 'em or nuttin – but it keeps goin' round and round, always changin'. And the whole thing's about seeing where it all ends up."

Lucifer looked up at the sky. "If you want us to understand, why are you talking to us through a minor demon?"

"Never mind," said Chesney. "I know what it is."

Of course Chesney knew. He'd been working with such things all of his life, particularly after he began to study probability theory, and especially since becoming an actuary. Before Joshua Josephson had inadvertently changed his condition, the development and consideration of what Xaphan was describing had been his chief joy – a pale and abstract joy by comparison with the physicality he had found in the embrace of Melda McCann, but a joy nonetheless. Even as he grasped what the demon was talking about, and prepared to enlighten the others, he realized that he had not indulged in that old pastime for quite some time; and he further realized that he missed its pleasures dearly.

"It's a mathematical model," he said. He saw comprehension on some of the faces around him, though not on all. Denby and his mother looked blank, while Simon and Melda appeared to be reaching for understanding but not quite getting there.

"A set of algorithms that models a complex system and mimics how it behaves," he said. "Once you've got it working, you can change some of the parameters and that lets you see how the system would respond under the new conditions."

Lucifer frowned. "You're saying we're nothing but a

gaggle of numbers?" The news apparently did not come as good tidings to the Devil.

"Is that any different from being a collection of randomly associated atoms?" Chesney said.

"I am not formed of atoms," said Lucifer. He indicated the demons and the angel. "Nor are they. We are made of finer stuff."

"Fine," said Chesney. He didn't feel like responding to the Devil's prickly pride. Now that the matter of numbers had come up, and imminent death was not in prospect, he was coming out of the funk that had enveloped him when Blowdell had been about to feed him to the Chikkichakk. He was feeling a surge of desire, though not of the physical kind; more like a craving to hear once again a favorite piece of music.

"Xaphan," he said. "Put the knowledge in my mind."

"Okey-doke," said the demon. "Better brace yourself. It's a doozie."

Chesney thought his skull would burst. His head felt as if it had been suddenly inflated to a huge pressure, as if it had swelled to the size of a hot-air balloon. He staggered and sank to his knees, lost sight of the place and people around him. All he could see was the immense, infinitely complex, mathematical construct that filled his mind – indeed, overfilled. He could not hold it all, or even a large portion of it, in focus.

But then, as his singular mathematical ability applied itself, the numbers began to sing to him. He listened and translated elements of the song into comprehension. He found that he could isolate strains and particular harmonies, as if he were concentrating on the woodwinds in a full-blown orchestral performance, then switching instead to hearing the strings.

But such an orchestration! It made the New York Philharmonic sound like a kid with a kazoo. Here was all of Creation rendered in numerical relationships. As Chesney concentrated on one huge, unwinding algorithm, he suddenly understood quantum mechanics. When he turned his attention to another spiraling mathematical worm, he grasped exactly the rules that governed how clouds formed over oceans. A glance over in another direction, and he knew how fingerprints formed.

But all that was background noise, he realized. The demon had said, "It ain't workin'." Chesney doubted that that statement had anything to do with the gravitational constant or the apparent inability of photons to decide whether they wanted to be waves or particles. He was sure it had everything to do with people.

He refocused his awareness, hunting among the math melodies, sorting and slipsiding, until he came to that part of the model that delineated mortals. It took up a lot of room in the model, like an orchestra within an orchestra, with each of the apparently individual instruments breaking down into its own complexity of tones and frequencies. It was a matrix of interrelating numerical values to challenge even a Chesney Arnstruther.

But Chesney had once lived to meet such challenges and now he found himself being more himself than he had been for months. He plunged into the music, swam in it, reveled in it, let himself be swept this way and that by its currents and movements. And, gradually, then more swiftly, then at a full-bore velocity, he heard the grand song that was the deity's representation of humanity – not only heard it, but understood it. He knew how it worked.

He also knew when it didn't. He heard the false notes, the disharmonies and clashes. He followed them to their source. And found himself and the people assembled on the top of the Chikkichakk priest-king's platform. Then he went back and pursued other threads, investigated parallel strains in the mingling of melodies. But, one after another, they brought him back to where he stood.

And showed him, time after time, that his demon assistant was right. It wasn't working. The notes were wrong, the harmonies discordant. The numbers just didn't add up right.

Chesney's vision cleared. He got to his feet, looked at the people and other beings around him and said, "We've got a problem."

"Speak for yourself, mortal," said Satan. "I create problems. I do not suffer from them."

Chesney knew that debates with Lucifer were not about getting to the truth. They were about getting to the Devil's victory. But he was spared from having to respond by the glowing figure in white.

"If you think you don't have a problem," it said, "try leaving this Creation."

Lucifer gave the angelic being a look that would have curdled blood, if angels had any such in their veins – or if they had veins, for that matter. But the glare's recipient returned only the blandest of smiles. The Devil then sniffed eloquently, elevated his scimitar of a nose, and disappeared. A few moments later, he reappeared, wearing an aspect of outrage compounded by injury.

"I want to know what is going on," he said.

"So do we all," said the heavenly being, "so I believe we had better listen to the mortal."

Chesney ordered his thoughts, which fortunately allowed him to look away from Lucifer, whose face was not pleasant to see. Then he began. "So it's a mathematical model, a very, very complex model. And God keeps tinkering with it."

His mother raised an admonishing finger and was about to speak. She was not the kind of woman who would let her deity be spoken of lightly. But the figure in white gently shushed her and she subsided.

"He has always made changes in the model," Chesney said. "Sometimes major, sometimes minor." He gestured to the stone town and the forest beyond. "This was one of the major changes. The Chikkichakk date from before He decided to create souls – that is, before He began to invest certain elements of the model with His own… substance. It dates, in fact, from before He created Heaven and Hell and their inhabitants."

Lucifer glanced about him in evident displeasure then gave the sky a murderous look. His precedence was being slighted.

But mostly, Chesney went on, as the model had become ever more refined, its designer had been content to make small alterations then see how things worked out. There had been a phase when He had created charismatic individuals – three of them were gathered here – and another when He had fostered political mass movements.

Lately, though, He had been experimenting with creating special types of persons and seeding them through the general population. After the initial trial with Shakespeare had worked well, He had made a raft of genius poets, artists, and composers – Mozart, Beethoven, Rembrandt, Picasso. Then He had tried working with engineers and inventors for a while. After that had come a phase for political leaders of various stripes.

The results had been mixed, but interesting. New ideas had flourished, societies had made great leaps or undergone paroxysms, individuals had been beset by new moral dilemmas. Then He had let things quieten down. Into this new, relatively placid phase, the deity had decided to introduce new nodes. He created some types of person that could exist within humanity without being fully part of it. He made a large number of psychopaths, including a subset of serial killers. And, as a contrast to the well socialized majorities in the now generally placid societies, He began creating more and more autistic persons. "Including me," said Chesney.

Chief Denby spoke up. "Why?"

"The simple answer," the young man said, "is 'to see what happens.'"

"And the complicated answer?" the policeman said.

Chesney looked to the heavenly being, and received in reply a shrug. Next he looked to Xaphan.

"Keep goin'," the demon said.

"He created me," the young man said, "and I did what was natural to me. The result was that things started to go wrong. To see if it would stabilize the model, God allowed some of us to become aware of the larger picture. Not completely, because we were supposed to think we were characters in a book – a book He was writing, as Billy Lee proposed, to learn about right and wrong."

But the model didn't stabilize. Tensions built up and discrepancies began to appear. Nodes that had been left behind in previous iterations of the model – the "discarded drafts" – were reintroduced into the current version.

Major nodes, like Lucifer and Barabbas, began to rewrite their own algorithms. The results were disharmonious.

"The model has become so unstable," Chesney said, "that He's thinking of rewinding it all back to when He started ramping up the number of autistics. He'll edit out that change. Which means that I would either never have existed, or I would be... normal."

"Can He do that?" said Melda.

"It's His model," said Chesney. "We're just nodes, mathematical functions."

"That's not fair," she said. She turned to the angelic being. "What do you have to say about this?"

"I have no will but His." It looked toward Xaphan. "But the demon seems to be speaking for Him."

She rounded on Xaphan. "Are you?"

The fiend looked like a weasel that has discovered a peculiar sensation in its innards. "Looks that way."

"So when I'm talking to you, I'm talking to God?"

"Yeah, and I'm thinkin', don't get Him hot under the collar. I don't wanna burst."

"Well, strap yourself tight," Melda said, "because somebody needs to say something here."

She stuck out her chin in a way Chesney had seen once or twice before. He wanted to warn her to go easy, but he got no further than "Um," before she was talking.

"You're going to cancel Chesney, take away his whole life, just because You don't like the way he worked out? When it was You who made him like that?"

Xaphan said, "In a nutshell, yeah."

"But that's not fair."

The demon's face took on the uncomfortable look again. "He don't have to be fair," it said after a moment's introspection. "He can't be. If He was fair, the machine – the model – wouldn't run right."

"But He expects *us* to be fair, to be good. If we aren't, he sends us down to this guy's place," – she waved a hand toward Lucifer – "and we get punished."

"No," said Xaphan, "He don't expect youse to be fair, just to be… yourselves."

"But, but…" Melda put her hands on her head then thrust them up toward the sky.

Chesney had never heard her splutter before. He decided it was time to step in. "I think what Xaphan's trying to say," he said, "is that *we* have to deal with right and wrong, because that's part of the model. God doesn't have to, because He's not part of it – even though He's written a little of Himself into each of us."

Now she turned on him. "God doesn't have to do right? I mean, what the hell?"

Xaphan spoke. "You're missin' the point, sister. He didn't make youse for youse. He made youse for Him."

"What, so we could worship Him?"

"Nah, He don't pay no attention to that stuff. Youse all came up with that on your own."

"Then what," said Melda, her hands back on her head, "are we for? Why did He make us at all?"

"I told ya. To see what happens." The demon shrugged. "And now that He's seen it, He don't like it. So He's gonna call it a dead hand and deal the cards again."

"The Lord," Letitia Arnstruther put in, "does not gamble."

"Not any more, perhaps," said Lucifer. "But I remember one wager He took. A man called Job." He gave Chesney's mother a side glance freighted with condescension. "And

I recall that when poor Job complained of being ill-used, he received much the same answer as your son's mistress just heard."

Letitia gave Satan a look that would have shriveled many a mortal. "The Devil can quote scripture," she said.

Lucifer's condescension became positively toxic. "Of course I can."

"But Job," the woman countered, "was not a wager. It's not a wager when it's a sure thing."

"You think He knew the outcome?" the Devil said.

"Of course."

"Then why didn't He know how this latest escapade would play out?" Lucifer looked up at the sky with a mischievous air. "Messed it up again, have You?"

"Never mind the points-scoring," Melda said. "Chesney's life is on the line here." She turned back to Xaphan. "And what about the rest of us?"

"The mortals stay here," the demon said. "Me and the Boss and Adramalek, we go back into the machine." It darted a worried glance at the Devil. "Cept we get our memories messed around with."

Lucifer glared at the sky. "You can't do that to me!"

Xaphan put its hands over its mouth but the words came out anyway. "He's done it before, after He's made big changes. We just don't remember. 'Need to know,' He calls it."

Satan raged about the platform, stamping his feet, and thrusting his fists here and there. Adramalek, as the largest and most inviting target, shrank itself in size and hid behind one of the dead Chikkichakks – unfortunately, it chose the one that its master decided to kick in a long, high arc that lifted it off the platform and down to land on a mud roof, through which the corpse and the archduke crashed.

"Stay here?" Melda said. "How long would we last in a world full of dinosaurs?"

"Not long," said Xaphan, "specially since in a little while, a rock comes down outta the sky and wham, bam, the whole neighborhood gets barbecued."

"We die?" said Chesney's mother. Now she looked up at the sky with a less worshipful cast to her face.

"And back in the machine," said the demon, "youse all get canceled out."

"Do we go to Heaven?"

"Nah, that's just for what your boy calls 'nodes.' None of youse is nodes anymore."

Letitia was having difficulty taking it in. "He's already edited us out? Even before giving us a chance to argue our side?"

"Yep."

"So where do we go?"

The demon's face puzzled for a moment. "Nowhere, I guess," it said. "There's no youse to go anywhere, cause youse never was."

The woman could not restrain herself. "That's not fair!"

"We done that one already," said the fiend.

"When," said Chesney, "does the asteroid hit us?"

"It actually hits a couple thousand miles that way," Xaphan said, pointing to the southeast. "But the hot stuff–"

"The plasma shockwave," Chesney corrected it.

"Yeah," said the demon, "it gets here a little under a half hour after the big smasheroo."

"And when exactly is that?" Chesney said.

The fiend held up a stubby digit that said, *Wait for it.* Two seconds later, there was a bright flash far below the southern horizon. "There ya go. Once that's rubbed out all the Chikkichakk, He's gonna close the whole shebang down."

Letitia Arnstruther said, mostly to herself, "And we don't go to Heaven. *I* don't go to Heaven."

Billy Lee put an arm around her waist and pulled her to him. "It will be quick," he said. "Like being hit by a pyroclastic flow from a volcano. We'll be dead before we know it."

She was trembling. He said, "Don't be afraid, Letitia."

"I'm not afraid!" she said, pulling free. "I'm goddamned furious!"

She stalked up to Xaphan, seized the fiend by its pinstriped lapels, and hauled it close until her nose almost touched its muzzle. "I spent my whole life doing what I was supposed to do, never doing what I wanted to do! I fought your fights, championed your causes, wore grooves in my fingers writing letters against evil-doers for your sake! And now you tell me I was some kind of goddamned mathematics mistake?"

"Lady," the demon began.

"Don't you 'lady' me, buster!" She shook the half-sized demon so that its head rattled from side to side like a bobble-headed doll on the back window of a low-rider. "You know what this is? This is crap, is what this is! And I'm not taking it!"

"Mother–" Chesney began.

She dropped the demon and rounded on him. "And don't you 'mother' me. You're the one got us into this mess! I should've known, all the way back when your father said I couldn't get pregnant the first time, that—"

At that point, Letitia's brain caught up with her mouth and she stopped speaking. Hardacre tried comforting her again, but she was even angrier than she'd been at the start of the episode. She thrust him away and went over to the nearest dead Chikkichakk, which she began kicking, to a muttered accompaniment of "Damn, damn, damn, damn it all."

Chesney watched her for a moment. Then his eyes went to Melda. She was hugging her elbows, her chin tucked in, but she was looking at him from under lowered brows. He could read her expression. It said, *Do something*, and at the same time, *There's nothing we can do*.

He surveyed the others, each sunk in his or its own emotions. Billy Lee Hardacre looked like a man who was thinking hard but not getting anywhere. Denby was shell-shocked; he'd heard from Chesney about angels and demons and arguments with the Devil, but being plunged into the middle of it all had apparently taken the stuffing out of the policeman – not to mention being dead. Barabbas was sunk in his own rage; Chesney doubted he could even hear what was going on. And Blowdell was not much different.

There was no help to be got from the citizens of Hell or the angelic being waiting blandly to be sent elsewhere. Even Xaphan had been co-opted.

Do something and *There's nothing we can do*. Chesney was strung between the two polarities – and still a little dazed by his sojourn through the mathematics of Creation. Whatever he might do now, as a thousand-degree-centigrade blast wave rushed toward them all, it didn't matter.

Billy Lee spoke. "It's not right. Call us nodes, mathematical functions, whatever – we're still playing the roles of characters in a story. And one thing I know about stories is: you give the characters what they deserve."

He gestured to the southeast, where the sky was lighter than it should have been. "We don't deserve this. We didn't make the mistake. We shouldn't have to pay the freight."

He looked at the sky, then at Xaphan, "Wherever you are, if this is the best you can do as a god, you shouldn't be allowed."

The demon hitched its shoulders. "Youse all gotta die," it said. "It's what youse owe for livin'."

"It's not about dying," said Hardacre. "It's about the how and the when, and especially about the why."

That won him another fiendish shrug. The Devil said, "Are we done? I think I've put up with just about enough–"

"Shut up!" said Chesney. "Just shut up!"

The monarch of Hell turned a disbelieving gaze on the young man, then drew himself up to his highest degree of dudgeon. "I think," he said, "before we say goodbye, I'll just let Barabbas here have one last meal. I understand it's a particularly awful way to go."

The Devil gestured toward the man in the bubble, but Xaphan held up a hand. "Sorry, Boss, but He says nah. The kid don't deserve it."

Chesney wondered if he was supposed to be mollified by the deity's concession. Because he wasn't. If anything, he was angrier than when he'd shouted at the Devil. He turned his face to the sky, feeling the heat of rage in his cheeks. He had a passing thought that this was the first time in his whole life that he'd ever been really ticked off, and then he let fly.

"'The kid don't deserve it?' You know, you got a lot of damn gall telling us who deserves what! You do whatever you please to us – rig the game, stack the deck – and we're just supposed to take it and say, 'Thy will be done.'

"Well, forget it!" He gestured to Hardacre. "The Reverend here thought you were trying to figure out good from bad. He was wrong. God knows what it is you're really trying to accomplish!"

He stopped to consider what he'd just said, then let it go. "But Billy Lee's idea was a lot better than whatever this problem is you're trying to work out – by putting us through all this misery!

"You just ought to be ashamed of yourself! If you can't treat people decently, you shouldn't be allowed to have them in the first place!"

The southeastern sky was brighter now. Xaphan was looking at him as if the demon expected something more. The fiend's expression drove the young man's rage to a higher level and he emerged into a new state of consciousness. He almost felt as if he was surrounded by one of those clear pools of light that autism used to shed for him.

"What?" he shouted. "You expect me to work it out for you? It's simple! It's what Billy Lee said: you give people what they deserve – you treat them with some common decency!"

"Youse can't go back inta the machine," Xaphan said. "Youse made it all screwy. So what's He supposeda do with yez?"

It was on the tip of Chesney's tongue to tell the demon,

It's His universe, let Him figure it out, but at that moment his glance fell on Melda. Behind her the southeastern sky was a roiling blaze of reds and oranges, reaching higher and higher. But all he saw was the look on her face, that sudden wild surmise that said, *Tell him!*

And then it came to him – not all the details, but the general shape of it – while he seemed to stand in the clearest pool of light he'd ever known. "OK," he said, "since You ask."

It was a learning experience. He'd never made a universe before, not even a little one. But he'd had a close-up look at the one that had used to contain him and Melda and the others. He'd heard the tunes, the rolling math-melodies for which he was blessed with perfect pitch. He understood them intuitively, to begin with. And the more he worked with them, the more refined, and the more powerful, his abilities grew.

God had started him off with the equivalent of a cleared building lot: a flat piece of solidity with a dome above it to keep in air and warmth, a hot glowing disk to pass over it during the day and a few stars to brighten up the night. Chesney had gotten down to work right away, making some ground and some grass, then a river and a few trees. They were all generic – like something from a Bugs Bunny cartoon – but he'd add the grace notes later.

He'd made houses: they were just huts, really, but he hadn't yet made any elements they'd need protecting from. He was going to wait until he was more practiced before he tried making it rain, let alone conjuring up a storm. And he made food, finding that he had a talent for textures and flavors.

In fact, he had a talent for all of it. Especially since he'd tweaked his own algorithm and restored himself to the Chesney he'd been before Joshua Josephson had fixed him. He had only to listen, and all of Creation sang to him in harmonies and rhythms. He had only to exert himself a little to make a new tune.

He did it now, sitting on the grassy slope that led down to the clear, winding river. A moment's concentration, and a small yellow flower sprouted between the green blades. He thought about it, and its color deepened to gold, with red stamens and pistils at the center.

Nice, he thought, and made a few more, then a sprinkling of blue ones along the far bank. Melda would like them when she came with the picnic basket. He was pleased with the pickled eggs – he'd got them just right – although he'd made the first batch of Mexican beer too strong.

Tomorrow, he would expand the universe some more. He was going to try to make a kind of heaven on the other side of some hills – after he made the hills. It would be the kind of place that would fit his mother's ideas of what the afterlife should offer the deserving. He imagined there would have to be a long process of tinkering to get that project just right, but they had all the time in the world.

Chesney knew that Billy Lee Hardacre was content enough as his assistant. The author had had more experience in creating worlds and enjoyed seeing his ideas literally come to life. Joshua Josephson was collaborating with the preacher; his only suggestion was not to make any sheep.

Simon was full of suggestions, too. He kept urging

Chesney to get started on a Las Vegas, but the magician understood that it would have to be a while before the young man could throw up multi-story hotels with fountains, casinos and all-you-can-eat buffets.

"I'm still just a god-in-training," Chesney told him.

There was the question of what to do with Barabbas and Nat Blowdell. He had studied their algorithms, listening to the discordancies. He was going to wait until he was better at the finer points of people-shaping before he woke them out of the long sleep he'd put them into and tried to remake them into decent human beings. Or, he might divide them up and redo them as insects and spiders.

It was all very complicated, but fascinating. He made a few more of the gold and red flowers then looked up. Melda was coming up from their hut, swinging the picnic basket and smiling a smile that even the old Chesney could read.

ABOUT THE AUTHOR

Matt Hughes was born sixty years ago in Liverpool, England, but his family moved to Canada when he was five. He has made a living as a writer all of his adult life, first as a journalist, then as a staff speechwriter to the Canadian Ministers of Justice and Environment, and – from 1979 until a few years back – as a freelance corporate and political speechwriter in British Columbia. He is a former director of the Federation of British Columbia Writers and used to belong to Mensa Canada, but these days he's conserving his energies to write fiction.

He's been married to a very patient woman since the late 1960s, and he has three grown sons. Of late, Matt has taken up the secondary occupation of housesitter, so that he can afford to keep on writing fiction yet still eat every day. He's always interested to hear from people who've read his work.

archonate.com